HARD DUTY

J.B. TURNER

HARD DUTY

A **JON REZNICK** THRILLER

THOMAS & MERCER

Text copyright © 2024 by J. B. Turner
All rights reserved.

Published by Thomas & Mercer, Seattle

www.apub.com

Amazon, the Amazon logo, and Thomas & Mercer are trademarks of Amazon.com, Inc., or its affiliates.

ISBN-13: 9781542039840
eISBN: 9781542039833

Cover design by @blacksheep-uk.com
Cover image: © Viorel Sima © SFIO CRACHO © Ivan Kurmyshov / Shutterstock

Printed in the United States of America

HARD DUTY

One

It all began, as it often did, when he least expected it.

Jon Reznick sat on his back porch, bottle of cold beer in hand, as night fell. The heat and humidity had been as suffocating as he could remember for a summer in Maine. Sweat stuck his T-shirt to his skin, his throat was parched. But it was all about to break. The radio had warned a storm system was approaching. He stared out across the murky waters of Penobscot Bay. The lights of a lobster boat twinkled as it returned to safe harbor in Rockland. Black clouds slowly rolled in over the water. In the distance, low growls of thunder. Then the first flashes of lightning streaking across the darkening sky, illuminating the steel and chrome of Reznick's trusty Beretta handgun, within reach on the table.

The rain would come, cooling the temperatures, bringing welcome relief after a brutal and mercifully rare month-long heatwave across the northeast. Lawns had gone dry as a bone, then burnt, then dead. The thunderclaps rumbled on, louder and louder, as if the sky itself were about to explode, threatening to shake Reznick's old wooden colonial to its foundations.

Reznick watched and waited, taking a sip of his beer. He always enjoyed the start of a gathering storm. He loved nature in all its raw, terrifying glory. Birds took flight from the oak trees shrouding his property. Even they sensed the danger. He remembered sitting with his father as a boy, watching as bad weather rolled in. Sometimes they'd be waiting for a storm in late summer, like just now. Or maybe a nor'easter blowing in a huge blizzard of snow or sleet in the depths of winter. It didn't matter. He had loved sitting with his father. The elements of nature at play. It was awesome to watch.

He remembered his father used to have an old barometer. A beautiful, wooden device handed down from generation to generation. He had shown Reznick how the air pressure changed during different climatic conditions. Reznick had listened, fascinated. His father loved all that sort of stuff; he had been able to look out over the waters and sense, almost through instinct, what storm front was on its way. Maine was invariably hit hardest, and Reznick and his father would enjoy hunkering down during those storms. If it hadn't abated by first light, Reznick would watch from his bedroom window as his father wrapped up, head down, and trudged down the dirt road to begin an early shift at the sardine packing plant— now long since closed down.

His father had lost his license after being caught driving under the influence by his best friend. He wasn't allowed to drive for a year. He'd been angry. But he'd known he was in the wrong. There was no bitching, no moaning. He'd just shrugged and gotten on with it. When Reznick's father had returned from Vietnam, he'd been broke, an alcoholic, and then he'd lost his wife. He'd struggled to find reasons to keep going, year after year.

Reznick found that the more the years rolled by, the more he thought about his father. He thought of the struggles his father had endured in war, but also back home, working a brutal, thankless, low-paying job with no end in sight. But his father had never once griped. He'd never taken a day off work. He'd endured. Always endured. From a sense of duty. A sense of place. He was a man who was flawed, like every man, but who'd worked like a dog all his days, even when the return was paltry. His only legacy was

Reznick—and the wonderful wooden colonial, built to last, that had withstood numerous storms.

Years earlier, Reznick had had the house rewired, repainted, and a new kitchen put in. But it was still the same tough, beautiful New England home his father had envisioned and built for them after he'd returned from Vietnam. Reznick remembered his own daughter Lauren as a child, gazing out from her upstairs bedroom across Penobscot Bay as a nor'easter rolled in. She had told him that the house always made her feel safe. And happy. She would inherit it when he was gone, as he had inherited it from his father. That made him happy. Lauren living in the house one day, hopefully with a family. It was nice to think that future generations would still be living there.

Truth be told, he didn't know when he'd see Lauren again. She was based on the opposite side of the world, in Indonesia, working at the CIA station. He rarely heard from her. But that was understandable. Nevertheless, he missed her. The trips down to New York to see her when she was working at the FBI's field office in Lower Manhattan seemed like so long ago.

Leaves rustled as the wind picked up, branches creaking and groaning as the storm got nearer.

Reznick's gaze wandered to the dirt road. Lights were heading toward his home, snapping him out of his reverie.

He put down his beer as a truck rumbled toward his porch. A FedEx truck, headlights picking out the clouds of dust in their full beams. Reznick got up and went around to the front of the house. He wondered if the driver was lost. He wasn't expecting any deliveries.

The truck screeched to a juddering halt and the driver jumped out quickly, package in hand, glancing around. "Mr. Jon Reznick?"

"That's me."

"Just a quick signature, buddy. And some ID."

Reznick showed his driver's license and signed his name on the delivery sheet.

The driver handed over the package. "You take care. Looks like we're in for a bad one."

Reznick tipped the driver twenty bucks.

"Appreciate that. Have a good day, man."

Reznick watched the guy reverse out of his driveway. He waited until the truck was out of sight before he headed back inside and locked the door. He had an inkling of what might be in the package.

He went upstairs to his small, second-floor office overlooking the bay. The storm was edging closer, trees swaying and creaking as the wind changed direction. He took out a knife and slit open the cardboard, then reached inside and pulled out a pristine MacBook Air. A handwritten note read: *We want to talk to you.* It was the way he was sometimes approached. Other times people were a little more direct.

He sat down at his desk. He had no plans lined up for the foreseeable future. He had hoped to maybe head down to Florida and kick back for a couple of weeks. But that might have to wait.

He opened up the MacBook and switched it on, and it booted up in seconds. Familiar security screening questions flashed up on the screen.

Reznick first entered his Langley password—*coldbracelet1*. A ping, and he was prompted to enter two all-too-familiar follow-up passwords.

The first was *OfwaihhbTn*, case-sensitive initials from the first line of the Lord's Prayer. Then *DNalKcOr*, or *Rockland* spelled backward. Then he had to answer two subsequent security questions: the maiden name of his grandmother on his father's side, *Levitz*; and Reznick's blood group, *Rh negative*.

A few moments later, a FaceTime screen appeared. He clicked to accept the call.

A middle-aged woman's face came into view, unsmiling. "Hi Jon. I was wondering when the package would arrive."

"Two minutes ago."

"Very good."

"Who am I talking to?" he said.

"My name is Fran. And I'm pleased to meet you."

Reznick nodded. "How can I help you, Fran?"

"You know who I work for, I assume."

"The Agency?"

"Correct. Listen, we have a situation."

"What kind of situation?"

"The kind that requires someone with your skill set."

"Off the books?"

"And then some."

"I'm listening."

"I wanted to first reach out to you and introduce myself. I hope you don't mind. It's irregular, I know."

"I'm an irregular kind of guy."

Fran smiled. "So I've heard. Here's the thing: I didn't want to waste your time or my time by asking you all the way down from Maine unless you could definitely help us. Or at least be interested to talk to us."

"That's very considerate of you."

Fran stared at him. "Does that pass for sarcasm?"

"It does where I come from. Before we go any further, where do you fit in at the Agency?"

"What do you want to know?"

"Your position? Your title?"

"I headed up the Directorate of Analysis, formerly the Directorate of Intelligence. My name is Francine Petersen. I've also worked in Operations, formerly the National Clandestine Service."

"I've worked for them in the past."

"I know you have. We know quite a bit about you. But we seem to have lost touch in the last few years."

"What do you do now?"

"Right now? I'm working on what I would call a special project. And I'm hoping you can help me."

"How did you get my name?"

"It doesn't matter."

"It does to me."

"It's my job to know things. Truth be told, I know all there is to know about you, Jon Reznick. And I believe you're the perfect fit."

"Do you want to answer my question? What do you do exactly? I can't move forward if I don't have a handle on this."

"I've specialized in analyzing foreign politics, intelligence, and military threats. I do the CIA daily briefing for the President. I have worked in intelligence, deniable psychological operations, and various paramilitary activities." She turned and pointed to the corner of the room she was in, as the camera panned around, showing a besuited man. "This is the general counsel for the CIA. Peter Berger."

"You got lawyers involved. It must be serious."

Petersen nodded. "This is serious business. And that's why we're reaching out to you. I read your file. You know how this works. You know your way around. You've done it all and then some."

"I've got the scars to prove it."

Petersen laughed. "I've worked in some interesting places over the years too."

"Where?"

"Syria, Iraq, Somalia, Libya. But this isn't about me."

"What is it about?"

"A time-critical project. A special access program. Highly, highly classified."

Reznick was intrigued, not only by what she'd said but what she *hadn't* said. "What exactly do you want?"

"I want to talk face-to-face. But before we talk, I need to know if you're available."

"Available?"

"I know you worked alongside the Feds for a few years."

"That's over."

"Well, I've got an opportunity."

"Is there no one in-house who can help you out?"

"There are plenty in-house. But we've gone down that route before. We ran into problems."

"What kind of problems?"

"It didn't work out. It was a shitshow."

"I see. Was there a reason for that?"

"There was a reason."

"You want me to do a time-critical job for you? I'm reporting to you?"

"Correct. So, are you in or out?"

"And you can't give me any further details at this stage?"

Petersen shook her head. "Not yet. Do you want to hear more? This is a matter of national security."

Reznick nodded. "That's a given."

"What I'm going to ask you to do is somewhat out of left field. But I have personally requested you for this mission. The Director is aware of this initial approach."

Reznick stared out of the window as the storm closed in, rain lashing against the windowpane, lightning bolts erupting in the black sky.

"I had a shortlist of three men who I believe are best suited to the job," said Petersen. "You are number one on that list. I believe you are a man of integrity and I want you to work for me. You will report to me. No one else."

Reznick reclined in his seat and sighed. "When do you want to talk?"

"Tomorrow morning. 0800 hours."

"That soon?"

"We're on the clock. A plane will pick you up at 0500 hours from Owls Head airport. Don't be late."

Two

The Gulfstream almost skimmed the treetops as it banked steeply and swooped low over the glistening waters of the York River, just outside Williamsburg, Virginia.

Reznick stared down at the place he knew so well. He recognized the familiar landscape and topography, and of course the secret facility surrounded by barbed wire. It was officially known as Armed Forces Experimental Training Activity (AFETA), but most people referred to it as Camp Peary—a covert CIA facility on a nine-thousand-acre bit of land, under the auspices of the Department of Defense. Students, also known as career trainees, learned tradecraft and intelligence-gathering, as well as some of the darker arts. But its specialty training program was in clandestine warfare. In particular, it trained American and foreign paramilitary forces in black ops work, including assassinations and the myriad forms of psychological warfare. Tens of thousands of foreign intelligence officers from dozens of countries had passed through its well-guarded gates over the decades.

The plane touched down in the brilliant sunshine of the late August morning. Reznick descended the stairs, sunglasses on, baseball cap pulled low. He climbed into the back of an SUV with tinted windows and was driven half a mile to a two-story redbrick administration building.

Two armed men holding submachine guns were waiting to escort him inside.

Reznick wondered if this wasn't overkill. But then again, perhaps it was an indication of how serious the CIA was taking this. He passed through a biometric security check, which scanned his retina. Then down a long corridor with gray vinyl flooring, up some stairs to an executive office.

The door was ajar.

Reznick was shown inside. Fran Petersen sat behind a polished mahogany desk alongside Peter Berger.

"Glad you could make it," Fran said. "Take a load off."

Reznick pulled up a chair opposite. The door was locked. An awkward silence stretched between them for a few moments. "Well, this is cozy," he remarked.

"I appreciate you taking the time to see us. And apologies for the early start."

Berger leaned across and shook Reznick's hand. "Nice to meet you, Jon. I've heard a lot about you."

"So," Reznick said, "what's this all about? I take it you didn't invite me down here to talk about the weather."

"We invited you down here because we have a proposition for you, Jon. Couldn't really go into that on a video call. I hope you understand. But first, we just wanted to set some ground rules."

"Fair enough."

"Whatever we tell you during this meeting is, of course, highly classified. National security. We are working under the auspices of an unacknowledged special access program. Two people at the Pentagon know about it. The President knows about it. And the various heads of directorates at the CIA. And of course Mr. Berger. We would all deny its existence."

"Before we get to it, why aren't we meeting at Langley? Why are we here?"

"People talk, even at Langley," Petersen said. "At this stage I would like to keep things as low-key as possible."

Reznick nodded. "I'm assuming this discussion is not being recorded?"

"What makes you say that?"

"Just need to know the ground rules."

"No, this is not being recorded in any shape or form. This is merely a preliminary discussion. It's an opportunity to hear what you have to say. Throw ideas around. At the end of it, you can either head back home or you can sign up. No hard feelings."

"Sign up for what exactly?"

"I'll get to that. We're talking a clandestine mission. You might not survive. The probability of survival is twenty percent at best."

"Not great odds. I'm not a betting man. But still."

"We believe you're the person who can do this. I've been looking at your file. It makes interesting reading. I've talked to people I know and trust to discuss options in the last few days. Your name is a recurring theme. Which is unusual in itself."

"Why's that?"

"No one doubted that you were the logical number one choice. The opinion was unanimous. And they all said the same thing about you—he's the best. They told me you're a machine. You don't fuck around. You do what it takes—whatever it takes. You're a maverick, a lone wolf. But you're the guy they'd all want."

"Why not send Delta or SEAL Team 6?"

"We don't want a team for this operation."

"Why the hell not?"

Berger cleared his throat. "You see, Jon, the Agency has tried this once before, using a special forces team."

"When you say tried once before . . . are you saying they failed?"

"Sadly yes."

"What kind of team was it?"

"It was a carefully assembled team of our best. Delta, SEALs, Rangers. But we failed. I don't think I would be exaggerating to say it was an unmitigated disaster."

Reznick shifted in his seat.

"So we decided to try a different tack," Berger said. "Asymmetric, so to speak. A bit unorthodox."

Reznick struggled to decipher what the hell he was doing there. "I'm not sure this is a great sales pitch. A special operations team, comprised of the best operators in the business, I'd imagine, and they failed. But now you're talking to me? I don't get it."

Petersen perched in her seat, her hands clasped in a contemplative mood. "You will."

"You're doing a lot of talking. But you still haven't gotten to the point."

She exhaled. "Everyone said you were a straight talker."

"Still waiting to hear the offer."

"We want you, Jon, to neutralize an American counterintelligence expert."

Reznick took a few moments to contemplate the magnitude of that information. He was beginning to understand that this sounded fucked-up in the extreme. "Why? Where? You need to be a hell of a lot more forthcoming."

"This man was one of the best in his field, if not in the world. It's a shadowy existence, as you know only too well. He worked for us at the CIA for decades."

Reznick shook his head.

"What is it?" Berger asked.

"Are you serious? You want me to kill one of our own? An American?"

"Correct. He's retired. Has been for several years. But since then, he's gone rogue. Dangerously rogue."

"Why not just arrest him?"

Petersen picked up a remote control and pressed a button. Electronic blackout blinds slowly closed over the windows. A huge screen on the wall appeared. "I'll tell you why. You have the highest level of security and intelligence clearance. So we're good to go in a legal sense."

Reznick stared at the screen. It showed a grainy color photograph of an elderly man smoking at an outdoor café, cup of coffee on the table, dark brown sunglasses.

"I knew this man personally," Petersen said. "He was a distant figure in many respects. But I worked with him in the early years of my career."

"So this is personal?"

"Absolutely not. This is business. National interest."

Reznick studied the photograph closely. "Where was this picture taken?"

"We've checked the metadata. Sousse in Tunisia, North Africa. Three weeks and one day ago."

"Who got it?"

"A French tourist visiting Tunisia. Purely random. He was taking a photo of a street scene and inadvertently captured this old American guy. The image was downloaded as a digital file to the guy's computer and saved to the cloud. A facial recognition program run by France's Directorate-General for External Security pinged. They had a match. They informed the NSA."

"Interesting. You said you knew this guy. You worked with him."

Petersen nodded. "This was a tough call. CIA veteran of thirty-five years. Very old-school. Tough, feared, pretty terrifying character when I think back. He had a tight-knit group of friends and colleagues. Cold War CIA types. They liked to drink. And plot."

"And you want me to kill him?"

Petersen stared straight at Reznick. "Is that a problem?"

"What's he done exactly? I need to know more."

"I'll lay it out in broad strokes. He retired seven years ago. But we've discovered, eventually, that he accumulated a vast treasure trove of classified intelligence. We believe this was written longhand in many cases—code names, details of operational networks across Europe—but also copied via flash drives."

"How was he able to do that? How is that even possible?"

"Sadly, systems that we have since put in place were not adhered to so strictly a decade or so ago. This is the end result."

"How much data did he get?"

"A lot. Terabytes worth of priceless intel, in addition to the copious notes he took over the years. He was a great notetaker. He wrote down everything. Could be a meeting. Could be diary entries he made. We know he kept diaries through his decades of service. But that's only something we have belatedly realized."

Reznick sank down in his seat, arms folded. "It's an intelligence failure. And you want me to deal with the fallout."

"Precisely. He is betraying Americans as we speak. He has already blown the cover of some of our finest spies and security assets across the globe. But we believe that dozens more undercover intelligence operatives are at risk if he divulges what he knows."

"And what does he know?"

"The real names and identities of Americans, some using the cover of private energy consultants, who are in fact CIA agents tracking weapons proliferation in Russia and Eastern Europe. This is a critical national security issue. He needs to be stopped. Forever."

"Who's his close protection?"

"This is where it gets complicated. But it also makes perfect sense."

"How come?"

"His personal bodyguards, as far as we know, are all hardened ex-Wagner mercenaries. Russian private military contractors. Think Ukraine. These guys were in the thick of it."

"You're kidding me."

Petersen shook her head.

"This leads back to Moscow?" Reznick asked.

"Where else? We don't mind if you kill one or all of the Wagner crew to get to the target. We have no qualms about that."

"What about collateral damage that might occur?"

"Absolutely not. We don't want anyone else losing their life. You can wipe out the Wagner crew and the target, but no one else. Those are the rules. Is that a problem?"

"Not at all."

"We just want you to be aware of that fact. We need you to neutralize this threat once and for all. We don't care how you do it. Just do it."

Reznick stared at the photograph. An old man, protected by thugs and killers, but mortal all the same. "What's the target's name?" he asked idly.

Petersen and Berger traded a look before she answered. "William Crenshaw. That's your target."

Three

Reznick sat quietly as he absorbed the information. He sensed that Petersen wasn't being completely forthcoming about why she had reached out to him. It all seemed a bit off. It was one thing to neutralize a jihadi threat overseas. It was quite another to kill an American citizen, traitor or not. He had more questions than answers.

Petersen shuffled some papers. "What are you thinking?"

"Something doesn't add up."

Petersen flushed crimson. "I don't understand."

"Why don't you just press charges against Crenshaw, and take him to court? Put him on trial. International arrest warrant. Isn't that the way we usually do it?"

"It is. But this is different."

"How?"

"I'll get to that."

Reznick realized there was a lot more to this operation than had been divulged so far. He looked across the desk at Berger. "A legal move would be the typical, obvious response, right?"

Berger rubbed his face. "I hear what you're saying. And that is correct. But as general counsel, I'm here to guide the Agency as to what it can and cannot do. As it stands, as far as I'm aware, the target isn't even in America. Hasn't been for quite some time."

"Extradition?"

Berger shook his head. "That's not going to happen."

"I don't understand. Correct me if I'm wrong, but America has extradition treaties with more countries than it doesn't."

"One hundred and sixteen," Berger said.

Reznick shrugged. "So?"

"The problem is that there are dozens of countries with which America does not have extradition treaties. For example: Saudi Arabia, the UAE, Bahrain, Libya. Countries that Crenshaw has been known to frequent."

"Do you see our problem?" asked Petersen.

"I do now."

"We know you're a patriot. We've looked at your file. You've been in the thick of it for years. You've specialized in black ops. Plausible deniability missions. You work alone, or damn near as alone as you can get. I believe this operation will suit you."

Reznick said nothing.

She continued, "We know you're not working for the FBI anymore. You told us yourself you don't work for them."

"That is correct."

"We know exactly what you can bring to the table. The extradition route is not, sadly, open to us. We believe we have no other choice. And we are convinced your skill set can help us on this one-off job."

Reznick looked again at the image on the screen of the old man. "So this was the CIA's top counterintelligence guy for decades?" He exhaled. If he was going to be tasked with playing hunter, he wanted to learn about his prey before he agreed. "I'd like to know a lot more about the target. Background."

"Top of his class at Yale, back in the day. Brilliant analytical mind. But something happened over the years and he changed. He turned."

"In what way?"

"People who knew him said that he became, in his latter years at the Agency, a paranoid, sick old man."

"What do you mean, *paranoid*?"

"He saw threats everywhere."

"Wasn't that part of his job? To see threats, emerging threats?"

"That's true. But he began to distrust those around him in the CIA. His closest friends and confidants. He began to think his colleagues were spies. He saw plots, both real and imagined. He began to point the finger at people in the Agency. I believe this was to throw the Agency off his scent. Maybe he was becoming unstable, we just don't know for sure. And it was felt that his retirement was best for everyone."

"So he was retired earlier than he planned?"

"By around two years, yes."

"So he could be embittered. Angry."

Petersen cleared her throat. "I believe that's correct. But we are where we are."

"He's been sharing his knowledge of operations and intelligence with the Russians, is that right?"

"And so much more. Assets we have abroad, for example. He has compromised numerous operations overseas. Europe in particular. The Middle East."

"Why? He can't just be pissed that he was eased out the door."

"Money, influence—wanting to be part of the secretive world he used to know. It's mostly about money. Status. But he also nurses grievances, real and imagined. Against individuals in the CIA who slighted him. There was a disaffection with his place in society."

"Is that the whole story?"

Petersen shifted in her chair. "Shortly before he retired, he spoke off-the-record to a journalist who specialized in intelligence, a source of his for thirty years. Crenshaw alleged that the then director, Charles Katz, was under internal investigation for dereliction of duty. The journalist printed the story online. And it sparked a storm on Capitol Hill. We believe this was classic disinformation deployed by Crenshaw—dirty tricks used to destabilize and sow doubt in America's foreign intelligence service."

"And it wasn't true?"

"Absolutely not."

"That was a disciplinary offense, right?"

"Exactly. And that's probably what tipped Crenshaw over the edge. He was reprimanded, officially. It humiliated him in front of CIA officers who had previously revered him, and he was forced to retire."

"So we've got an angry old man."

"His work was his life. And then it was gone, with no way of getting it back."

"What else can you tell me? I'm not buying that he became embittered and that sent him into the arms of the Russians. Or that it was mostly for a little more money."

"Very perceptive. It's only in the last year that the true scale of his years-long deception became apparent. We have subsequently learned, since his retirement, he wasn't sharing intel from Mossad and Shin Bet with his colleagues. He kept it all to himself. During our investigation, we interviewed a number of his former colleagues, and they testified that Crenshaw showed signs—way, way back—of becoming more and more erratic. Indiscreet. He had always been a heavy drinker. But three months after he retired, we found classified intel on a flash drive stashed away in a secret room, a sub-basement, in his house. He had already abandoned the house—left for what we think was Iran."

"What kind of intel?"

"The deepest classified intel we have. Special access programs. Unbelievable that this was in an unsecured environment."

Berger chimed in. "He's also known to have provided classified intel to Colombian and Mexican drug cartels. They love him. He gets a slice of the pie, believed to be up to five percent. Serious money."

"How exactly has he helped them?"

"Among other things, Crenshaw has supplied lists of DEA agents across South America who work alongside the CIA. Mexico too."

Reznick felt sick hearing about the extent of Crenshaw's betrayal of fellow Americans.

Petersen continued, "That's only the beginning."

"There's more?"

"Throw into the mix African arms dealers, Middle East arms deals, and cozying up to foreign governments hostile to the United States. And the real killer—hard intel being passed to the Russians. Believed to be cutouts in the Middle East. Everything he is doing is weakening America, strengthening Russia. I could go on."

"What a résumé. But back to my previous point, why didn't you find him and haul him into the courts while he was still in the US?"

"It was too late, he was gone. Disappeared."

Berger leaned forward, hands clasped tightly. "I admire the fact you're gathering as many facts as you can, Jon. You're not just taking it on faith."

"Thank you. So what else?" Reznick asked.

"We've been building up a picture of Crenshaw," Berger said. "There was a concerted attempt to protect him. Maybe misplaced loyalty. We don't know. But this is stuff that just gives you a fuller picture of the man you're dealing with."

"I'm listening."

"Crenshaw is a sadist. He has a predilection for violence. We had no idea. We thought he was a cerebral agent. But, one example, we learned he had a meeting roughly fifteen years ago with station chiefs in Baghdad and then Riyadh. Crenshaw took a very, very keen interest in interrogations in these countries. Brutal interrogations. Extracurricular. He insisted on being a part of it."

"Stuff like that happens in war. It's not nice. But it happens."

"He watched three detainees be tortured to death at a facility near the Syrian border. Al-Qaim. You've heard of it?"

"I've heard of it."

"We learned that he overruled one of the CIA lead contractors during the interrogation. He insisted these three men be tortured in his presence. Tribal elders. He pulled rank. Wanted to send a message to the village. But to complete the picture, he filmed the whole thing on his BlackBerry for what we can only conclude was his own personal gratification. There's no intelligence explanation. He took a souvenir. Gruesome. We only found out about that when his cloud servers were examined nine months ago."

Reznick shifted in his seat.

"That's the backdrop to this," Petersen said. "Any further questions at this stage?"

"Have we got a fix on this guy?"

She shook her head. "That's the frustrating part. He's smart. As are his protectors. The men he uses as bodyguards love him. They have great loyalty to him. So he stays on the move. We've learned that he was staying at the safe house of some Palestinian academic with pro-Russian sympathies, but he moves all the time, and always with his same team." She pressed the remote and a collection of six photos appeared on the screen. Six tough-looking soldiers.

"Who are they?"

"This is the core leadership of his bodyguards, these six. You remember all the hellish stories about the tens of thousands of lives lost in Bakhmut in eastern Ukraine?"

Reznick nodded.

"These six guys were in the thick of it. Deranged, battle-hardened. All six are Russian citizens. Heavy links to Russian intelligence. They've been with Crenshaw for eighteen months. Three of the Russians were in the French Foreign Legion at one time. They've fought in Africa, Eastern Europe, wherever and whatever it takes. They don't take prisoners. And if they do, it's to torture them. Then kill them."

Reznick studied the photos. "How many men does he have around him?"

"It varies. They rotate. Ordinarily there's a minimum of a dozen guys with him. This gets beefed up when he's on the move. Vehicle up front. Maybe two."

"This is pretty sketchy intel."

Petersen nodded. "I agree. But it's the best we've got. William Crenshaw is like a ghost. He appears. He disappears. Crosses borders. Then he's gone."

Reznick pointed to the photo on the screen. "Crenshaw has links with MI6 and Mossad, right?"

"Very close ties. Very worrying. They want him erased too."

"What else did he do before he headed up counterintelligence?"

"Way back in the 1970s and 1980s, he was head of station in Athens, Vienna, Rabat, Baghdad and . . . Moscow."

"Now that is interesting. You think they got to him decades earlier?"

"We have no proof of that."

"What about leverage? Did the Russians have something on him? Something incriminating?"

Petersen said nothing.

"Guys, here's how it's going to work. If I'm going to go after this guy, I need to know everything. You either lay your cards on the table or I walk."

Petersen looked briefly at Berger, who nodded. "There is more."

"How much more?"

"Three years ago, we found out about a pedophile ring in Rabat. It was set up in the late 1970s by Crenshaw. Boys, girls— he's a fucking monster. It began as an elaborate trap to snare North African politicians, businessmen, military men, and entertainers who visited Morocco for sex. He wanted to exploit and blackmail these people."

Berger picked up a file from the desk. "Inside are hundreds of photos. Depraved, disgusting photos. If you don't believe me . . ."

"I believe you."

"Legally, we can open up extradition talks with a foreign country we believe is hosting or protecting Crenshaw. But this could take months. Maybe years. It would go through diplomatic channels. The State Department. And Crenshaw would invariably disappear. We don't think he's currently in a country with an extradition treaty with America."

"What about input from the NSA?"

"They intercepted a cell phone conversation with one of the six members of Crenshaw's praetorian guard," said Peterson. "It suggested that the Yankee—that's how they refer to him—has been making final plans to wind up his interests. He's sick of traveling. Sick of being on the run."

"So he's going to ground?"

She nodded. "In effect, he's dropping off the grid."

"So he'll disappear for good?"

"We have scant intelligence that Saudi Arabia might be his final destination."

Berger added, "And once he's there with protection, he might never be seen again. You might remember the genocidal Ugandan dictator, Idi Amin. After he went into exile, he was given sanctuary first in Libya, then Iraq, and finally Saudi Arabia."

"I hear you."

Petersen nodded. "We believe Crenshaw will disappear entirely soon. Maybe a matter of weeks. Maybe less."

"When exactly?"

"We don't know, that's the truth."

"I don't know . . . this all sounds flaky. One guy to take down this crew. . . I'm assuming Predator drones were considered?"

Petersen blushed momentarily.

"You need to spit it out."

She stayed quiet.

"What happened?"

"With regard to using Predator drones?"

Reznick nodded.

"Considered and used."

"Well, now we're getting somewhere . . . What happened?"

"It got messy."

"How messy?"

"The intel we had on the target was false. We were fed a line. It was bullshit intel. Disinformation."

"What happened?"

Petersen lifted the remote control. The huge screen showed grainy nighttime footage from a drone tracking a fast-moving vehicle convoy. The action slowed down. A Predator drone was shown honing in on the convoy. Closer and closer. Then impact. Explosions obliterating the vehicles; fires raging into the night sky. Not a sound.

"Bad intel?"

"Big-time. We ended up destroying a convoy of vehicles. Innocent men, women, and children were killed. The convoy contained Algeria's Minister of Energy and Mining and his entire entourage."

Reznick groaned.

"Complete and utter shitshow. And you can imagine what the Algerians thought of it. A disaster for the CIA."

"False intel from within Crenshaw's security detail?"

"That's what the analysis showed. No question. Old-school disinformation. That's what he used to specialize in. So now here we are."

Reznick shook his head. "This is the best we've got? We don't have any other options?"

"We've even reached out to one of the Wagner guys, on the periphery of the core six. We offered him ten million dollars to assassinate Crenshaw. If he was killed, the money would go to his family."

"So what happened?"

"Before the operative got to Crenshaw, his inner circle got wind of the plan."

"What do you think happened to him?"

"We have drone footage showing the guy being taken out to an oasis in the desert. Far south of Algeria. Then shot. Then thrown down a well."

Reznick contemplated the scale of the task ahead. He could see a ton of hurdles.

"So," Petersen said, "what are your thoughts?"

"My thoughts . . . About what?"

"The mission?"

"I think it's bullshit. It's a suicide mission, no question."

"It's challenging, I'll give you that."

"Challenging? Give me a break. It's a nightmare. This is not a one-man job. Never in a million years."

Reznick closed his eyes for a few moments. His main concern was his beloved daughter. Ironically, Lauren was now a CIA agent based in Jakarta. He would be working as a contractor for the Agency one more time. What would she make of this?

He wasn't a young man in his twenties anymore. He wasn't that fearless, headstrong Delta warrior who didn't care whether he lived or died. He was older. Maybe even wiser. And what the CIA was asking him to do was an ultra-high-risk mission, almost certainly resulting in his death.

"You thinking about your daughter?" Petersen asked.

"Do you blame me?"

"Not at all. I know she works for us. I know how much she means to you. I had to factor that in before I approached you."

Reznick considered what lay ahead.

"I figured you'd be thinking about how this high-risk operation might or would impact her. How you might not return."

He nodded.

Petersen pointed at Reznick. "Crenshaw must be stopped. Sooner or later. We will get him—that's a promise. One way or another."

"If not?"

"Failure is not an option. You know that."

Reznick twisted in his seat, staring up at Crenshaw's haunting image on the screen.

"Let's cut to the chase," said Petersen. "Are you in or out?"

"I need time."

She shook her head. "No can do. You're either in now, or you're out. We need to have the operation up and running within the next forty-eight hours."

Reznick felt himself being drawn closer into the vortex of the shadowy world of Crenshaw. He knew the dangers.

"You walk away from this, no hard feelings," said Petersen.

"Where was he last seen? Best analysis."

"Dubai, almost certainly. A phone belonging to one of the Russians was pinged in the city. That was a day after Tunisia. But no photo."

"What is the mission? Parameters. Precise aim."

"Kill him. Within the next week."

"That's not possible."

"Needs to happen."

"You want him dead in seven days?"

"That's the window we have. After that? God knows where he'll be. This is the best chance we've got. This needs to happen."

"So just me? I'm on my own?"

Petersen steepled her fingers. "No, not just you, Jon. I agree this is not a conventional clandestine operation. You can use two operatives."

"What?"

"The first can be an American, but they must have top Pentagon security clearance. Someone to provide logistics backup. Real-time intel, that kind of thing."

"What about the second operative?"

"This is where it gets tricky. We've decided that, if you use an accomplice, they must not be on active service or even recent active service for US special forces in any capacity. Ideally someone with no connection to America."

"Plausible deniability?"

Berger nodded.

"Are you serious? This is insane."

"There are geopolitical pressures on overt American hard power. Those in the corridors of power don't want the government of the United States to have our fingerprints all over this."

"Of course."

"We can't afford another fuckup in the desert. We want to make this right. We want to put that fucker out of business. But we want it handled as quietly as possible."

"We need to have a far bigger team. Three people is not realistic. You should have a dozen operatives, minimum."

"Not an option."

Reznick exhaled heavily.

"Like I said, we don't want any trace of American government involvement," said Berger. "It is considered highly dangerous."

Reznick shook his head. "What else do I get?"

"You will be provided with fake IDs and passports. We've already taken the liberty of setting up a fake bank account, and a fake name, for the duration of the operation."

"Very presumptuous. You want me back in the arena? Me and two others?"

"The geopolitical tectonic plates are shifting under our feet. We don't want this bastard thinking he can sell classified American secrets to the highest bidder. We don't want a war erupting."

Reznick's instincts told him to decline the offer. It was clear they were working on the assumption of hope over expectation that it would be successful.

"You in or out?"

"Do I have a choice?"

"We've all got choices, Jon."

Reznick stared back at the CIA attorney. "And this is all legal?"

"From an American government standpoint—yes, this is legal. We don't know anything about it. You'd be on your own. So, what do you think?"

"I think this is a crock of shit."

"Are you in?"

"He's a traitor, right?"

"The worst kind. He's cost the lives of untold American intelligence operatives so far. Who knows where it will end."

"Fuck it. I'm in."

Petersen clapped. "I knew you would be. We have secured a ten-million-dollar off-the-books budget for you."

"I'm not doing this for money."

"It's on the table anyway. For you. And for expenses and for the two operatives who will help you."

Petersen and Berger then both got to their feet and shook his hand.

"I wish you all the best," Petersen said.

"I very much admire you taking this mission, Jon," Berger said. "One week?"

"You're on your own," Petersen instructed. "Find him. And neutralize him. The clock is ticking."

Four

It was late August in Libya, one hundred degrees in the shade.

William Crenshaw sat in the back of a four-wheel-drive SUV headed south on a sand-strewn desert road. He swigged some water from a bottle, trying to quench his thirst. The air-conditioning growled low but seemed to have given up the ghost so far as providing any actual coolness. He felt drained by the days of moving, traveling. It was grueling at his age.

His frail eighty-eight-year-old body struggled to cope. His bones and joints hurt. He also felt grouchier than usual, and thought he was coming down with the flu. To top it all off, the merciless, punishing North African heat nauseated him. He was getting too old for this shit. Moving around. Long drives. Long flights. Country to country. And all the time trying to evade detection by intelligence services.

What he wouldn't give for peace and quiet, calm reflection, sitting by a pool, overlooking the ocean, not a care in the world. Retirement, never to be seen again, money no issue—this was what he had been striving for since he left the CIA.

Crenshaw gazed at the endless, shapeless, shifting sands of the desert as his driver sped toward the godforsaken town of Sabha in the Sahara Desert. The town where Colonel Gaddafi had grown up and been educated. The town where the military dictator and ruler, as a young man, had become radicalized in the ways of Arab nationalism.

The arid landscape seemed to go on forever. Time dissipated under the sun and the sand and the flies. Mile after goddamn mile. The inhospitable desert was home to only Bedouin tribes and the fearsome Tuareg militias roaming between villages and towns to their next port of call.

He had grown to loathe this part of the world. It was unfathomable. Unbending. Unchanging.

He hated the sickening, punishing sun, blistering from dawn to dusk. The never-ending, blinding heat. The filth. The smell of decay. When would it end?

A world with no beginning and no end. The smell of rotting animals strewn by the side of the road, entrails exposed. Crenshaw hated the hideousness of people eating rancid goat curries and camel meat with their nicotine-stained fingers, swatting away flies. He kept antibacterial hand gel in his pocket at all times. He was terrified of catching some gastrointestinal infection. They didn't wash their hands like people in the West did.

The country had descended into a dystopian hellscape. The corruption. The killings. The barbarism.

The SUV's AC switched to the maximum setting, and he felt it finally begin to cool his skin. He was pleased with small mercies. But his throat was still dry as a bone.

He swigged a few gulps of warm bottled water, getting some slight relief.

Dimitri, his scar-faced personal bodyguard, sat beside him—a man of few words. His protector. His confidant. The six-foot-three Russian mercenary mostly stared listlessly out the window as they drove. Past dusty desert ghost towns. Past decrepit, rusting old cars, long since abandoned to be reclaimed by the desert, the minarets of distant mosques glinting in the fierce North African sun. Dimitri knew this part of the world well. He had fought in sub-Saharan African wars for the better part of a decade. He was a brutal, murderous man, prone to temper tantrums, even with his own men. To Crenshaw, though, he was a respectful and reassuring presence.

Dimitri took his cell phone out of his pocket and scrolled through the encrypted messages.

"Anything interesting?" Crenshaw said. "Updates?"

"My friend . . ."

"From Moscow?"

"Precisely. He has indicated that it is imperative that you meet up with him tonight."

"Why the hurry?"

"I'm not sure; he didn't say."

"Do you think that seems a bit out of character? Such short notice?"

"Perhaps. But if he is asking to see you, it is best to see him."

"Where?"

"Sabha . . . some place."

Crenshaw knew the city well. A bleak, low-rise sprawl, Sabha had sprung up and expanded in the 1970s and 1980s because of the oil boom and the patronage of Colonel Gaddafi, who had ordered the rapid development in the heart of the desert. But since his overthrow, migrant shanty towns had sprung up amid the mud houses. It was now a shell of a city, virtually ungovernable, with the majority of the residents not Libyan but rather migrants from Chad, Niger, and other African countries.

"How long till we're there?"

"Before sunset. I'll say we'll meet at eleven p.m."

Crenshaw nodded. "Do you think there's anything to worry about?"

"There's always something to worry about."

"I know. But in this case, should I be worried?"

"If there is any concern about your safety, Maxim will pass on what he knows."

"You respect him, don't you?"

"Maxim? I respect him very much."

"But do you trust him?"

"I'm Russian. I don't trust anyone. Least of all Maxim."

His hotel was located not far from the heart of Sabha Old Town.

Crenshaw was relieved that his simple room was cool. *Small mercies*, he thought again. The air-conditioning unit rattled in the background. He was lucky. He knew the electricity supply was fitful at best in this godforsaken part of the world. It had a dysfunctional quasi-military government with a semblance of authority across the region. But tribal loyalties, memories of the civil war, blood oaths, and primitivism were never far from the surface. Sabha was a stopping-off point for people from countries like Chad, and for impoverished Africans in general, to escape unbearable poverty. It wasn't much better than where they came from, but Sabha was a crucial destination for those who were trying to get to Zawiya, on the northwest Libyan coast, hoping to connect to human smugglers who would get them into southern Europe. The promised land. Many died en route. Many died in Sabha, buried like dogs in unmarked graves on the edge of the city. Those who made it to Zawiya and onto an overcrowded boat were lucky if they didn't drown in the Med.

The more Crenshaw thought, the more he wondered why on earth he had taken so long to disappear for good. He wondered if part of him still hankered for the vague excitement that came with being on the move. Shadowy. Clandestine. He wondered if he needed that excitement in his life. Maybe that was it.

He showered and changed into a dark linen suit, a Savile Row shirt, and Italian boat shoes. The Africans in particular he'd encountered seemed to respect white men like him who dressed well.

He stared at himself in the mirror—his lined, tanned face and rheumy, bloodshot eyes. He'd run his race. Not long now and he could finally live out the rest of his days in peace and seclusion, shielded by the ghastly Saudis. High walls to protect him from nosy neighbors. He would swim every day at dawn. He would write his memoirs. He would eat food imported from Italy. And behind the high walls of his gated community, he would discreetly enjoy the finest wines, away from the prying eyes of Saudi citizens.

The more he thought about it, the more appealing it sounded. A country with absolute order. Where things worked. Medieval in belief, for sure, but its infrastructure was decidedly twenty-first-century, especially in the cities. It was a grand life for an expat. Who cared if the country was ruled by barbaric laws and methods of punishment? He didn't. He was past caring. He sensed Saudi Arabia was headed in a new direction. The appearance of golf tournaments, concerts, Formula One motor racing, boxing, and other sporting extravaganzas meant that Western societal norms were now spreading to the previously closed, medieval state of the Kingdom of Saud. They attracted visitors with dollars. Euros. Pounds. *Sportswashing*, some called it. He called it *progress*. The country was looking beyond a world of gas and oil. Its vision was fixed on a future of Saudi Arabia as a winter destination for well-heeled European and American tourism. Tightly controlled. High-end. Upscale.

Crenshaw was going to be OK. He had done well for himself. He had accrued two hundred million dollars, payment for his services over the years. It was a fruitful nest egg for his retirement, and it might be more. He hadn't checked for a while. The money was spread over myriad accounts in Switzerland, Grand Cayman, the

British Virgin Islands, Panama, the United Arab Emirates, Russia, and, of course, Saudi Arabia. His property portfolio was worth one hundred million dollars. Penthouse apartments in Russia, Riyadh, Dubai, and gated beachfront villas in Doha. It was time to enjoy the fruits of his labor in his retirement. The sacrifices he had made for his country had left him looking forward to a meagre CIA pension. But he'd realized he couldn't rely on Uncle Sam. He needed to look after number one.

Crenshaw put on the new Maybach shades he had picked up in Dubai. He adjusted his miniscule hearing aid to the right volume. Then he headed downstairs. His security detail escorted him to the SUV parked outside. Bulletproof windows, cell-jamming technology activated, as per usual.

He climbed into the back seat, sat on the white leather upholstery, and was whisked away following the lead car. The convoy headed into a rundown part of town, centered around an old, abandoned grain warehouse.

The SUV pulled to a stop. There was the sound of raised Arab voices. Then agitated shouts.

Crenshaw got out of the car. The smell of cigarette smoke and stale sweat hung heavy in the air. He could hear a crowd nearby.

Crenshaw followed Dimitri toward the drab concrete building. Inside were packed hundreds of older Arabs, waving dollars in their fists, screaming and shouting, the din almost overwhelming. He moved through the crowd to the periphery of the large stage. Young black men and women, fear in their every reaction, were standing shackled in chains, in filthy jeans and ripped T-shirts. A couple of the women on the stage, heads bowed, began to cry.

The auction was a great opportunity for Crenshaw to buy fresh slaves for the European market. Crenshaw turned to Dimitri. "You like it here?"

Dimitri spat on the ground.

Crenshaw chortled. He was instrumental in facilitating human smuggling from Libya. He organized routes. Entry to Italy via Sicily, assuming the migrants survived the choppy waters of the Med, especially in the winter months. But once there, they'd find it wasn't the freedom they craved. He'd always thought that Africans did as they were told. They smuggled large quantities of cocaine. The drug was flown in from South America to sub-Saharan Africa airstrips, then shipped across the Mediterranean in container ships, fast boats, yachts, whatever was available—flooding the multibillion-dollar European cocaine market. Fashionable society in Milan, Rome, as well as Munich, Zurich, Paris, and London. Everyone wanted to do blow.

Crenshaw's associates raked in vast sums each and every year. His cut had amounted to seven million dollars in fees in the last three months alone. He lit up a cigarette. The blue smoke mingled with the putrid air. A Russian associate near the front made a final bid, securing twenty strapping young men from Sierra Leone and ten fine-looking girls from Nigeria. Crenshaw didn't even have to lift a finger. But he still controlled it all.

He watched the young Africans get a number branded onto their arms. The mark of ownership.

He finished his cigarette, threw it on the ground, and walked back to the car.

Dimitri said, "He's been in touch. He's waiting for you."

"All in good time."

"He's not a man to be kept waiting."

"Dimitri, relax. You worry too much."

Crenshaw was driven through a warren of dusty backstreets in Sabha until the vehicle stopped a few blocks from the rendez-vous point. He was escorted past barefoot children hurrying to the nearby mosque, answering the sound of the last call to prayer. Crenshaw turned a corner and walked past an open sewer, dogs drinking from it, as Dimitri escorted him toward a roadside café.

The Russian was sipping a Turkish coffee, a bottle of water on the table.

Crenshaw gave a polite nod.

The Russian looked up. "Nice of you to join me."

Crenshaw sat down and took in his surroundings. He ordered two coffees, and a bottle of water for himself. "You haven't been waiting too long, have you?"

The Russian shook his head as he nursed his coffee for a few moments. "I have all the time in the world."

Crenshaw studied the man's features. He was a flinty-eyed, fifty-something Russian colonel who worked out of the embassy in Tripoli. He was one of several cutouts who were the back channel to Moscow. The man transmitted messages that needed to be heard. The exchange of information, classified or otherwise, happened as and when required. It always took place at a different café, restaurant, or bar. Maybe an apartment building. Whenever and wherever they deemed necessary. It was a tight-knit operation which had kept Crenshaw safe and protected for years.

"I have some news," the Russian said, "which should be of interest."

Crenshaw took out a packet of cigarettes and offered the Russian one.

"No, thank you. Don't you know they are not good for you?"

Crenshaw lit up. "Does that pass for Russian humor?" He sucked hard on the cigarette, enjoying the nicotine hit. "So . . . down to business. You say you have some news?"

"Rather urgent news. Troubling news. I wanted to bring it to you first-hand."

Crenshaw knew how the Russians liked to operate. They liked to keep you on edge. Maybe there were good reasons for it. But a lot of the time it seemed to him that it was simply a way to quietly create an air of fear, so the subject did exactly what they wanted.

"Our analysis is pointing to a renewed attempt to kill you."

Crenshaw dragged hard on the cigarette, blowing the smoke away from the Russian. "I thought you told me they tried and failed. Are you going to tell me they still want to target me?"

"William, shut up and listen. We are very concerned for your safety. And we want you to pay close attention."

"Relax . . ."

"I don't relax. Relaxation will get you killed."

"I'm listening."

"We have it on good authority, through impeccable sources in the French and German foreign intelligence services, that your friends at Langley have not given up trying to neutralize you."

"Are you sure?"

"Positive. The French contact told us that they are still resolved to kill you once and for all. But the threat this time is potentially the most worrying."

Crenshaw pondered this revelation for a few moments. "Correct me if I'm wrong, but I thought you told me a month ago that it had all blown over."

"It had. But things have changed for the worse."

"In what way?"

"They have grown exasperated. So much so that they are trying a high-risk strategy."

"You got any details?"

"The CIA is reaching out to one of their former operators—a very dangerous man. A man we know all about."

Crenshaw inhaled another lungful of cigarette smoke. "Are you sure? I mean, that this wasn't disinformation to be consumed by your friends in Russian intelligence? It wouldn't be the first time."

"Quite sure. The man's name is Reznick."

Crenshaw felt his stomach tighten. He knew the man's reputation.

"Does that name mean anything to you?"

"Vaguely. I do remember the name. Yes, he worked for us for several years. Was working for the FBI, last I heard."

"The FBI, huh?"

"He worked, if my memory serves me correctly, under the auspices of Assistant Director Martha Meyerstein."

The Russian scribbled down the name on a napkin. "Go on."

"I've heard she's no longer there."

"So the FBI is hiring assassins?"

"Not as such. But he was an exception. He worked as a consultant."

The Russian smirked. "A consultant? You Americans have a very dry sense of humor. Well, it appears that this man Reznick is back with his old gang. And you are the man he has been sent to kill."

Crenshaw sat impassively. His work demanded a poker face, not giving the game away or showing any weakness. "So, what do you suggest?"

"Your work is done. You are a very wealthy man. If it were me, I'd disappear for good. I mean right now. Tonight. Head to your beachfront villa in Doha and you'll not have to worry about any threats. You can live your life in peace, comfort, and security."

"If I didn't know you better, I'd think you were trying to startle me. Get me frightened. Is that what you're doing?"

The Russian gave a dead smile, eyes impassive.

"I have a few loose ends to tie up before I'm done. Papers to sign, final goodbyes. A few days, that's all."

The Russian shook his head. "Are you not listening? Forget about papers and goodbyes. The only goodbyes will be said by your ex-wife and your children at your graveside. Don't you get it?"

Crenshaw shifted in his seat, unused to being spoken to so brusquely. "So where is he at this moment?"

"We don't know."

"You don't know? Gimme a break."

"Heed my advice. A man like Reznick will find you."

"You don't even know where he is. Is he even in this country?"

"He will be soon. William, our job is to look after you and your interests. Disappear tonight for good, before it's too late."

Five

The operation got underway. The Cessna with Reznick on board touched down at SouthWest Florida International Airport after a three-hour flight from Camp Peary. Reznick was now on the clock. He understood the gravity of the situation but he needed to get the first part of the jigsaw in place—recruiting ex-NSA cybersecurity expert Trevelle Williams for the classified operation.

The problem was that he had no idea if Trevelle would be able to help. Maybe he was busy. Maybe he was out of town. But he also had to consider if Trevelle was in the right frame of mind. It had been less than a year since Trevelle's girlfriend was killed on the New York City subway, pushed under an oncoming train. Was he still deep in grief, mourning her loss? This operation would push Trevelle to the limits, more than he had ever been pushed before. The time constraints and the added responsibility of providing logistical support would ensure a high-pressure environment. But the reality was, Reznick considered Trevelle Williams as critical to the mission.

Reznick understood the logic of the three-man team. It was all about need-to-know. The fewer people who knew, the better. But the fact remained that three people was not enough. The risks were at the top end of the scale.

He picked up a rental car from the Avis lot and drove straight across to Captiva Island where Trevelle had moved his base of operation. It was a speculative visit. Trevelle was one of a handful of people Reznick trusted to work on top-secret government assignments. He didn't know Trevelle's precise address, since his friend had only moved there six months earlier. He just knew it was on Captiva. But he hoped that the flying visit could persuade him to join Reznick's team. It was an all-or-nothing approach.

A few miles before he got to Captiva Island, Reznick texted Trevelle, giving a heads-up for his imminent arrival.

I'm nearby. And I want to talk. Are you available?

The reply was swift. *You're here in Florida?*

Yes, I am, Reznick texted back.

Are you alone? Trevelle asked.

Correct. Where are you?

Trevelle texted an oceanfront address in Captiva. Reznick headed across the causeway to the beautiful, secluded island, lying off the turquoise waters of San Carlos Bay. It was less touristy than its sister island, Sanibel. The car's GPS guided him along the beach roads and single track to a private road on the north side of the island.

Reznick figured Trevelle was looking for seclusion, as well as peace and quiet. It was a perfect place to escape from it all. Or maybe his friend simply wanted solitude, shutting out the world after the devastating loss of his girlfriend. Perhaps that was the real motive for sequestering himself in Captiva.

He drove on under the shade of towering palms, swerving to avoid those that were partially blocking the roads. He figured the damage was probably the result of a previous hurricane.

Finally, Reznick turned a corner and saw huge electronic gates. As he drove on they opened automatically, and he headed slowly down the driveway until he saw the house. The elevated pink Art

Deco–fronted home was shrouded by foliage and palm trees, set back from the single-track road but overlooking the ocean. It would have been near impossible to find without instructions. Reznick turned off the engine and watched Trevelle descend from the third floor to greet him. He stepped out of the car and walked up to his friend, hugging him tight.

"How the hell are you, Trevelle?" Jon asked. "Hope I'm not disturbing you."

"This is crazy! I can't believe you just turned up like this."

"Long time no see, my friend. I hope you don't mind?"

Trevelle beamed. "Not at all. Reznick . . . when was the last time?"

"Probably New York."

Trevelle gave a wan smile. "Right, yeah."

"You OK? This a good time?"

"It's fine, Jon. To be honest, it's nice to have some company."

Reznick detected a terrible sadness in Trevelle's voice. He wondered if his friend was on medication, seeing the dreamy, zoned-out, faraway look in his bloodshot eyes. "Listen, if this isn't a good time . . ."

"Forget it. It's fine. Besides, I need to take my mind off things."

Reznick felt awkward. He cursed himself for not reaching out to Trevelle before he'd made the journey down. Maybe it was too early for him to be entrusted with such a responsibility. Maybe it all still felt too raw. Amy's death had been a catastrophic event, and it was likely still weighing on Trevelle's mind.

Reznick wondered if he had been too impulsive, only thinking of the mission and not considering Trevelle might be in a fragile emotional state. He pushed those doubts to one side as he followed Trevelle up the stairs and inside the pink home. He looked around the stunning interior. Whitewashed walls, huge modern artworks.

Light flooded through the floor-to-ceiling windows, which overlooked the turquoise waters of the Gulf.

"Are you kidding me, Trevelle?" Reznick said. "What an amazing place. I'm blown away by this."

"It's custom. It's quiet. It's set on pilings so it's built to withstand just about anything—flooding, wind, storms, whatever the Florida weather can throw at it. And I can work undisturbed." He turned and grinned at Reznick. "Usually."

Reznick put up his hands in mock surrender. "Well, apart from me turning up unannounced and shattering your peace and quiet."

Trevelle chuckled. "I was going to say, apart from hurricane season . . . and Jon Reznick."

Reznick's gaze wandered round the ultramodern interior, which was like something from *Architectural Digest*. High ceilings provided a feeling of infinite space, and light bathed the whole house. "This is quite something."

"It's great, isn't it? It was designed by an architect, a friend of a friend, who owned the home. Super high specifications. So much so that it was one of the few houses to escape the worst of last year's hurricane."

Reznick patted Trevelle on the back. "You've done well, man."

"The thing is, the house even managed to withstand the storm surge, with the way it's designed—so no foundations underground. It was only palms being blown over that shut an access road to this property. Unfortunately, all the nearby houses were wiped out. People lost everything."

"Is that right?" Reznick said.

Trevelle showed him into the open-plan kitchen—black granite worktops, German appliances. "Can I get you a drink? I make a mean Mojito."

"It's five o'clock somewhere, right?"

Trevelle grinned and began to carefully make the drinks. He handed a Mojito to Reznick and raised his own glass. "To friendship," he said.

"To friendship." Reznick took a gulp of the cocktail. He felt the liquor hit hard. "That is one strong drink, my friend."

"It's Florida measures. Listen, how about we go out and sit by the ocean and shoot the breeze. We can catch up."

"I'd like that."

Reznick followed Trevelle through the large French doors and out onto an elevated wooden deck. Reznick was about to take a seat when Trevelle beckoned him farther down, to a deck at beach level, directly by the ocean. The balmy island air, infused with salt and mangroves, wafted around them.

"I could get used to this. Someone must be making big bucks to afford this house."

Trevelle slumped down into a wicker armchair. "I've got the Department of Defense and the NSA to thank for some pretty nice contracts."

"God bless excessive government spending."

Trevelle stared out over the waters. "I've been lucky in my work life. But . . ." His voice trailed off and he paused. "I haven't really been working these last few months. It's been difficult."

"I understand." Reznick sat down beside his friend. He leaned over and patted him on the shoulder. "I'm sorry, man. I mean, about what happened."

"I'm not over her. Maybe I never will be."

Reznick knew all about loss and the sort of pain that Trevelle was enduring. It was impossible to appreciate unless you'd been through it. But what made Trevelle's loss doubly shocking was that his girlfriend had been murdered by operatives working for the Chinese government on American soil. A place where she should have been safe.

Trevelle forced a smile. "It's still not getting any easier. I guess it's finding ways of coping. A way of navigating my path through it, day by day, week by week."

"I shouldn't have come."

Trevelle shook his head. "Don't beat yourself up."

"I thought you might be able to help. I should have called first."

"So what's this all about?"

"Listen, I think I misjudged this. I realize I've been too quick reaching out to you. Way too quick. Maybe I wasn't thinking straight."

"Jon, what are you talking about?"

"It doesn't matter."

"Jon, I'm hurting still, but what do you need? You've helped me out big-time in the past. What do you need? Tell me. Talk to me."

Reznick shook his head. "I forgot about your loss. Amy, I mean . . . That doesn't sound good, does it?"

Trevelle took a sip of his Mojito, shielding his face from the sun. "Maybe I need to get back to doing what I do. Work is a good distraction."

Reznick knew better than anyone that it took time to grieve. Not days, not weeks, not even months. But years. It was true that time healed. But slowly. The lingering, gnawing emptiness never faded completely. It would always be there.

It was clear being face-to-face with Trevelle that he was still feeling his loss intensely. The exuberant, live-wire hacker genius had been subdued. It was like his friend was a different person. But he needed the old Trevelle. The guy who came up with solutions. Who was on his A game all the time.

"Tell me exactly what you want me to do," Trevelle insisted, "and I'll see if I can help you. And I don't want to hear any more about Amy. I'll work through my loss, no matter what."

Reznick put down his drink. "Very well. I want your help. Your expertise. But the problem is, I'm seriously up against the clock."

"Time frame?"

"One week to complete a top security assignment overseas. And the first person I thought of was you."

"One week? And that's supposed to give you enough time to get intel, head overseas, and complete the mission?"

"It is what it is."

"That's not possible."

"I agree. But I said I'd do it. National security."

"So you need my help for the next week?"

"I need you around the clock, all the time. If that will be a problem, you need to let me know now."

Trevelle finished his drink, putting his glass on a wooden table. "Listen to me. You know what I can do. I'm very good at what I do. And if I can help you in any way, I want to help you. Coffee and amphetamines are my standby."

Reznick grimaced and shook his head.

"What's this about exactly?" Trevelle asked.

"Before I tell you, you need to know the rules. My rules."

"I know the rules, Jon. Classified. Top secret. Need-to-know. I don't share anything with anyone. My clearance is still at the highest level, despite me not officially working for the government anymore. So, are you going to tell me what you want?"

"I want you to be my eyes and ears. I need you to gain access to real-time satellite imaging. I need you to track down a target. I need you to gain access to systems around the world. I want it all. And I want it yesterday."

Trevelle nodded. "Interesting."

"I need a fix on someone."

"Why?"

"I need to track down and neutralize a guy. An American."

"Abroad?"

Reznick sighed. "No idea where. What I do know is that the guy has gone rogue. A spy, selling classified intel on American operatives throughout the world and the technologies we use. It's as bad as it sounds."

Trevelle was quiet.

"Listen, if you haven't got the stomach to get back into it, I understand. Believe me."

"I told you . . . I'm in. What else is there? You got a name?"

"William Crenshaw. He's a former head of counterintelligence at the CIA."

"Are you fucking with me, Jon?"

"No, I'm not."

"And this Crenshaw dude, where is he?"

"Like I said, I don't know. That's where you come in. You need to find him."

"Hang on a minute. Are you saying the NSA haven't been able to locate him?"

Reznick shrugged. "The CIA mentioned the Middle East. He's on the move. Constantly on the move. Has interests in Africa, the Gulf States, and most notably Russia. I need you to pinpoint his location. And fast."

"Might be easier said than done."

"Whatever it takes. And you need to work alone. You can't reach out to anyone else on this. That's part of the operational security."

"I hear you. If I had to say where in the world he might theoretically be, where do you think I should start?"

"He might be in the Middle East . . . they believe he has property interests in Saudi Arabia."

"Why don't we just send in SEAL Team 6 and kill him? Predator drones?"

Reznick sipped some more of the impossibly strong Mojito. "I asked the same thing. Apparently, there was already some fucked-up mission along those lines. I was told the political sensitivities in the Middle East geopolitical world are at play. So that option, the most obvious option, is off the table."

"So is this an off-the-books assignment?"

"Completely. If this goes south, we're on our own. The American government will deny all knowledge."

"That's nice of them."

"Plausible deniability. It's the name of the game. If you've got a problem with that, maybe this isn't the job for you."

"Fuck that, I'm in. All the way in. Here's the thing though, Jon, I'm going to be up-front. If this dude used to be in counterintelligence, he's going to know all about dropping off the grid. He's not going to be easy to find."

"That's where you come in."

Trevelle pinched the bridge of his nose. "Holy fuck, it's like a needle in a haystack."

"Pretty much."

"What else do I need to know?"

"The main thing is to get eyes on this guy."

"And then?"

"I need to isolate him, get his GPS coordinates. But I'm also going to need you to step outside your comfort zone."

"In what way?"

"Logistics. Setting up, procuring, and delivering equipment overseas at short notice. Weapons, guns, ammo."

"I know people. What if they ask the reason?"

"It's a training exercise. Military contractor client of yours. NATO. Leave it at that. If they want to know more, find someone else. Got it?"

"Got it. And your job is to neutralize him?"

"That's the plan. Let me ask you something. Your computer work, that stuff, it's all here?"

"It is."

"How secure is this?"

"Rock-solid. There's a specially constructed room. Huge space. Biometric access. Voice analysis, fingerprints, only I can get in. Fireproof, even hurricane-proof."

"Are you sure?"

"It's secure."

"What about storing intel? What about off-site cloud storage?"

"There's no third-party access. I use in-house servers. I have physical control. Critical data can't be accessed."

"That's interesting. So there's no way for an outsider to access the encrypted data which is stored here?"

"Correct. The servers I used to use for sensitive government data operations were held in secure military-grade cloud data locations around the world. I made the decision in the last few months to install state-of-the-art data and server racks here. Shipped it all in."

"All eggs in one basket?"

"No chance of getting hacked," Trevelle said with pride.

"But it does make this data vulnerable if you have a power outage."

Trevelle nodded and cocked his head. "Let me show you the setup."

Reznick followed Trevelle back into the house and up a couple of flights of stairs to an attic level. "It's like James Bond in here."

Trevelle laughed as he headed down an LED-lit corridor, the AC purring gently. He pressed his face against a biometric scanner beside a steel door. Then his thumb. Then he pushed the door open. "Fingerprint and facial scan required before it opens."

Reznick looked around. Walls of floor-to-ceiling racks of servers, lights flickering as information was relayed, containing untold secure data.

"Emergency power generator kicks in during storms. Power for thirty days if need be. Doors locked and vacuum-sealed to prevent water corrosion."

"And what about the wiring?"

"It's linked from this server room, through the floor and walls, to the room behind this. Where I operate."

Reznick stared at the thick wooden door.

"It's my high-tech playroom. You want to have a look?"

"Why not?"

Trevelle looked up at a camera on the door. "*This is Trevelle Williams, please open the door to my playroom.*"

The voice recognition microphone opened up the door.

"I change the password once a week."

Reznick's gaze bounced around the beating heart of Trevelle's operation. A bank of jumbo-sized monitors, a leather operator chair, real-time satellite tracking systems showing desert regions, screens displaying news feeds from Europe and Africa. "This is fun. Very cozy."

"This is where the magic happens. So, if you use me, no one will know what I'm doing. There will be no digital fingerprint of how I access backdoor systems in the cloud. Any data I download is stored here. Any questions?"

"I'm going to need encrypted cell phones."

Trevelle opened a drawer and pulled out two phones. "I always like to be prepared. We can charge them here and then you're good to go."

"One more thing."

"What's that?"

"I also need you to find a friend of mine. A guy I want to help me on this assignment."

"Who?"

"Ex-SAS. Mac. David McCafferty. UK citizen."

"The Scottish guy?"

"That's the one. Last I heard he was based in a little hamlet called Cala San Vicente in Mallorca. Scuba instructor. But I lost touch with him."

"So technically he could be anywhere too."

"I think he'll be in the Mediterranean."

"That's a big fucking place, Jon."

"I know. That's your job. Find him. And quick."

Six

After Reznick dropped off the rental car at the airport, he headed straight for the main terminal. One of the new encrypted cell phones Trevelle had given him rang for the first time.

"Hey Jon," he said. "Glad to see your new phone works. It was also nice seeing you again."

"Appreciate you being on board."

"I have something for you."

"Already?"

"This is what I do. You wanted a fix on Mac, right?"

"Sure."

"David McCafferty is on the Greek island of Crete. He changed his cell phone six months back."

"You got any idea what he's doing there? Who he's working for?"

"Scuba instructor, apparently . . ."

"That sounds like Mac." Reznick wondered the best way to get there. "While I've got you, you know any direct flights to Crete?"

"Get yourself to JFK. Delta goes direct to Athens. Then catch a flight to Heraklion, Crete."

"Thanks, Trevelle."

"Stay safe."

After landing in New York, Reznick headed to Terminal 4 and managed to catch a direct Delta flight to Athens. The flight was interminable. He napped and received four texts from Trevelle as his hacker pal attempted to get a GPS fix on the "Old Man," the code they were using for William Crenshaw. The flight dragged on for nine and a half grueling hours.

When he finally got to the modern terminal in Athens, he felt stiff, having sat in one place for so long. His cell phone rang almost immediately.

"Jon?" Trevelle said. "You in Greece?"

"Yup. Any luck so far?"

"I'm still working on it. I need a bit more time."

"We don't have time. You need to track down this mother-fucker. You need to get me something."

"I'm on it. Anyway, I just wanted you to know that I got an exact fix in real time for Mac."

Reznick checked the departure board and saw an Aegean Airlines direct flight to Heraklion. "Make it quick."

"He's in a bar in the port of Agios Nikolaos."

"Figures. It's definitely Mac?"

"Affirmative. I checked the bar's surveillance footage. It's him alright. He's a fearsome-looking dude."

"Is he alone?"

"He's alone."

"Good work. Let's hope he's still there when I arrive. But in the meantime, you need to find the old man. That's imperative."

"I'm on it."

"I'll be back in touch."

Reznick bought a ticket for the flight. Mercifully, at fifty minutes it was a relatively short one. The skies were cobalt blue as the plane descended, over the Sea of Crete, and landed in Heraklion on the north coast of the island. When the plane touched down mid-afternoon, Reznick was the first to disembark. He headed into the stifling terminal through security, flashing his fake American passport. A few quizzical looks from security and passport control, but no resistance. As he left the terminal for the taxi rank, the heat hit him full on like a hairdryer. It was an hour-long journey along a winding, coastal road, past whitewashed villages and towns overlooking the deep blue sea. Eventually, the cab arrived in the center of the town of Agios Nikolaos. He paid the driver one hundred euros.

Reznick got out of the cab, the wall of heat hitting him again. It was like a furnace. It was high summer in Crete—peak vacation time for many visitors from northern Europe. He turned and shielded his eyes from the blinding sun. As if on cue, his cell phone rang. "You need to head to Giannis's Bar. It's not far."

"Copy that."

Reznick checked his maps app on his phone. He walked round the corner, searching for shade, sweat plastering his T-shirt to his skin. He headed down the bustling street, past tourists eating burgers, jewelry shops, men smoking as they drank coffees on the sidewalk, fancy seafood restaurants, cafés, little grocery stores, a couple of Greek banks, and a handful of tucked-away bars.

He looked about a hundred feet ahead. Sitting alone at an outside table, shaven-headed, neck burnt red as if he had been out in the blistering sun, was the fearsome-looking Mac, glowering and staring off into the distance as if lost in his thoughts.

The Scot was nursing a bottle of beer.

Reznick walked over and sat down opposite him. "Well, what do you know . . ."

Mac stared at him hard. "Fucking hell . . . Jon?"

Reznick grinned. "How you doing, man?"

"Holy Christ!" Mac got up and they hugged like old friends. "Reznick. What the fuck? You're the last person I thought I'd bump into here."

Reznick signaled to a waiter and ordered a couple of cold bottles of Fix Hellas, a Greek lager.

Mac slumped back down in his seat, shaking his head. "What are you doing here? You on holiday? You retired?"

"Not quite. I'm out here on business."

The waiter returned with the beers; Reznick handed him a twenty-euro bill. "Thank you, sir."

Mac picked up his beer and took a couple of large gulps, surveying the people walking past with a menacing stare. He waited until no one was within earshot. "What kind of business?"

"That's what I wanted to talk to you about. Maybe you could help me."

Mac stared at him with cold blue eyes. "I'm listening."

"I'm looking for a certain individual. Someone with your skill set."

Mac shrugged. "I've not been active for three years."

"You look pretty lean and mean to me."

"Are you hitting on me?"

Reznick laughed.

"I look after myself. Apart from quenching my thirst from time to time."

"It's allowed, right?" Reznick watched the pedestrians walking past. "Is there somewhere we can talk in private?"

"Inside the bar. There's no one inside apart from the bartender. He's deaf and dumb."

"Seriously?"

Mac nodded. "So I heard."

"Can he lip-read?"

"I fucking hope not."

56

Reznick picked up his beer and backpack. They picked a table tucked around the corner, in a private, screened-off area set apart from the main bar. "This OK?"

Mac pulled up a chair. "Perfect. So, what's on your mind?"

Reznick leaned closer, watching the bartender cleaning glasses. "I've got a proposition. I want you to join me."

"Join you doing what?"

"It's a take-it-or-leave-it job. I need to know by the end of today if you're in."

"Sounds urgent."

"*Time critical* would be more accurate."

"Why me?"

"Good question. The job entails a certain type of person. I know what you can do. You've worked in difficult places."

Mac gulped some beer, leaning forward. "Why me?"

"You've worked extensively with Delta, Seals, Marines. NATO stuff, sometimes black ops with military contractors in the Middle East. You know the drill."

Mac sipped his beer. "How many on your team?"

Reznick winced. "This is where it gets complicated."

"Spit it out."

"The fact is, Mac, it's barely a team."

"*Barely a team?*" Mac parroted. "What's that mean, exactly?"

"It means it's me and one other. Hopefully that one other will be you. And we also have a cyber expert and logistics support guy."

Mac laughed. "Are you fucking out of your mind? Three fucking people? Are you serious?"

"Deadly."

"I don't know . . . that sounds like a suicide mission if you're going after a high-value target . . . I'm assuming it's a high-value target."

Reznick nodded.

"Who would I be working for?"

"Me. You'd report to me."

"Small chain of command. And who are you working for?"

Reznick sat in silence.

"The Agency?"

"Would that be a problem?"

"I've worked alongside you guys before. I know how you roll. But why not pick one of your fellow countrymen?"

"That wasn't an option."

"Why not?"

"It's complicated . . ."

"Plausible deniability?"

"Pretty much."

"So we'd be on our own if the thing went to shit? A Brit and an American, our balls hanging in the wind."

"You got it. This is not on the books. We've both got extensive military experience, but if we wind up dead, then this has nothing to do with the American government. Just a couple desperadoes, mercenaries, out to make a quick buck."

"Well, that's just fucking great."

"It is what it is. Like I said, it's a take-it-or-leave-it job."

Mac rubbed his face as if weighing up Reznick's offer. "You remember what happened back in Mallorca? The guy you were after, he killed my sister Catherine."

Reznick recalled what had happened very well. He still felt a twinge of regret that the operation—which had centered on targeting a rogue American special forces medic, Adam Ford—had backfired, resulted in Ford killing Mac's sister.

"That took me a while to get over. Actually, you never truly get over something like that, right?"

"Mac, Catherine's death was the fault of that maniac I was after."

58

"I know it was, you don't have to tell me."

"If you blame me in some way for her death, I wouldn't hold it against you. You've got a right to be angry with me."

Mac shook his head. "I'm not angry with you, Jon. And I certainly don't hold it against you. I know for a fact you tried to save her. But hey, life's full of regrets. She was the smart one. Top lawyer. Me? I was the violent fuckup in the family."

Reznick sipped his beer as the bartender looked over toward them. "I'm sorry . . . about what happened to Catherine. But if you can't help me, I need to know. No hard feelings. And I'll move on."

"Not so quick. Let's get back to this mission. I need to know what it's all about."

"What do you need to know?"

"I was always told to have a plan B. I take it you have a person who could take my place?"

"There is no other person on my list. I want you. You're my first and only call."

Mac looked up at the ceiling and shook his head.

"Listen, I want you with me," Reznick said. "But if this isn't something you can commit to, and who can blame you—this is a beautiful part of the world—then I need to get on with my mission."

"Give me more detail."

"It's a high-risk operation. High-reward. High-value target."

"Well, now we're getting somewhere."

"How much does your scuba instruction pay?"

"Peanuts. You got a better offer?"

"A lot better. How does three million dollars sound? Maybe a week's work."

Mac gulped some more beer. "That's a lot of fucking money. I'm assuming that I might not be coming back."

Reznick stared at Mac. It was an astute observation. "I think that's a fair assumption. Me, you, we'll be the tip of the spear. Helping us from the States is the tech guy."

Mac leaned in close, eyes hooded. "I need to know more. A lot more. What you're giving me is a broad brushstroke."

"I can't give you a lot more at this stage. This is just a preliminary inquiry."

"How many are we to neutralize?"

"One man."

"But there might be more of his guys around, right?"

Reznick smiled. "You've done this shit before, haven't you?"

Mac nodded.

"There will be protection around this guy, sure."

"Who's providing the protection?"

Reznick took a gulp of cold beer. "This is where it gets interesting."

Mac stared back at Reznick. "Tell me."

"You really want to know?"

"Try me."

"Wagner crew"

Mac shook his head. "Fucking hell, Jon. Seriously?"

"Oh yeah."

"I've run into those guys. They're animals."

"They also know what they're doing. And they're backed by the intelligence of a nation state. We've got our hands full."

"Break it down for me, money-wise."

"Equal shares. Three million each. And we have a million to play with. Expenses, weapons, costs, logistics, that kind of shit."

"Where is this guy?"

"That's what we're trying to find out."

Mac shifted in his seat, beer bottle in hand, and grimaced. "Hang on, you don't know?"

"It's all up in the air."

"Fuck off. You can't be serious."

Reznick sat in silence.

"You're kidding me. You don't even know where this guy is?"

Reznick shook his head. "We're working on it."

"Well, that's just great."

"Like I said, this isn't gonna be a walk in the park. Everything about this job is tough. Locating him is going to be tough."

"Sounds like a challenge."

"Not insurmountable."

"Tell me more about the target."

"He's smart. High IQ. Resourceful. He knows a lot of government secrets. American as well as European. Highly, highly classified. And he's been sharing them with the enemy."

"Anyone in particular he's been sharing with?"

"Usual suspects. Iran, Russia, China, African countries, Middle Eastern states. And that's just the beginning. Bottom line? This guy has cost the lives of American operatives as well as British. And soon, very soon, he's going to be disappearing forever."

"And we won't be able to lay a glove on him then, is that what you're saying?"

"That's exactly what I'm saying. At this moment, we believe, he's out in the open somewhere with his Wagner thugs protecting him. There's a window of opportunity. But for how long, we really don't know."

"Do you have any timescale?"

"I've been given a week to pinpoint and neutralize."

Mac grinned. "That's batshit crazy. You do know that, don't you?"

"What do you think?"

"We don't know the first thing about where this guy is in the world and we've got to find him and kill him in a week?"

"That's the deal."

"This guy is American, isn't he?"

"Born and bred. He's been working with the Russians since he retired. Maybe before. He has in his possession, we believe, highly classified intel on operations the West is running, networks of spies in foreign countries. And that's why he must be eliminated."

Mac was quiet for a few moments.

"What are you thinking?"

"I'm thinking about my son. I want to be around when he grows up."

"Like I said, this isn't for the faint-hearted. I can't sugarcoat it. This is going to be high-risk."

"What if I'm taken out during this operation? I need to know that my son will be taken care of financially."

"My tech guy has been instructed that your fee be sent to your loved ones if you don't make it back. Where does he live?"

"In Glasgow, with my ex-wife."

"What's his name?"

"James McCafferty. Bit of a tearaway. But he's a good kid at heart. And I want my ex to have whatever she needs."

"That's not a problem. We can arrange that."

Mac downed the rest of his beer. "I was never around when he was growing up. It's only now that I regret that."

"He'll be taken care of, I give you my word."

"Just me and you and the tech guy?"

"You in?"

Mac's craggy features cracked into a smile. "Damn right I'm in."

Reznick reclined in his seat and sipped his beer. "I knew you would be."

"Any rules before we head off?"

"First, we can't travel together. That would be a red flag. But once we're on the ground, we can formulate or finalize any plans. We'll be flying by the seat of our pants. Hour to hour, day to day."

"This is going to be a crazy ride, Jon."

"Let's get to it."

Seven

Fran Petersen was already running late for her meeting as she gathered up her papers. It was not unusual for her to be juggling numerous projects along with back-to-back meetings and briefings. But this was no ordinary meeting. It was a briefing in the seventh-floor office of CIA Director Jorge Mendez—an update on her "special project."

She knocked on his door and walked in.

Mendez didn't look up. He sat behind his desk, reading a summary of the daily briefing he was about to give to the President. He looked exhausted, dark shadows around his eyes. Large screens on the wall showed real-time developments around the world. Ukraine, Gaza, and Chad had special placement in his eyeline; other geopolitical hotspots were on less optimally placed monitors. He was only a few months into the job and rarely left his office. Some people questioned if he ever went home. But Mendez reveled in the daily challenges and critical importance of the Agency's work.

He looked up from his papers and sat back in his chair. "Sorry about that. Still coming to terms with every facet of the job."

"Tell me about it."

"Fran, I'm hoping you've got good news for me." He indicated for her to sit down. "Please."

"Rough day?"

"Isn't anyone civil anymore?"

"This is the Agency, sir, with all due respect. People get very agitated when it comes to national security."

"Point taken. So, where are we with your special project?"

Petersen pulled up a seat opposite and sat down. "It's finally underway. I got a message from Reznick that his two guys are on this."

"I thought they might be in position, ready to neutralize the fucker."

"These things take time."

"We're out of time."

"Not quite."

Mendez rubbed his eyes, looking as if he had the weight of the world on his shoulders. "I have to say, Fran, this worries the hell out of me. Legally, ethically, politically, it's not good."

"This is the route we've chosen, Jorge. We've gone through our usual special activities scenarios, and you indicated we couldn't fuck up again. Hence, this skeleton crew and this unorthodox method. There were no good choices."

Mendez stared at her. "Starting to get a bad feeling about this, and it hasn't even started yet."

"We need to see this through. This is asymmetric warfare, unconventional. Turning our usual special forces role into a more low-level track-and-kill operation."

"Let's get down to the nitty-gritty. What are the actual chances of this succeeding? I mean really."

"It depends on what you define as success."

"Oh, for God's sake. Can no one give me a straightforward answer in this place?"

"It's complicated. My analysts say, as it stands, from the outset, it's fifty-fifty at best. Only two think it has more than a fifty-fifty chance of success."

"What about you, Fran?"

"What about me?" She shifted in her seat.

Mendez jumped through the hoop of asking her the question outright. "What do you think our chances are?"

"Very difficult to put a figure on it. I trust Reznick. He's operated on his own or at least predominantly on his own, with only tech support, for years. He's the go-to guy for any black ops. I like what I've heard. He's been over the course before, numerous times."

"What are we calling this?"

"*Leviathan.*"

"Who comes up with these stupid code names?"

"Some guy deep in the Pentagon."

"Figures."

"I've formally requested the establishment of an unacknowledged special access program with the Pentagon. This is a high-risk strategy and there could be blowback if the shit hits the fan. So, we need to keep the CIA and the US government safe from any fallout."

"Who's the guy Reznick's taking with him?"

"McCafferty."

"One of ours?"

"No, Scottish. Ex-SAS. Tremendous operator. Behind enemy lines in Iraq, Afghanistan, Syria. He's been all over. Tough as nails."

"I'm guessing MI6 might want to know about this?"

"They already do. I've liaised with London. They appreciated the heads-up."

Mendez nodded and stared at Petersen. "I'm only three months into this job. I'm still finding my feet. I feel uneasy about this extra-judicial killing shit."

"You better get used to it. Things get messy."

"My background is Harvard law. Government. Ethics. Morality. Accountability."

66

"This is a different ball game, sir, with all due respect."

"Shit." Mendez rubbed his face.

"Welcome to the CIA."

Mendez glanced briefly at the screen showing Al Jazeera footage from Gaza. "How can I justify these two trained killers being let loose, possibly in the Middle East? It's a tinderbox as it is. How can we justify it?"

"You don't justify it, that's the point. We don't know anything about it. They're on their own."

Mendez reached over and picked up a file from his desk. He took a few moments to leaf through the contents. "I had a look at this earlier. Jon Reznick. Ex-Delta, CIA, worked for the FBI on highly classified operations. He was the guy that upended the bioterrorism plot against the Pentagon orchestrated by the Pakistani intelligence services."

Fran nodded.

"I remember reading about that. But I didn't know he was involved in preventing that."

"He was there alright. In the thick of it. He was on a DC Metro train as he fought to track down and kill the leaders of the operation."

"Reznick took them down?"

"He took down the whole thing. He'd hooked up with the FBI. It was a complicated operation."

"That's interesting." Mendez leafed through a couple more pages of Reznick's file. "So he's a trained assassin who has neutralized countless jihadists and funders of terrorism."

"It's a stellar résumé."

"But now he's being tasked with killing an American."

"Sorry to be pedantic, sir, but William Crenshaw is a traitor."

Mendez nodded. "Yes, he is. And he must be stopped at any cost."

"Indeed he must."

"This file on Reznick . . . notes from the CIA Inspector General, concluded that Reznick has never failed. Not once. Cold as ice."

"That's why we're using him. I believe, against all the odds, he can pull this off."

"And if he doesn't?"

"Not a trace of US government involvement. Just a wacko ex-American special forces guy and his British pal, working as military contractors in the Middle East, or Africa, who got in above their heads. That's how we'd frame it if asked."

"These guys are expendable, aren't they?"

"They know how this works. These are big-boy rules. They're on their own."

Eight

The Greek taxi driver sped along the coastal road toward Heraklion Airport at breakneck speed. Reznick was sitting in the back seat, buckled up tight, concerned that they weren't going to complete the journey. His cell phone pinged. A text message from Trevelle. *The old man has left Libya, believed to be en route to Hurghada, Egypt. More to follow.*

Reznick called Mac. "We're on the move."

"Where?"

"The old man is en route to Hurghada. I'm going to catch a direct flight."

Mac cleared his throat. "I've just packed my bag. I know there are flights to Sicily. So, to keep us separate to start with, I'll head there. And then head down."

"Excellent. You good for this?"

"Oh yeah. Right in the fucking mood."

Reznick smiled. "Nice to have you on board, Mac. See you in Egypt."

"I'll be there before you. You'll see."

It wasn't until the following morning that Reznick's delayed plane finally touched down in Hurghada. He picked up a tactical backpack at a luggage locker outside the airport. Then he caught a cab to a traditional Egyptian restaurant in the old town where they had arranged to meet up. When he arrived, Mac was already eating goat curry and drinking a beer. He signaled Reznick over.

"How the hell did you get here first?"

Mac laughed. "Didn't I tell you I'd arrive before you?"

"Yeah . . . But how?"

"I got lucky with connecting flights. Why are you so late?"

"Technical problem with the plane. Delayed for hours."

"Nightmare."

Reznick's scrutinized the flaking paint on the walls; the insects buzzing the lights. "This is off the beaten track."

Mac leaned in close. "Not quite a Michelin-starred restaurant. But it's part of the attraction."

The young toothless waiter bowed. "Heineken?"

Reznick nodded. "Make it two. Cold."

The kid went to a nearby fridge, took out a couple of beers, opened the tops, and placed the bottles carefully on the rickety table.

Reznick handed him a twenty-dollar bill. The kid held the note in his hands and trembled. It was like Reznick had given him a million dollars. "Thank you, mister, sir. Very kind."

Mac shook his head. "Poor bastards."

Reznick swigged his beer. "So, the latest intel. He headed here. We just need to get an exact fix on his location."

Mac wolfed a mouthful of an unappetizing-looking goat curry. "It's a big place, Hurghada. He could be arriving and climb on a yacht. You thought about that?"

"I am now."

"You should try this."

Reznick looked at the unappetizing meal. "I think I'll pass."

"Listen, Jon, he could be anywhere in the city."

"I get that."

"So the kid doing the hacking shit, he's got our back? I'm assuming he has."

"If anyone can find the old man, it's him. His name's Trevelle. Ex-NSA. Amazing skill set. And absolutely, he has our back."

"Let's hope the kid narrows down this search or it'll be like a needle in a fucking haystack."

Reznick spotted a tactical backpack lodged at Mac's feet. "I see you got your delivery."

"DHL package, delivered to my hotel."

"Courtesy of Trevelle. I got the same."

Reznick's phone rang. "That's him." He answered the call.

"Jon?" Trevelle checked in.

"What's happening, man? I was about to call you."

"The target has touched down in Cairo."

Reznick closed his eyes. "He what?"

"Cairo."

"Cairo? What the fuck? I thought you said Hurghada."

"I did. But he changed his plans."

"Well that's just great. We're hundreds of miles away. That's bullshit, Trevelle!"

"I know."

"So he's in Cairo? You know that for sure?"

"Definitely."

"Where in Cairo?"

"City of the Dead."

"What the hell is that?"

"There's a market there. Packed with hawkers. People selling animals, food, fish, whatever you want."

"Why's he headed there?"

"I assume this is business. That's all I know."

"When did he land?"

"Three minutes ago."

"Trevelle, this is fucking bullshit. Not good enough."

"I don't know what happened."

Reznick ended the call, almost shaking with anger. He looked across at Mac. "The old man is in Cairo!"

Mac dabbed his mouth with a napkin and finished his beer as he got to his feet. "Well, that's just great."

"Intel he had was bad. It might have been disinformation."

"Jon, it's bullshit. Either your guy isn't as good as you say, or the old man suspects someone is on his tail and he's feeding bad intel to whoever is eating. Either way, we're getting played."

"Listen, let's head up to Cairo. We need to get this back on track before the old man leaves the country."

Nine

Trevelle slumped down in his seat, heart pounding. He stretched his arms, desperate to untie the knots in his shoulders from being hunched over his computer screens for so long. He squeezed a stress ball, still shocked that he had fed Reznick and Mac wrong information. He had messed up. He owned this setback.

He needed to find out what had happened before he could move forward. The flight log of Crenshaw's plane had clearly showed that it was en route to Hurghada.

So what had changed? Was it a deliberate attempt to mislead by uploading a fake flight plan? That made sense. It was simple. It was smart. But then again, maybe Crenshaw had just changed his plans at the last minute while they were in the air.

However, that would mean that Crenshaw was operating on a whim. Trevelle knew from the intel they had so far that their target was a thoughtful man. He didn't make rash decisions. Trevelle had to assume they'd been purposefully duped.

He was angry with himself. He was responsible for providing impeccable intel to Reznick, the way he had in all the previous assignments they had worked together on. This was the first time he had gotten it so wrong, and it stung.

He felt overwhelmed by waves of tiredness. He stifled a yawn as he realized he hadn't slept since Reznick had turned up at his house. Not even an hour's sleep. He self-diagnosed that his sleep deprivation was affecting his sharpness.

The more he thought about how he had been deceived by Crenshaw or his men, the more agitated he felt. He carried the weight of an enormous responsibility on his shoulders.

He reached over to the top drawer of his desk and took out a bottle of Adderall. The medication had been prescribed by his doctor for his ADHD. The drug was supposed to work by allowing him to focus better and not be so distracted. It made him more awake and more calm.

Trevelle had been using the drug non-stop for the last three years. Only his doctor knew he was using it. But it had slowly but surely turned into a low-grade addiction. Taking the drug was a ritual he adhered to morning, noon, and night.

Trevelle was plagued by a cacophony of voices in his head, all whispering doubts. The drug usually organized the frenzy of ideas ricocheting around his head. He began a few deep breathing exercises he used when he was stressed out. A way to center himself. After a few minutes, he felt calmer. He wanted to do his best for Jon.

He shut his brain down for a few moments as he waited for the prescription amphetamine to kick in. In his mind, he saw Amy again, smiling. He always remembered her smiling. He had felt good when she was around. Without her, he was hanging by a thread, and the distraction of his work was all that was keeping him going. Sometimes, he asked the mirror if this was what insanity felt like. Forces outside his control closing in. He had no one to turn to. No one to talk to.

He wished Reznick was the sort of person he could open up to. But he wasn't. Not by a long shot. Reznick was a closed book. He didn't emote or share his feelings. But Reznick knew all about loss. He had lost comrades on the battlefields of Iraq, fellow Delta operators in the white heat of battle. Reznick had lost himself in his work, burying himself in special ops and overseas postings. Year after year.

He presumed this was a way for Reznick to stay sane after learning that his wife had died on 9/11. For more than two decades he had led a terrifying existence, working in the shadows. He did the dirty work to keep Americans safe. But then out of the blue, a couple of years ago, Reznick had had to cope with the shattering news that his wife had used the New York City terror attacks as a ruse to disappear for good, having been secretly recruited by the CIA to work for them in Switzerland. Trevelle doubted how anyone could deal with such devastating news.

The man he knew was formidable. Reznick killed for a living, working alone or in small groups on special forces deployments. Reznick was a man he admired. Trevelle saw the humanity in him. But he also feared him. Occasionally, very occasionally, he saw glimpses of the stone-cold killer. The icy blue eyes could be intimidating and he often felt unnerved in Jon's presence, knowing what he did about the man. But sometimes he saw Reznick in a different light. A patriot, a man of integrity and honor, a family man. He liked that side of Reznick.

More than anything, he wanted to reach out to him. To talk about how he was feeling. The anxiety he felt. The hopelessness and despair he felt, knowing Amy had been murdered. But now wasn't the time. Reznick was on a mission and he was relying on Trevelle. Which made today's setback all the more upsetting.

Trevelle got up and walked over to his coffee machine. He fixed himself a double espresso and gulped it down. A short while later, the amphetamines and caffeine were coursing through his veins.

Trevelle felt focused. He sat back down at his desk, alert, his attention glued to the huge screens in front of him. He felt like his old self, and he had work to do. He needed to use all his ingenuity and experience and guile to track Crenshaw down. He couldn't afford any more missteps.

His skill set gave him backdoor access to the 'constellation' of US surveillance satellites around the world used by the NSA and the CIA. His time at the NSA had included a specialized intensive course in space intelligence, learning from the country's foremost experts. The satellites allowed critical coverage of foreign ground forces, secret missile sites, and naval targets. He was also able to access electronic activity through these highly specialized satellites using a complex web of monitoring stations across the world. The Five Eyes in particular—the United States, Canada, New Zealand, the United Kingdom, and Australia—offered him global coverage and real-time intelligence.

Trevelle ran his software, accessed via a secure cloud server in Darwin, Australia, to get a real-time fix on Crenshaw's location. He was using cell phone location-tracking technology aligned with social media surveillance across the globe. It was a new way to gain intel. A gigantic crawl of hundreds of thousands of cloud servers and data farms from Boston to Brisbane, Minsk to Pretoria. He estimated that he could access billions of cell phones worldwide and averaged between forty and fifty location pings for every cell phone, every day. It exploited thousands of applications used or needed by cell phone users all around the world. He was essentially buying private data anonymously from countless social media companies, which they had on each anonymous cell phone user. And with his program he could extrapolate where an individual was at any moment in time.

It was early-stage technology that Trevelle was privately developing and hoped to license to the Pentagon and the CIA next year, if it worked in real-time, real-world situations.

He ran the program for a few minutes. A set of results flooded in.

Suddenly, one of the monitors flashed. Out of nowhere, he had a hit.

Trevelle stared at the geolocation on a huge main monitor, pinpointed on a map of North Africa. "OK, what have we got?" He had, within a matter of seconds, finally pinpointed all three vehicles, tracked by a satellite belonging to NASA, headed through Cairo's crowded streets. "There you are, you old bastard."

He hit a few more keys and accessed the thousands of surveillance cameras that had recently been installed in the Egyptian capital. He synchronized the satellite imagery geolocation and almost instantly, he had a second real-time fix on the cars as they sped through the congested streets.

Trevelle stared at the screen, breathing hard. He had Crenshaw in his sights. It was a breakthrough. But Reznick and Mac were still hundreds of miles away from their moving target. He called Reznick.

"What've you got?"

"I think I've got a direct fix on the moving target in Cairo."

"And that's them?"

"It's them, alright."

"How can you be so sure?"

"It's a new technology. If a member of the old man's team has a social media account, even if it's set to private, it can provide a real-time GPS location."

"That's better, Trevelle."

"Listen, I'm sorry about the detour to Hurghada. Hopefully this will get you back in the game."

"Good work, man."

Then the line went dead.

Ten

It had just gone midday. A burnt orange sun beat down on the dusty streets of downtown Cairo.

Reznick drove into the city, at the end of a grueling four-hour journey from Hurghada.

"Wake up, Mac!"

Mac roused in the back seat. "We there?"

"Cairo, yeah."

Reznick quietly dumped the car in an alley half a mile from the market. They picked up their tactical backpacks, lightweight travel backpacks stuffed inside, and headed across to the market where Crenshaw was last seen. He checked his cell phone for directions and headed in the direction of the Al-Tonssy flyover, also known as the Autostrade. It was located close to the Southern Cemetery in the Khalifa district, south of the Citadel. Barefoot children ran alongside them, tugging at their jeans for cash. Mac threw them a handful of coins and the kids fought over the pennies.

They got closer to the market, the sights and smell of rotting flesh, flies buzzing around filthy meat, chickens crammed into filthy wooden cages, and live animals hanging from hooks growing more present with each step.

Mac had a large telephoto lens. His cover, if he was stopped, was that he was a photojournalist from the UK. He took photos of random people, of old men smoking cigarettes or chewing khat, of wide-eyed children staring at them.

Reznick walked on. His cell phone buzzed. "Talk to me, Trevelle. Is he still in Cairo?"

"Correct. The latest intel shows a fix on three cars on the other side of the market."

"So he's still here at the market? Right now?"

"You're in luck. They're still there."

"What else?"

"There's bodyguards with him. Spread out. Twenty, maybe more."

"So he's here on business?"

"I don't know. I'm surprised he's still in the same location as this morning. I'm guessing he stayed somewhere close. Maybe meeting up with a contact or handler."

"Trevelle, I'm walking around here blind. I need hard intel!"

"Two hundred yards northeast, under the flyover. Right now!"

Reznick ended the call and began hurrying through the crowds. "We're going to fucking lose them."

Mac climbed up onto a wall and surveyed the scene with his camera. He and Reznick had earpieces in so they could communicate with each other—and with Trevelle—at all times. "Due north, Jon, three cars. Target is being escorted into one of them. Fuck, we're going to lose them!"

Reznick pushed through the throng as Mac jumped down from the wall and caught up with him. They barged past men on donkeys and burka-clad women. In the distance, he caught a fleeting glimpse of the three-car convoy as it edged through the crowds, turned into an alley, then disappeared from sight. "No no no. I can't see them, Mac."

Mac climbed onto another wall. "Negative. Fuck."

A kid on a motorbike, smoking a cigarette, weaved his way through the crowds toward them.

Reznick hauled him off the bike, dropping a hundred-dollar bill on the ground. "Sorry, kid!"

The kid stood and shouted at Reznick.

Reznick ignored the crowds approaching him and, getting on the bike, accelerated through the gathering throng, sending people diving for cover. "I'm going after them, Mac."

"Copy that, Jon."

Reznick turned into the dusty alley and rode hard. He squinted against the grit in his eye. He turned sharp down one street. When he emerged, all of a sudden he saw them—the three-car convoy turning into a major intersection.

The convoy headed onto the highway, speeding fast through the other traffic.

Reznick was in pursuit as he rode west through the city, weaving around cars, until he got on the Cairo–Alexandria desert road. Faster and faster, trying to keep up with the high-speed convoy. They seemed to be accelerating.

In the distance, he spotted the surreal and magnificent sight of the Pyramids of Giza.

Reznick shouted, hoping he would be heard above the traffic. "Trevelle, talk to me! Where the hell am I?"

"Got to be heading toward the airport!"

"Copy that."

Reznick rode on for a few more miles. He saw that further ahead, through the smoggy, blue sky, a plane was descending into the city.

He spotted a sign for Sphinx International Airport. He wondered if the convoy had taken another turn.

He sped alongside a chain-link fence.

Reznick caught a fleeting glimpse of the convoy before they quickly disappeared from sight as they headed through an electronic gate and into a secluded part of the airport—perhaps a VIP entrance. He pulled up beside the fence, got off the bike, and pulled a monocular from his tactical backpack. He watched the convoy pull up on the scorching asphalt beside a Cessna plane. *And there he is.*

The old man wore aviator sunglasses, a Panama hat, and was smoking a cigarette as he boarded the plane followed by two tattooed bodyguards. Reznick searched the plane for markings and glimpsed the tail number painted in bold black letters. N3782. He committed it to memory and felt himself balling his fists in frustration as the plane taxied on the runway before taking off.

Reznick called Trevelle and gave him the tail number.

"It's a Cessna."

"Copy that, Jon."

"Find out where it's going."

"Bear with me . . . OK, I'm in!"

"Already?"

"Flight plan shows it's headed to Muscat in Oman."

"Son of a bitch! Are you sure?"

"Affirmative."

"This isn't more disinformation, is it?"

"Let's hope not. But why Muscat? What's in Muscat?"

"We don't know. Yet. But we know that the old man has a lot of interests in the UAE. Right?"

"True."

Reznick shielded himself against the sun as the plane became a speck in the brilliant blue sky. "Motherfucker!"

He called Mac and relayed the news. "Oman?" Mac said.

"I want you to go to Dubai."

"Why there and not Oman?"

"I don't want us to be seen together at airports or transport hubs if at all possible. Also, remember to dump the tactical backpack before you arrive at the airport. We'll get a fresh delivery from Trevelle."

"Where you going?"

"I'll head straight to Muscat. I just think it might be useful if we hedge our bets in case there's a sudden change of plan again."

"So he's headed for Oman," Mac said. "But that's not a million miles away from—"

"Dubai. So we've got both bases covered. Any questions?"

"We need better intel, Jon. This is bullshit. We're running about like headless chickens."

"Trevelle is working hard on it, around the clock. We need to get lucky."

"We need more than luck. We need to find the bastard, Jon, that's what we really need. And then we nail him."

Eleven

William Crenshaw stood on the private beach of the Ritz-Carlton, staring out over the Gulf of Oman. He knew his bodyguards were watching from a respectful distance. It was nice to get some time to himself. The traveling, at his age, he found exhausting.

He mused on where the time had gone. The years. What had it all been for?

He felt the humidity in his chest, breathing becoming a bit difficult. He heard a wheezing, whistling sound and realized it was his own body. It was the fifty-year cigarette addiction.

Sweat stuck the back of his linen shirt to his skin. He lit up another Gauloise, coughing as he did so. The French cigarette brand had been a favorite of his since his posting, as a young CIA operative, in the febrile atmosphere of 1960s Paris. Student protests, riots, the shadow of the Algerian independence movement. A revolutionary fervor in the air.

Crenshaw's mind flashed back. It was hard to believe how fast the world had changed. He had changed too. He reflected on his idealistic younger self—the patriotic, clean-cut American. It had all been new and exciting work then. He'd been in the thick of it, at the height of the cultural revolution sweeping the West. Undercover as an American postgraduate economics student, his job had been to infiltrate the higher echelons of one of the Marxist student groups. His cover was plausible, as he already had a master's degree in economics. He was a good listener. He'd blended in.

He'd soaked up all the intel he could. He'd ingratiated himself with the wide-eyed Paris radicals; gotten to know them and their names. Their addresses. Their backgrounds. He'd drunk cheap red wine with them, smoked with them. He'd learned about their families. They were the sons and daughters of privilege. Captains of industry, journalists, bankers, socialites—his new friends were the children of the bourgeoisie. He'd poured wine down the throats of the indolent offspring of diplomats, senior civil servants, socialist politicians as they'd led their student army of protesters under the red banner of the French Communist Party. Anarchists. Useful idiots, as Lenin would have dubbed them.

Crenshaw had watched and waited. He'd fed all he learned back to the French secret service—and, of course, the CIA's station chief. He'd abhorred the French penchant for street rioting, revolution, and lawlessness. His very first experience in France was as a twenty-five-year-old rookie CIA operative during the Paris massacre of 1961. He'd watched, and taken notes, and observed everything. He'd compiled reports that were suppressed by Langley. At the time, the French police still had many officers who had been part of the Vichy collaborationist regime during the Second World War.

It was a brutal time. A different France.

He'd watched as some of the protesters, many Algerians living and working in Paris, were picked up, hands tied behind their back, and thrown into the Seine. Some had drowned, screaming for help. Others were never found. It was absolutely shocking. His gut reaction at the start had been revulsion. But over time, over years, and then decades, he had come to view those events in a different light. He'd borne witness in 1962 to police killings of the CGT trade union members—mostly working-class communists in Paris seeking shelter in the Charonne metro station. They were clubbed to death, their skulls fractured, or had suffocated. The same punishment as was meted out to civil rights protesters in the Deep South of his own country.

Crenshaw dragged heavily on his cigarette as he snapped out of his dreaming. He turned and saw Dimitri approach, cell phone pressed to his ear.

"What time?" Dimitri said to the person on the other end of the line. "We'll be there."

Crenshaw looked over at his trusty aide. "Was that your countryman?"

"Forty minutes, he will see you."

Crenshaw laughed softly. "You Russians are a strange bunch, aren't you?"

Dimitri stared at him with cold indifference. "What do you mean?"

"We think we know you. At least we convince ourselves we do. But we'll never really know you, will we?"

"We bleed like everyone else."

"I know you do. We can scratch the surface of the facade, but we'll never ever get you."

"I could say the same about your countrymen."

Crenshaw finished his cigarette. "You're probably right."

The winding alleys of the ancient souk in Muscat guided Crenshaw and his men to a backstreet café. He headed inside, and the smell of steamed chicken and smoke, heavy in the sticky air, replaced the stench of the city.

Viktor Mozorov, a senior operative within Russia's Foreign Intelligence Service, sat alone at a table. He was drinking Turkish coffee and smoking an unfiltered cigarette.

"There he is," Mozorov announced when he saw them.

Crenshaw walked over and sat down opposite the Russian.

Viktor was Crenshaw's main handler. His first and last point of contact. The senior controller. Had been from the beginning. A decade earlier, the Russian had taken the first, tentative steps to cultivate and befriend Crenshaw. Crenshaw was only a few years from retirement then with an eye to the future. Viktor was a patient man. He played the long game. It was the Russian way. He massaged Crenshaw's fragile ego. But he also knew when to tighten the screws. The trap had been set. All Viktor had to do was wait until his patience was finally rewarded.

Crenshaw had been slowly but surely reeled in. He had been cultivated after accruing massive debts. Then he'd been targeted in a classic Russian honey-trap operation. He had been compromised. They had him in their icy grip. It wasn't long before he traded intelligence worth its weight in gold.

Viktor smiled. "You're late."

"Apologies. My security detail, your fellow countrymen, were being more cautious than usual. A more circuitous route." Crenshaw tapped a cigarette out of his metal case and lit up nonchalantly. "What do you want?"

Viktor stubbed out his own cigarette, screwing up his eyes as the gray smoke filled the fetid air. "I have some news for you. That's why I was keen to speak to you face-to-face. I would like to get my hands on the intel you've been promising."

"I thought we agreed when the handover would be."

"Events have overtaken us. You're a wanted man. We think it best if you give us what you promised."

"In case I'm neutralized?"

"Precisely."

"All in good time."

"William, time is of the essence. We need to ensure the safe delivery of the intel."

"I don't have it on me."

Viktor closed his eyes for a few moments, as if disappointed by Crenshaw's answer.

"You'll get it. But as and when we agreed."

"You have talked in generalities. Give me cold facts."

"It contains a list of hard intelligence. The kind of intelligence you won't find on WikiLeaks."

"Do you want to be more specific?"

"It names every foreign operative in Eastern Europe sent from Britain, Poland, and, of course, America, operating not only across Ukraine but also a major base on the outskirts of Warsaw. It also contains NATO operatives, and the names, blood groups, and dates of birth of twenty-three CIA operatives in Georgia and Estonia. I thought you might find that quite useful with this ongoing military operation of yours."

Viktor stared at him, unsmiling. "It didn't have to be this way. But you Americans will never learn. Foreign interference in our sphere of influence never works. The CIA is still adhering to the Dulles playbook from the 1950s. It's grown tiresome."

"Russia is the least of our problems these days."

"China?"

"Indeed. Maybe the Middle East generally. Access to oil. Saudi Arabia in particular. They have, last I checked, proven reserves of more than two hundred years. The UAE, nearly three hundred years. And that's assuming no more significant finds."

Viktor smiled. "You seem to have overlooked Venezuela."

"How much do they have left?"

"Over one thousand years. Do you understand why not only us but China is keen to foster relations with the country? Russia has anything from sixty years to one hundred and fifty years. Assuming we don't make any further discoveries. Which we will."

Crenshaw dragged on his cigarette. "You do a lot of business with Venezuela?"

"They are not only an important military ally in Latin America, but one of our most significant partners in trade in the Americas. And there is the small matter of oil. That's why Venezuela has spent billions of dollars building up their defense capabilities, with our help."

"You have significant military assets based there?"

"We have interests in that country. We help them monitor comings and goings of Colombian intrusions. We advise them on how to deal with it." Viktor was quiet for a few moments. He took in everything and everyone in sight.

"You play a very, very long game."

Viktor said nothing, as if he had shared enough information with Crenshaw. "I need the intel very soon."

"As I said, you'll get it."

"Things have changed. The timetable has been brought forward."

"Let me think about that. First, I believe you have some news for me?"

"William, I speak as a friend. But you need to listen. I'm the second person that has alerted you. You need to heed the warning. I can't stress the gravity of the situation you are facing."

"I know."

"Don't be complacent, William. Pay close attention. Listen to what I have to say. We have already told you about a former CIA operative being tasked with neutralizing you, right?"

"Quite a compliment."

Viktor shook his head. "Don't be so cocky. We've done some more digging. Jon Reznick is the most dangerous of men. And we have new intel that concerns us greatly."

"What's that?"

"Reznick has company."

"Who?"

"A former SAS man. A Scot. Ultra-dangerous. You don't want to be around if they find you. Reznick has him on board. And they are looking for you."

Crenshaw rolled his eyes. "Reznick, huh? I know all about him."

"Trust me, you don't know the half of it. I'm here to tell you that he is closer than you think. He was in Cairo. He's getting close. So we need the intel you have!"

"How did he know where I was?"

"It doesn't matter. You had a close call. Only a few hours ago, he came within yards of getting to you."

"He's tailing me?"

"We understand there is assistance from an ex-NSA operative in America. You need to heed our advice or you won't be able to enjoy that retirement you've dreamed of."

"Viktor, I very much appreciate your interest in my well-being. You'll get what you're looking for."

"When?"

"When I decide."

"Don't abuse our hospitality, William."

"There's no need to be overly dramatic. The Russians have never struck me as demonstrative people."

Viktor shook his head. "I will be reporting back that you are reluctant to pass on what we were looking for. I will also be reporting back that you received a second warning about a threat to your life. We can only do so much."

"I don't like being dictated to, Viktor."

"No one is dictating anything. Only offering advice. Take it. Give us the files. Then you can disappear for good, before it's too late."

Twelve

After countless, infuriating delays, and cursing his dumb luck, Reznick sat in the back of a taxi, stuck in slow-moving traffic in Muscat, Oman. It was down to a crawl, the taxi driver speaking into his phone, babbling in Arabic, smoking up a storm. Reznick was beginning to feel cursed. He wound down the window to get a blast of humid air.

He was essentially chasing shadows in pursuit of a ghost. William Crenshaw seemed to appear and disappear like the wind. They were behind the curve, being reactive. It was a stop-start-stop operation, dogged by either poor intel or bad luck.

To compound matters, the flight from Cairo had had to return to the airport when a passenger got sick. The flight had taken off again for Muscat, but after going through security and customs, now he was running four hours behind.

The operation was beginning to feel like a bad idea destined for a bad end. He needed a dozen operatives, minimum, working around the clock. He needed full operational and logistical backup too. What he wouldn't give for a dedicated Delta sixteen-man troop with full technical backup.

The taxi driver turned on the radio. Some crazy station playing what sounded like techno.

Reznick tapped on the glass partition to get the driver's attention. "What's causing the holdup, buddy?"

The driver shrugged and lit up another cigarette. The traffic crawled for another twenty minutes before it finally got moving.

Reznick eventually checked in to the Grand Hyatt using his fake passport. He gave his fake credit card details and headed to his seventh-floor room, travel backpack slung over his shoulder. He swiped his room card and opened the door, switched on the lights, and turned the air-conditioning up to high. Before he could catch his breath, his cell phone rang.

"You're late," Trevelle said. "What the hell happened?"

"Dumb fucking luck, that's what. The flight was delayed. We had to turn back and get a woman some medical treatment. Hours later the plane eventually took off. And then, to top it all off, the cab in Muscat was caught up in traffic. Complete nightmare."

Trevelle sighed. "This isn't going well."

"Tell me something I don't know. Got any updates on Crenshaw? Tell me you have something."

"I believe he's in town."

"You believe?"

"That's what I said. Listen, I need you to do me a favor. Count out loud to ten. I need to upload software onto your phone."

Reznick did as he was told. "Trevelle, you've already told me he was in town. That's why I'm here. But where is he exactly? That's the question."

"I'm still trying to track down his current location."

"Come on, Trevelle. Seriously? I need a break here. What's going on? I thought you had him."

"I did. I don't know if they've switched their phones. I know they're using some radio jamming, so Bluetooth, Wi-Fi, GPS, all radio communications are in a dead zone. It's tricky."

Reznick took off his backpack and placed it at the bottom of the closet. "I don't want excuses. I want a location. I need to find this guy."

"First things first. Your bellhop is headed up to your floor with a fresh delivery."

A knock at the door. "Speak of the devil. Got to go."

Reznick ended the call and answered the door. The bellhop had two UPS packages. Reznick tipped the kid twenty dollars, then carefully shut and locked the door. He placed the packages on the bed, opening the first package. It contained a folding AR-15 rifle, night vision scopes, a 9mm Beretta handgun along with silencer, and ammo for both guns. He arranged the items precisely on the bed. Then he opened the second package and pulled out a tactical backpack, specifically designed for the military as it was robust and able to carry heavy loads. He deliberately placed the items from the first package into the heavy-duty backpack and zipped it up. He knew it was high-risk, walking around with weapons on his person. If he was stopped by cops or his hotel room got visited by the Oman secret police, he was fucked. He'd be disappeared, never to be seen again.

He showered, freshened up, and put on a fresh set of clothes.

His cell phone rang again. He answered it on the third ring.

"Jon, it's Mac." It was good to hear his voice.

"How are you?"

Mac groaned. "Twiddling my fucking thumbs, drinking a beer in Dubai."

"Lucky you."

"What are you doing?"

"I'm in Muscat. Still trying to get a fix on the old man. Trevelle believes he's still in the city."

"There's no precise fix? Oh, for fuck's sake, what is going on? Jon, I'm telling you, this is not how to do a job like this. It takes a team. We need logistical support to the tune of dozens of people."

"Mossad regularly operates in small teams."

"I know they do. But this is different. There's only fucking two of us, chasing our tails. We're taking commercial flights. It's bullshit. We're running here, there, and everywhere. And still fuck-all."

"Mac, listen to me. Sit tight. You knew when we took this on what it would entail."

"I want to get the bastard, Jon."

"I know you do. So do I. But let's just show patience. Restraint. We'll find him."

"And if we don't?"

"Let's have faith. I think we're getting closer. It's just a matter of time."

A few hours later, a text from Trevelle buzzed Reznick's phone.

Beach club in Muscat, down at the Marina. Ray's Beach Bar. Frequented by wealthy Arabs and American tourists. The old man on yacht!

Reznick grabbed the tactical backpack stuffed with essentials. He caught a cab waiting outside and headed directly to the marina. He tipped the driver fifty bucks. He walked through the marina wearing sunglasses and a baseball cap he had picked up at the hotel gift shop, emblazoned with *Product of Oman*, his backpack on like he was just another tourist out and about.

His earpiece buzzed. "I think I have precise GPS," Trevelle said.

"Where?"

"Just got a visual from a drone, run by a PR company. One hundred and fifty yards due northeast of you, sitting on a fucking yacht, cool as you like."

Reznick walked casually over to where the luxury yachts were moored, bobbing in the swell. He studied the fancy yachts of the ultra-wealthy. On the decks was an assortment of people. Men wearing traditional Arab garb, taking calls on the deck. Mingling with them were a scattering of Westerners. Some drinking Coke or no-alcohol spritzers. At least he assumed that's what they were drinking. A few models pouting who appeared to be hanging on the every word of the wealthy patrons. But his gaze fixed on one of the biggest yachts at the far edge of the marina. He saw what looked like a family, women and children on the deck. Then he spotted them. *The crew.*

Shaven-headed heavyset guys wearing black polo shirts and dark jeans. He counted five in total. But then he saw the guy, sitting on the deck. The target. *The old man.* William Crenshaw was languidly smoking a cigarette, sitting on a leather chair.

His earpiece buzzed again. "Face recognition is running. The drone was hired by the marina to promote an international exhibition of real estate in Oman. Pure luck. You got a fix on him, Jon?"

"Are you sure it's him?"

"I've run the footage. This is him. One hundred percent."

Reznick knew that if he took out the rifle or weapons of any sort in full view, he would be taken out before he could get a shot off. Besides, he couldn't rake the boat with gunfire with women and children on it. Fuck. He watched one of the bodyguards lean over and whisper in Crenshaw's ear.

Reznick had seen enough. A germ of an idea began to form.

He looked over at the lights of the fancy hotels and apartments around the marina, overlooking the water and luxury yachts.

Reznick turned and took one last look at the yacht. The man in white, Crenshaw, was sitting quietly, still smoking his cigarette. Reznick walked over to a nearby boutique hotel. He headed down a side street and accessed the rear of the building, pushing open an emergency door.

He made his way through the hotel kitchen, smiling as some chefs and waiters shouted at him. He took the service elevator up to the top floor, then walked down a corridor until he got to the door to the roof terrace. He pushed it open, stepped out into the stifling night, and looked around. No one there. Perfect.

He took up position at a perimeter wall overlooking the water. The marina was in full view.

He crouched down and unzipped the tactical backpack, knowing he would have to work fast. He pulled out the foldable rifle and locked it open at its full length, attached the night sights. He evaluated the people on the yacht to try to find Crenshaw.

It was four hundred and ninety-five yards to the yacht.

Then he saw him. Crenshaw had his arm around one of his bodyguards like an old pal reminiscing with a friend. Reznick checked and rechecked the man's face. He zeroed the rifle's scope. He had his target in the crosshairs.

"Trevelle, give me a visual confirmation."

"Copy that. This is the old man. I repeat, this is the old man. I'm watching too, in real time."

Reznick steadied himself as Crenshaw slowly moved around the deck. He flicked off the safety catch. Crenshaw turned and spoke to a woman wearing a tight minidress, then pulled her close. *Fuck.* "Get out of the way," Reznick muttered under his breath.

His earpiece buzzed again. "Face recognition confirms target, Jon. Confirmation green!"

Reznick stared through the sights, his finger on the trigger. Suddenly, the woman wrapped her arms around Crenshaw's neck, hugging him tight. The line of sight was blocked. No clean shot.

He watched and waited. He worried whether he should risk hitting the woman. But that was not part of the assignment. Crenshaw was the target. No collateral damage, apart from the Wagner crew. Strict orders. And he followed orders.

Reznick watched as the woman, who was around the same age as his daughter Lauren, disappeared downstairs, the old man now out of sight. He felt a mixture of rage and frustration, and clenched his fist tight. "Motherfucker!" The bastard had gotten lucky again.

He got back in position, watching through the night sights of the long rifle. He might need to wait all night for the old man to reappear.

The minutes passed.

Suddenly, the bodyguards signaled to a guy on the quayside and the yacht was loosened from its moorings.

Reznick was about to lose them. "No, no, no!"

But the yacht quietly and deftly maneuvered out of the marina, away from the other boats. Then it sailed off into the night.

Reznick stared through the rifle's sights, helpless. The old man was below deck with the girl.

"He's getting away, Jon!" Trevelle's voice snapped.

"Copy that."

"Why didn't you take the shot?"

Reznick quickly disassembled the rifle and sights, shoving them into the backpack and zipping it up tight.

"I said why didn't you take the shot? He was there! You had him!"

"There was no clean shot. I repeat, no clean shot."

"But you had him."

"The girl moved in, blocking the line of sight."

"Shouldn't you have taken the shot anyway?"

Reznick growled. "I wanted a clean shot. A clean kill. No collateral damage on this operation. Do you understand? Those are my strict orders."

"Copy that."

"We'll get him. One way or another, we will get him."

The problem was that it wouldn't be tonight. Crenshaw was gone, maybe never to be seen again.

Thirteen

Petersen's cell phone pinged with an encrypted message at 1523 Eastern Time. She was at her desk in her seventh-floor office, reviewing details of a briefing for the President's national security advisor. She picked up her phone. A text from Trevelle Williams. Her heart skipped a beat in anticipation as she scanned the message.

Target got away. Oman. Destination unclear. More to follow.

Petersen's heart sank. There were no prizes for trying. It was a world of success or failure. Black and white. No gray.

She had so wanted to give the Director some good news. She knew he was skeptical of the whole operation. A setback or a close call, whatever she called it, was of no interest to him. And rightly so. Time was running out. Truth be told, she felt the pressure getting to her. She wasn't sleeping well. She wasn't going to the gym or the pool like she usually did before or after work. She had immersed herself in the operation. She knew whatever happened was technically out of her control. But her responsibility was to keep the Director and President's advisors in the loop. No one liked hearing bad news.

The more she thought about the course of action, the more concerned she got. Somehow, Reznick had gotten eyes on the target. That meant something. But she knew the Director wasn't interested in near misses.

The decision to recommend this course of action was hers and hers alone. Her reputation would stand or fall on the results of whether the operation succeeded or failed.

This news, meanwhile, couldn't have come at a worse time.

Petersen was due to give a special briefing to America's most senior politicians with responsibility for intelligence. She was due to speak within the hour at a sensitive compartmented information facility in the Senate. All eyes would be on her. A trip to the Capitol to speak to politicians was something she never looked forward to. She was more a behind-the-scenes person at Langley, most of the time.

She found the briefing room at the Hart Senate Office Building on Constitution Avenue, known as the SCIF room, intimidating. Today she would be speaking to the heads of the intelligence and armed services committees, including the chair and ranking members of both the Senate and House, in addition to the majority and minority leaders. The closed session ensured everyone would be listening to her every word.

In the meantime, she picked up her phone and called Jorge Mendez's direct number to give him the bad news from the Middle East.

The Director answered with "I hope this is good, Fran."

"Not exactly."

"What does that mean?"

"We tracked him down to Oman. Muscat."

"That's a start."

"It is a start. We did have eyes on him. But the target slipped away. He's proving very elusive."

Mendez groaned as if it was the last thing he wanted to hear. "You're speaking to the intelligence committee later I see?"

"In an hour."

"Be very careful what you say and how you say it. How you frame it. It might be a private audience—"

"I've done this before, sir. I've got this."

"I'm just saying . . . and keep me in the loop."

Petersen ended the call and fixed herself a strong cup of coffee. She checked her briefing paper for the committee as she enjoyed the caffeine fix. Then she headed into her executive en suite and quickly freshened up, reapplying her makeup and brushing her hair. She put on a smart black jacket and adjusted the Tiffany diamond brooch her husband had given her for their twentieth anniversary. She treasured it. It was a symbol of his love for her. Sadly, he hadn't seen much of her in the last month, with Fran focusing her time and energies on this operation.

She headed down to the basement with her team. Petersen slid into the back of the chauffeured CIA SUV as she was driven into DC, giving her time to reread the briefing. Her father had always instilled in her that preparation was key. The irony that her special projects operation was being led by Reznick, a man she had been told was the polar opposite, wasn't lost on her.

Petersen saw a few cameras and TV crews as she approached. The SUV turned sharply and headed down into the underground parking garage. She was escorted to a basement entrance of the Hart Building, then escorted by her CIA team to the second floor. She had been here before. It was not unfamiliar. But it was nerve-racking all the same.

The SCIF room contained a dozen committee members with the highest intelligence clearance, who would hear her classified briefing behind locked doors. No cell phones or electronic equipment allowed. Satellite-jamming technology was deployed in the room to ensure there was no eavesdropping of any sort.

Petersen took her seat, her heart occasionally skipping a beat, as she once again glanced over her papers. She perused a few highlighted passages.

The chair introduced her. Then, "Assistant Director Petersen, the floor is yours," he said.

Petersen locked eyes with each of the assembled committee members. Saw the inscrutable expressions on some of the most senior and powerful politicians in America.

"I'll keep this brief, ladies and gentlemen," she said. "I will take questions afterward. Just a reminder, if you need one, that we have a media blackout on what I'm about to tell you, for national security reasons. A few ground rules. Strictest security protocols are in place. You are in the most privileged position to have access to such highly classified information. What I am about to divulge is for your information only. There can be absolutely no on-the-record or off-the-record media briefings. No chats to staffers on this issue. No chats to loved ones. This is for you only. Just so we're clear."

The politicians all fixed their gazes on her with an air of solemn reverence.

She cleared her throat. "A retired American intelligence officer has been selling classified and secret information to our enemies. Russia, in particular. Also possibly to drug cartels and criminal syndicates in the Middle East, Far East, and Africa."

The fearful looks of the politicians around the table spoke volumes.

"We see this as an existential threat to America's national security interests. Accordingly, we have tried to neutralize this threat, as the target is believed to be overseas. But he is proving elusive. As you know, the geopolitical landscape is changing, getting reshaped and reformed far quicker than any of us could have imagined. Former close allies and partners like Saudi Arabia and the United Arab Emirates are peeling away from our sphere of influence. The

Middle East is a cauldron. Arab states are edging closer, year by year, to China, Russia, even Iran. This is unprecedented. Three months ago, I told the committee about an operation we carried out to neutralize this target. As I said at the time, it was not successful. Innocent lives were lost. Political fallout in the region was immense. We launched a series of Predator drones to kill this man and his protectors, as they traveled in a convoy. The intel we had been given by three separate sources turned out to be, according to our best analysis, old-school disinformation from the Russians. We got played. It doesn't happen often. But it happened. And we need to learn from that. Accordingly, we have decided to find another way to reach our goal—a new strategy. The traditional way of dealing with this threat using special forces has not been deemed either feasible or diplomatically smart, at least at this time. The events of three months ago played badly in Middle Eastern intelligence circles. Basically, we're having to think outside the box."

Petersen took a sip of water as the committee members sat quietly. "Today I'm here to tell you that a top-secret, high-risk operation, involving a three-man team, has been launched. This is off the books. We have not told our partners in the Middle East for the reasons I have already outlined. We believe some of the people in these governments have been compromised. In particular, we believe assets in Libya and Qatar, who are subject not only to Russian spying rings but Chinese too, have been compromised. So we're not going through the usual military or special ops channels. Essentially, it's two men on the ground, operating independently of the United States. These are highly trained and decorated soldiers, and they are using a cybersecurity expert here in America to locate and then neutralize the target. This is a loose, fluid, ongoing situation. It may or may not be resolved within the next week. The CIA can't officially acknowledge that this operation is underway or was authorized. I'm sorry I'm not coming to you with better news. But we believe that, in the democratic process, senior politicians, privy to highly classified intel, have a right to know about this."

Ben Schultz, the chair of the Senate intelligence committee, cleared his throat. "Assistant Director, this is both worrying and alarming. First, though, I want to start by thanking you for your candor and for sharing with us this highly classified briefing. I want to reiterate what Assistant Director Petersen has said. We can't talk about this outside of this room. We can't gossip about this. And we absolutely cannot share this intel with the media, friendly or not. There will be no reaching out to journalists to give them an off-the-record chat. Any such breach, in effect, is an unauthorized disclosure of confidential information, and will be punished severely. Mark my words. Ladies and gentlemen, this is national security, first and foremost. America's national security. And we are all in a privileged position to receive such information."

A few nods around the table.

Schultz turned and looked across at Petersen. "Assistant Director, I'd like to ask if you are able, at this stage, to divulge the identity of the target?"

Petersen paused, as if giving the question genuine thought. "Not at this stage, purely for operational reasons."

Gillian Marshall, a fresh-faced Republican senator from Wyoming, said, "Can you divulge where this operation is taking place?"

"The Middle East, that's all I can say. I repeat, the target is an American citizen. He is a spy. The Russians are in control of him. He is a formerly revered member of our intelligence community. This is not a foreign national."

Tom Gorton, a former Marine and now North Dakota senator said, "Assistant Director, who have you sent to kill the target? And has this been subcontracted to a friendly nation?"

"We didn't deem it to be the right move to subcontract this operation. I won't give specifics."

Schultz said, "I'd like a lot more detail, Assistant Director. I don't think it's appropriate that democratically elected politicians can't be privy to that."

"This is on a need-to-know basis. You know the bare bones. But nothing more will be forthcoming until further notice."

Petersen gathered up her papers and placed them carefully in her briefcase. She strode out of the room, escorted by her team, went back down to the basement and into the SUV, hoping and praying that Reznick would get another chance.

Fourteen

A burnt orange sun peeked over the horizon as dawn broke in Muscat. Shards of sunlight bathed the minarets and rooftops across the skyline, picking out particles of dust hanging in the air. All the while, the plaintive sounds of the call to morning prayer carried across the city.

Reznick headed along the promenade, crunching on a couple of Dexedrine after stopping for a coffee. The waters of the Gulf of Oman rippled out as far as the eye could see, bathed in an ethereal tangerine hue. He had hung around the marina, waiting to see if the yacht might return. But it had all been to no avail.

He felt frustrated after being thwarted the night before. He had spotted the old man. He'd had him in his sights. But despite Trevelle's best efforts throughout the night, the ex-NSA hacker seemed to have lost track of Crenshaw after the yacht ventured out to sea.

It was another worrying setback. Reznick had only caught a glimpse of the target in his crosshairs. Would his younger, hungrier self have taken the high-risk shot? It would have been rash to compromise the mission by killing innocents. Collateral damage, apart from the Wagner crew, was not allowed. Mercenary deaths usually went unreported, but a dead civilian would draw the sort of unwanted attention that could compromise not only the mission, but bring massive headaches to the government, who would have to deny that it was behind the operation to kill an American citizen. Still, it gnawed at him—the sense of failure. The one saving grace of the whole incident was that Trevelle had tracked down Crenshaw once. He would find him again. Reznick knew he would. The problem was that time wasn't on their side.

Reznick wandered down toward the beach. Fishermen wearing traditional clothes hauled a small boat up onto the sand, baskets of their nighttime catch being taken away. His mind replayed the night before as if on a loop. He wondered if he should have killed Crenshaw, to hell with any consequences. But even setting aside his orders, his moral code would not justify killing an innocent, even if the woman had been a friend or lover of Crenshaw. No, it had to be a clean kill. It would have been fine if the Wagner thugs had been partially blocking Crenshaw from sight. He would gladly have taken the shot then. But something about the young woman had dissuaded him. Maybe that she looked to be a similar age to his own daughter. Perhaps she had simply gotten caught up hanging out with shady rich guys on yachts. Perhaps she was just a party girl who hung with the wrong crowd.

The more he thought about it, the more he wondered whether this hadn't been an ill-conceived mission from the start. It was beginning to look like that. Jinxed even.

Reznick had been on numerous missions to neutralize targets—mostly terrorists or the financial sponsors of terrorists. Each one had taken planning, and time, and numerous operatives to bring it all together—all things he didn't have now. But something deep within him had stirred when he'd heard about the traitorous behavior of Crenshaw. Someone had to put an end to his treasonous acts. This spy had to be neutralized.

He needed to get close. Maybe even closer than he had already. But this guy had a team of bodyguards in addition to state-level protection, allowing him to glide in and out of harbors, ports, and cities, shrouded in secrecy.

Reznick got back to his hotel room, quickly showered, and put on a change of clothes. Then he called Mac, who was still in Dubai.

"We might never get a better chance," Mac said.

Reznick sighed. "I know. Mac, I'm killing myself over not taking the shot last night."

"Did you have line of sight? A clear shot?"

"No clear shot. Bodies in the way."

Silence stretched between them.

Reznick chewed over a question before he asked it. "What would you have done?"

"Exactly what you did. Nothing. The task is to neutralize the old man. Nothing more, nothing less. The people on the yacht, we're not at war with them. They're not in the arena. Don't beat yourself up over it. We've got a job. We do the job. And we do it properly. Sometimes there are no shortcuts. Let's just hope we get another opportunity."

"Still frustrating, Mac. I had a visual. He was in my sights. But he got away."

"Jon, you know how this works. You suck it up, we move on."

Reznick knew Mac was right. His cell phone pinged. "Hold on, Mac." He checked the message. It was from Trevelle.

Satellite phone conversation intercept. The old man is en route to berth at Dubai's Mina Rashid Marina. ETA ninety minutes.

"Mac, you still there?"

"Yeah, still here, Jon."

"The target is headed to Dubai."

"Dubai? I'm already at the marina. I'm looking at all the fancy yachts."

"That's where he's headed. The old man's yacht will be docking in ninety minutes. Do what you have to do."

"Count on it. What about you?"

"I'm in fucking Oman."

"Are you going to catch a direct flight to Dubai? It's only an hour."

Reznick weighed up the best course of action. "I get the impression this guy is one or maybe more steps ahead of us."

"You think Trevelle's intel is wrong?"

"No, I don't."

"Copy that. Listen, Jon, I was thinking about entry with a yacht. My experience in Special Boat Service training exercises . . . Maybe rig up a magnetic bomb to the hull of the yacht."

"Too risky. Collateral damage would be terrible."

"So you want me to get in close?"

"Whatever it takes. Or take him out with the rifle. Was that delivered?"

"Nice piece of kit. Yup, I got that."

"You have the tools, right? Set up on a rooftop overlooking the marina."

"Copy that."

"I'll be in touch."

The minutes dragged as he waited for news.

Reznick ordinarily would have jumped on a flight to Dubai. No problem. But he sensed it might be wise to have Muscat covered until he heard otherwise. He wouldn't put it past Crenshaw or his handlers to lay down a false trail, seeding disinformation about his whereabouts.

Ninety minutes later, Mac called.

"What's happening, Mac? You got eyes on the target?"

"Negative."

"What?"

"I was watching the yacht through the rifle sights, six hundred meters where it berthed. I observed plenty of young women on board, three members of the crew of heavies. Wagner guys. It's the same crowd of people."

"So the old man is still out of sight? I'm assuming he's below deck."

"I headed down to the marina to try and get closer, on the off chance that he would just step up onto the deck."

"Still no visual?"

"Negative. I don't know, Jon. I'm dying to step on board."

"Not the way to go."

"I know."

"Listen, this is frustrating. I'm going to call Trevelle. I would have expected the old man to go ashore, or at least surface."

Mac cleared his throat. "Precisely what I was thinking. I'm assuming he's keeping out of sight. Maybe he's been alerted to our presence."

"That's a real possibility."

"What are you going to do?"

"Well, since we have confirmation the yacht is in Dubai, I need to be there. I'll be in touch. But keep your eyes on this goddamn yacht."

"Copy that, Jon. See you soon, pal. I'll text you details of the Airbnb I've got."

When Reznick arrived at the marina in Dubai, he headed to the apartment overlooking the water. Mac was watching the yacht through a powerful telescope.

"Something is wrong, Jon," he said. "Still no sign of the bastard."

"Nothing at all?"

"Fuck all. Look for yourself."

Reznick peered through the telescope, which was trained on the deck of the yacht. The young women were taking in the sun while the Wagner thugs prowled the deck. He took over the surveillance. Hour after hour throughout the rest of the day. But despite a clear visual on the yacht, there was still no sign of Crenshaw. Reznick had expected him to take a walk into the city, maybe go to a nice hotel or a restaurant incognito. At least have a drink or two on the deck with the girls as they sunbathed. But there was nothing. Like he had vanished.

Night fell. The lights of the yachts bathed the dark waters of the marina.

Reznick needed to know what was going on. He watched and waited. His cell phone rang. "Trevelle, talk to me. What the hell is going on? We're stuck here in Dubai, no sign of him. Something is wrong. I can't believe he hasn't emerged from below deck at least once. Have we missed him?"

"Jon, that's why I'm calling. I think I've figured out what's happened."

"You told us Crenshaw was in Dubai."

"Gimme a minute. I'll try and explain. I've been checking the GPS track for the yacht leading up to when it berthed in Dubai. I thought it was strange."

"Thought what was strange?"

"The yacht I was tracking, or rather retrospectively tracking, stopped for ten minutes on the way to Dubai."

Reznick's brain was racing. "It stopped for ten minutes out at sea *before* it got to Dubai? Was it an electrical fault? Engine problems?"

"Not at all. I don't know for sure if they were just floating around or what . . ."

Reznick pieced together where Trevelle was going with this. "The yacht arrived in Dubai. Mac had eyes on the yacht the moment it arrived. The whole time. But nothing since."

"The yacht arrived . . . that is correct."

Suddenly it dawned on Reznick what had happened. The realization was like a freight train hitting head-on. "Motherfucker."

"You understand now?"

Reznick pursed his lips, annoyed by the brilliance. The simplicity. "Classic move. A switch at sea?"

"Bingo!"

"Explain how this went down."

"So, I've been analyzing the GPS track. I learned that Crenshaw's yacht made a maneuver that was very, very close to a megayacht."

"You figure Crenshaw was taken off one yacht and transferred to a second, bigger yacht?"

"Absolutely correct."

"What other details do you have?"

"This is where it gets interesting. The yacht, Jon, is truly huge. Built in Germany. And you're going to like this part . . . built to order for a Russian oligarch with interests in oil and gas."

"That is brilliant. Chilling. But brilliant."

"I did an analysis of that yacht's GPS route. This megayacht owned by the Russian, it was positioned within yards of where Crenshaw's yacht stopped. Literally yards."

"These guys are good. I mean, really good."

"They're running circles around us. It's almost like he knows there are people waiting for him in Dubai, watching him. I think there's high-quality intel prompting Crenshaw and his crew, or part of his crew, to take preventative action. It can't be a coincidence."

"That would make perfect sense too," said Reznick. "Crenshaw has been told, presumably by his Russian handlers, to avoid Dubai."

"Exactly."

"And after this warning, Crenshaw jumped aboard this monster yacht. Maybe got into a dinghy with an outboard motor for the transfer at sea, then he climbs aboard the big yacht. Out of sight. You got any more precise details about this ten-minute stop?"

"This all happened in the Persian Gulf, forty-three nautical miles north of Dubai. It's a gigantic yacht. But it's far away from UAE vessels in the area. Which is also very telling."

Reznick felt the anger rising slowly in him. "Which leads me to my next question. Have you got a fix on this megayacht that we think Crenshaw is on?"

"Affirmative."

"Excellent."

"I managed to get access to surveillance cameras hooked up to the deck and rooms on board."

"You did?"

"Yup. He's there. I see him right now. He's talking into a satellite phone."

Reznick's cell phone pinged.

"I just sent you a text message. Attached is a photo."

Reznick opened the message. And there he was, in near real time, a heavily suntanned Crenshaw on the teak deck, speaking into a huge satellite phone.

"Safely received?"

"Copy that."

Reznick studied the image. Crenshaw had a cigarette in one hand, the phone in the other, and a glass of wine on the table, as if he didn't have a care in the world. Sitting by his side in an easy chair was a heavily tanned guy who looked like he might be Slavic. "And the guy with him, is that who owns the yacht?"

"Copy that. You've got to hand it to him, the old man is smart."

"We need to up our game, Trevelle. Big-time. Don't fucking lose him now, OK? Where are they headed?"

"They're not moving at the moment. They're just sitting, anchored, nice and easy, three miles from Abu Dhabi. The GPS on the onboard computer shows the final destination as Qatar."

"This guy gets around."

"No kidding."

"So the yacht is *not* moving at this precise moment?"

"That is correct. I'm using satellite imagery. The GPS has stayed the same for the last couple hours."

Reznick ended the call and walked over to Mac.

"He switched yachts out at sea. He's anchored just off Abu Dhabi, just down the coast from Dubai. But his destination after this is Qatar."

Mac grinned. "So, as it stands, Crenshaw is down the coast?"

"Pretty much."

"So, what are we waiting for? Let's see if he's still there. Maybe give him a little surprise."

Fifteen

Crenshaw sipped vintage French champagne from a crystal glass with the reclusive Russian oligarch Andrei Levenko—part of an inner circle who had close ties to the Kremlin, the intelligence community, and the feared Federal Security Service. Levenko was one of the cutouts who had been tasked with looking after Moscow's investment. Over the past five years, Crenshaw had also found him to be a friend and confidant, as well as an all-around nice guy, and he was enjoying the lavish hospitality of his host. That included limitless bottles of Grey Goose vodka and Dom Pérignon, and whatever favors the aspiring models who hung around the yacht were offering.

Levenko tsked him. "You are very headstrong, William. I appreciate that trait in a man. Forthright, passionate. Very much like myself. But it's getting to the stage that my friends in the highest echelons of the security services in Moscow are growing rather concerned at the blasé attitudes you are displaying. Despite repeated warnings, you still have not disappeared as we had agreed. We don't know what to make of that."

Crenshaw sat quietly. Levenko wasn't a man to be interrupted.

"Please remember, our advice and guidance are for your well-being. I hope you realize that."

Crenshaw nodded. "It's very much appreciated."

"The intel we have is alarming."

Crenshaw felt his blood pressure hiking up a notch, as it sometimes did when he was stressed. He checked his new smartwatch. "My heart rate is four percent higher than it should be. That's also concerning."

"William, can you promise me that after Abu Dhabi you will disappear?"

Crenshaw was beginning to wonder if he could trust Levenko. His wealthy Russian friend was the latest to give him a warning. "Just a little more patience. I'm tying up the loose ends of some business."

Levenko studied Crenshaw, his piercing expression like an ice pick to the heart.

"I promise you, we're nearly there."

"Don't disappoint us, William. We don't like to be disappointed. You must understand what we're telling you. If they say they need the files sooner than expected, you need to trust them. They'll expect you to keep your word."

"And I will. Just a bit more concerned about this old heart of mine."

"I know a good doctor in Dubai. I'll get him flown out here."

"I appreciate that. But I just have another day or two. Besides, I don't want to speak to someone I don't know."

"I can vouch for him."

"It's very kind of you to offer."

Levenko leaned closer. "Tell me, William," he said, sipping his champagne. "Do you miss America?"

"Not so much. I miss my kids. They're all grown-up now. I guess I'll never see them again."

"What about FaceTime?"

"I mean in person. To hold them. To hold my grandchildren. I'm a grandfather to five children I've never seen or held."

Levenko finished his champagne, placing the glass on the table. "They could visit you in Jeddah."

"I'm not so sure. I had imagined my retirement in Florida. Visiting the Keys. I have a place down in Marathon. But I guess the Middle East will have to do."

"The house in Florida will probably have been sequestered by the Feds and the IRS."

"Probably."

"Was it worth it?"

Crenshaw felt a wave of sadness wash over him.

"I mean the money—was it worth the price you will pay?"

"I don't know. I don't have any regrets, if that's what you mean. Nothing that will keep me awake at night."

"You've changed, William."

"Everyone changes."

"But not that much, surely."

"I think I grew disillusioned."

"With America?"

"Yeah . . . with America. The country I grew up in was about exceptionalism. Being the best. Fighting the good fight. Sacrifices for the greater good so we could stay free. I bought into that. Everyone did. Or at least it seemed they did."

Levenko seemed to consider what Crenshaw had said, a slight tilt to his head.

"It was an incredible empire while it lasted. But, like all empires, we are doomed to a slow and painful decline. Not now. Not next year. Not in the next decade or two even. But this is the beginning of the end."

"I have a soft spot for your country. Its aspirations."

"We seem to care about everyone in the world apart from our own American citizens. You seen the homeless across the country? Even veterans have lost their homes. It's pitiful. I was one of the lucky ones. I could afford to pay medical bills, that kind of stuff. America seemed impregnable."

"You served your country very well for a long time. You sacrificed a lot. But what did you get in return?"

"A shitty government pension and the gold watch—a shitty one by the way—and thanks very much, now fuck off."

Levenko frowned. "You felt unappreciated?"

"That and many other things. I felt as if I had given everything, sacrificed so much, and for what? The last ten or twenty years of my life would be spent scraping by. Maybe writing a memoir."

"You became embittered?"

"I saw former colleagues of mine. Good men. And they ended up on the scrapheap. It was painful to see. Burnouts in their fifties. So, yeah, maybe I became embittered. Angry. Maybe I was angry with myself."

Levenko cheered. "You've taken a different path. You're looking after number one. I understand exactly where you're coming from."

"I don't want to die poor. Why shouldn't I be rewarded with more than a shitty watch and pension? Clipping coupons to afford to vacation in Europe. Waiting to die."

"We're all going to die."

"I had envisaged living out my days in Coral Gables. I like the sun. But I couldn't abide living in a retirement community. Talking about golf, getting driven around in a buggy, playing bridge. Fuck that."

"It's a big world. If you need sunshine, this part of the world has sunshine. And huge oil and gas reserves to last hundreds of years. And no tax."

"They have rules. They have laws. And their society works. I like it."

"Have you ever considered Hong Kong?"

"Too many British operatives still in place there. I want to relax."

Levenko edged forward, getting closer.

Crenshaw took a deep breath. "Life is full of regrets. Somewhere along the way I fell out of love with my country, the Agency, and our mess of a society. But we do what we have to do."

"It sounds like you don't believe in America anymore."

"The America I knew is gone for good."

"Take the advice of me and my friends and contacts in the Federal Security Service. We care about you. Don't let them get you now, at the eleventh hour. You need to hand over what you've got and disappear. Enjoy the rest of your retirement in the sun."

"It's all under control."

"You are being complacent. That can be deadly in our business. We Russians know all about danger. We know all about death."

Crenshaw stared out over the water.

"Do you know what Tolstoy said? He said, *The two most powerful warriors are patience and time.* Men like the American Jon Reznick have both patience and time. The window of opportunity for you is closing faster than you think, William. Don't wait too long."

Sixteen

Reznick and Mac watched as a young uniformed police officer hosed down the wooden deck of a fast patrol boat in the Dubai marina. Then Mac jumped on board as Reznick untied the rope from the dock, jumping down onto the craft.

The kid looked frightened. "Who are you?" he demanded in Arabic. He had a nametag which read *Khalifa*.

Reznick pressed the gun to Khalifa's head. "Shut up!"

"Please." The young officer's voice changed. "Don't hurt me."

"Good, you speak English. This is how it's going to work. You do as we say, OK? If not, I'll blow your fucking brains out over this nice new boat."

The cop nodded, blinking furiously.

Mac stepped forward with some nylon rope and a knife. He grabbed Khalifa's arms and tied them up, sat him down, and then tied his legs together at the ankles. Then he took away the cop's gun and sat him on the deck. "Don't move, son!"

The cop nodded.

"You understand English good?"

"Yes sir."

Mac kneeled down, face squaring up to his. "Do what you're told, and you won't get hurt. You don't want to get hurt do you, son?"

Khalifa shook his head.

Reznick quickly maneuvered the boat carefully out of the marina and pointed it toward the open water. He grabbed the throttle and edged it forward as they sped out to sea. Then he turned and looked at Mac. "Everything OK there?"

"Never better, Jon. Good as gold."

Reznick checked the GPS map. He needed precise intel now. He called Trevelle. Reznick gave the latitude and longitude coordinates of their current location. "Have you got a fix on where I am?"

"Yes, absolutely. You need to edge southwest for forty-three nautical miles. The yacht is still anchored off Abu Dhabi."

Reznick tapped the details into the boat's GPS system and adjusted the steering wheel. He was headed straight there. He turned around to face the young cop. "Khalifa, are there other uniforms, like you've got on?"

"Below deck."

Reznick nodded and Mac headed down the steps. A minute later he emerged with two scruffy and dirty uniforms.

"Put one on," Reznick shouted.

Big as Mac was, the uniform had been made for a giant. "It's too fucking big."

"Roll up the sleeves and the pant legs. It'll do."

Mac complied and then prowled the deck like a caged animal.

"Take the wheel," said Reznick.

Mac stepped forward and did so.

Reznick pulled on the other uniform, which was a slightly better fit than Mac's. "Stay on course."

They skimmed fast across the waters of the Persian Gulf, heading southwest from Dubai, following the blinking dot on the dashboard display that represented the target's boat. "I know this type of boat, Reznick. You could get fifty-five knots out of it. Fifty easy. I reckon it'll take us forty minutes."

"Well, get a move on!"

Mac pushed the boat faster and they picked up speed, smashing through the dark waters toward the megayacht anchored by the capital of the United Arab Emirates.

Reznick looked down at Khalifa, who had wet his pants. "Just do what we say and everything is going to be fine."

Khalifa nodded. "I don't want to die. I have a wife and two children who rely on me. And my mother too. They all need me."

"Then be a good boy and there's no reason to get frightened."

"Your friend frightens me."

"My friend has that effect on people. Don't worry about it."

Khalifa closed his eyes and began to say a prayer.

Reznick checked his watch. It was around half an hour until their ETA. He unzipped Mac's backpack and took out night-vision military binoculars, ammo, and a folding AR-15 semiautomatic rifle. He was locked and loaded in seconds.

Khalifa stared at the weapon. "What are you going to do with that? Are you going to kill me?"

"Listen, son, if you keep on talking, I might have to kill you. My advice? Don't speak unless spoken to."

Khalifa nodded, fast.

Reznick trained the powerful binoculars on the far horizon. The algae-green viewfinder showed the endless open waters of the Persian Gulf, an occasional dhow chugging away on the swell. Ten minutes. Twenty minutes. Thirty minutes. They were getting closer and closer.

Mac seemed to be speeding up the closer he got to the target. "We're a couple miles from the GPS point," he shouted.

Reznick spotted the lights of the huge yacht on the horizon.

"Nice and easy, Mac. Let's not frighten the horses."

Mac slowed down instinctively.

Reznick peered through the binoculars, scanning the horizon, checking out the floating palace. The yacht was enormous, with multiple decks. A helicopter squatted on a landing pad on the top deck. "I've got a visual!"

Mac steered the boat within half a mile of the yacht's starboard. "You got it, Jon?"

"I've got it."

"Fifteen knots. Closing."

"Copy that," said Reznick. Brutal-looking deckhands prowled the yacht. "It's our Wagner pals here waiting for us."

"That's nice of them," Mac said sarcastically.

Reznick analyzed the deck, looking for any sign of Crenshaw—or the Russian oligarch who owned the yacht, for that matter. He couldn't see either of them. He had to assume they were below deck. But he needed to make sure they hadn't sped off in another boat to Abu Dhabi. He turned to the Dubai cop. "Khalifa, you speak good English, right?"

"Yes sir."

"Get on the radio. Tell the captain and crew of the yacht to prepare to be boarded. Say it's for illegal contraband and weapons."

Reznick signaled for Khalifa to be freed.

Mac was quick to oblige. He took out a serrated hunting knife and cut the rope tying the kid up. Then he pointed at the terrified young cop as he led him to the steering booth of the patrol boat. "Just say what you were told, nothing else. Any funny stuff, and I'll behead you. Got it?"

Khalifa nodded frantically, clearly terrified of Mac. He picked up the radio, hand shaking. There was the sound of crackle and static on the boat's audio speaker.

"This is the captain of *Freespirit*," a voice said. "Who am I talking to?"

"This is the Dubai Police."

"Copy that."

"Prepare for us to board. We're looking for illegal contraband, weapons."

The radio went quiet for a few moments.

Khalifa spoke again. "Do you hear me? We are about to board."

"Copy that. I've been told that it will be ten minutes while we check your police credentials, sir, before I can allow you to board. I repeat, we'll need ten minutes. Security protocols we have in place for our guests."

"We need to board now. We have the authority. Do you understand?"

The radio went dead.

Reznick knew the crew were not going to comply. He urged Mac to edge the patrol boat closer, within fifty yards. Floodlights from the police boat illuminated some goons on the deck of the yacht, guns in hand.

Reznick picked up the AR-15 rifle as he saw some movement on the upper deck. He flicked off the safety as he zeroed in on the chopper. The rotor was moving. "Mac, movement on the upper deck. Chopper preparing for takeoff."

A gunshot cracked the patrol boat's windshield.

Reznick spread-eagled on the deck. "They're shooting at us."

Mac crouched down, gun in hand. "Let's get on there!"

Reznick took aim. He fired off two loud shots, killing the deck-hands who had semiautomatics across their shoulders.

The chopper suddenly took to the air, swooping low over the dark waters.

"They're getting away, Jon!" shouted Mac.

Reznick fired four, five, six shots at the chopper. The sound of the cockpit's glass shattering, then bullets hitting off metal pierced the roar of the engine. "Come on, you asshole!" He raked the chopper with more gunfire.

The chopper banked steeply as if hit. It flew low, veering just yards above the waves, lurching dangerously, about to crash into the sea.

Reznick fired more yet more shots. The helicopter struggled to gain altitude. But then it accelerated and swooped upward fast. It was gaining altitude. Getting farther and farther away. "Fuck it! Go after it, Mac!" He spotted more crew crawling over of the yacht. He raked the deck with a burst of rapid gunfire. He turned and fired up at the chopper as it disappeared into the night. The bullets just seemed to ricochet off uselessly.

He wondered if the helicopter was bulletproof or had reinforced armored plating. It would explain a lot.

Mac accelerated the police boat, trying to catch up with the chopper. It was headed toward the lights of the city skyline in the distance. Reznick watched as it banked sharply to the port side and disappeared off into the Arabian night.

Mac maneuvered the patrol boat and pointed it due south, the direction the chopper was headed. "The GPS says we're headed for Abu Dhabi, Jon."

"Copy that."

The last mile was through choppy waters.

Reznick strapped a life jacket to Khalifa.

"What are you doing?"

"Nothing personal, son."

He pushed the young cop overboard, watching him flail about then surface in the water. The kid would survive.

In the distance, the twinkling lights and high-rise skyline of Abu Dhabi rose up before them.

Mac opened up the throttle but the helicopter had disappeared among the residential towers and hotels.

Seventeen

Fran Petersen was getting it from all sides. She was being assailed by the Director about the direction of the operation. He was also feeding back to her dissenting voices at the Pentagon regarding her special access program. And if that weren't bad enough, she had been called in to the White House to brief the President's national security advisor in person.

She knew it wasn't going to be smooth sailing. Tough questions would be asked, which was appropriate. But she sensed the pressure was about to grow more intense as she followed a grim-faced staffer into the Cabinet Room in the West Wing, adjacent to the Oval Office.

She sat down at the highly polished mahogany table opposite the President's senior national security advisor, Brad Altman.

He didn't look up. He never did. It was par for the course for Altman, who enjoyed making people feel uncomfortable. He also liked to keep them waiting, showing them who was boss. He appeared disinterested as he leafed through some papers—probably her briefing about the diplomatically sensitive chopper incident in the territorial waters of the United Arab Emirates. She had an idea of what was bugging Altman. She knew the President was close to the UAE's head of state. He had known the sheikh since their Harvard days, and the President supported his mission to modernize the country. The sheikh owned a ton of land in the Scottish Highlands, swathes of central London, and prestigious brands and companies across the world. But what would be of most pressing concern to Altman was that the United Arab Emirates was geopolitically vital to American national interests. Oil and gas, but also military and surveillance operations across the country. The last thing the UAE needed or wanted was a corporate chopper being brought down in their waters, close to their maritime borders with both Iran and Qatar.

Petersen cleared her throat and continued to wait for an acknowledgment.

Altman was a major-league pain in the ass. A geopolitical expert, the kid considered himself a Henry Kissinger–type sage on the world stage. The reality was he was angling for a plum and highly lucrative position on a tech board on the West Coast. She knew all about that. It was her job to know political machinations. He wanted the money and the prestige but without the soul-destroying hours, days, weeks, and months away from home. He wanted to make a name for himself. She sympathized with that, but as it was, she was dealing with a fly-by-night.

He would invariably be gone within the year. The President had already gone through two national security advisors in less than eighteen months. The legacy of the Ukraine invasion, the mess in the Middle East, and the growing confidence of China and Iran had shaken the rules-based international order that had governed the world since the end of the Second World War.

Altman finally looked up. "So, let me start by asking you, Fran—whose idea was this operation?"

"It was my idea. And mine alone."

"You're taking full responsibility for this amateur-hour effort?"

Petersen could feel him getting under her skin. "The Agency, after much discussion, in light of the previous failures you authorized, decided on this course of action."

"I beg your pardon?"

"Previously, Seal Team 6 and the Predator drone debacle resulted in the killing of an Algerian politician and his family. You remember that, don't you?"

Altman stared at her, face blazing with indignation.

"So this time it was agreed that we should think outside the box."

Altman pursed his lips. "Just for the record, Assistant Director, you're talking to the President's national security advisor."

"I understand, sir."

"So enough of the sideswipes."

"That wasn't a sideswipe, trust me." Petersen saw that he was a little more thin-skinned than he liked to make out.

"It was faulty intel, right?" Altman said.

"Disinformation was what it was, Brad. And we acted on it."

"We are where we are. You say it was time to think outside the box . . . but Fran, seriously, are you fucking kidding me with this?"

"Do you mind—the profanity?"

"How did I not know about this mission?"

"You were copied in on the briefing. You were also invited to the meeting at the Hart Building."

"I had other matters to attend to. Israel, Ukraine, Pakistan, that kind of thing."

Petersen shrugged. "I also called you to give you a briefing ahead of time."

"When?"

"Do you want me to give you the exact time and date?"

"Doesn't matter. You don't need to be reminded that the United Arab Emirates is a trusted partner of the American government in security matters."

"I know."

"We value their strategic role in the Middle East. And now we have two operatives killing and running amok in UAE waters. Explain your thinking, please? Do you know the first thing about this Jon Reznick?"

"He's the finest operator in the arena, according to people in the know. I read his file. I talked to people. He specializes in difficult stuff. He knows the CIA and the FBI. He's a patriot to his very bones."

"According to people I know and trust, Reznick is unpredictable."

"We're all unpredictable. It's what makes us human."

"He doesn't take orders easily. He's a lone wolf. He's also a loose cannon. I don't like loose cannons or lone wolves."

"I know he's a lone wolf. But in this case, he has assistance from one other operator. A Brit."

Altman gave a patronizing laugh. "Have you read *that* guy's file?"

"Yes, I have read *that* guy's file. I was given access to it by MI6 via the Ministry of Defense."

"David McCafferty is a psychopath. He killed a man in a bar in Glasgow after he returned from service in Iraq."

Petersen felt uneasy. It was true. "He was found not guilty. He was attacked with a knife. An unprovoked attack. He was defending himself. A jury cleared him."

"McCafferty attracts trouble. He once single-handedly fought a squad of Irish guards on shore leave in Cyprus. And he put them all in the hospital. Four with broken jaws."

"Brad, what's your point?"

"My point is that putting these two fucking crazies in the heart of the Middle East at this particular juncture is just plain stupid."

"Are you implying I'm stupid too, Brad?"

Altman had the decency to blush and averted his gaze. "No, I am not."

"Well, that's good to know."

"This operation, if we can call it that, is a wild goose chase."

"The latest I heard from the tech guy, Reznick is close and getting closer. He saw the target's yacht. And the chopper."

"He saw the chopper! I got that intel too, Fran. You don't win any prizes for getting close. We need to neutralize the target. But he mowed down the Russians on that megayacht."

"I'm well aware of that."

"I'm not happy. It's a mess."

"Things get messy."

"I say we use a different strategy. Hell, why don't we launch drones from Qatar? The President seems willing."

"We've gone over this a million times. The geopolitical ramifications after the previous failed attempt make that impossible. It would be catastrophic for our relations with our partners in the Middle East, including Qatar and the UAE."

"I spoke to a member of SEAL Team 6 an hour ago. You know what he said?"

"What?"

"We should try again. He believes the end justifies the means. We eliminate Crenshaw, and to hell with our relations in the Middle East."

"It might work at the third, fourth, or tenth attempt. Until then, though, it would be both diplomatically and militarily a disaster. This low-key method offers plausible deniability. And a chance of success."

"The President is on board with this bullshit plan of yours . . . for now. But that might change. I need to warn you."

"Don't pull the plug on this. Give them a chance. They're on Crenshaw's tail. We need to not freak out at the first sign of trouble."

"You're not the one dealing with the UAE. The sheikh was apoplectic on the phone to the President. He seemed to believe the Ukrainians are involved."

"Which is good. That's our line. Ukrainian special forces mercenaries."

Altman shook his head. "I need this to work. I need this problem to go away."

"I hear you. We all want the same thing. Reznick is a very resourceful man. I believe in him."

"Blow Crenshaw out of the water on his yacht. Blame it on a gas explosion. Blame it on Russia."

"We already excluded that plan. Collateral damage."

Altman sighed.

"We need to get this right," continued Petersen. "We can't be too heavy-handed. You know how this works. Qatar, Libya, Saudi Arabia, the UAE, wherever Crenshaw's hanging out, they've threatened to slash oil and gas supplies to America and Europe if there is any 'significant' sign of the American military on their territory. Any 'significant' intervention whatsoever by American special forces or proxies on their soil would provoke them. The world is changing, Brad. The Saudis don't view us as the best medium- or long-term bet in geopolitical terms. They're hanging out with the BRICS. The Chinas, the Russias. The deal that the Saudis did with the Iranians, coordinated by the Chinese, left us completely blindsided. All I'm saying is Reznick needs just a little more time. Give him time to do what he does. He will find Crenshaw. I know he will. And he will neutralize him."

"What if he doesn't?"

"Then no one will be the wiser."

"Let's hope you're right. I want this finished. I want Crenshaw finished!"

Eighteen

The tension and frustration eating away at Reznick had been building since the latest near miss. It was all so close. Terrifyingly close.
But Crenshaw had gotten away. Again. Somehow, Crenshaw had
slipped away on the helicopter with seconds to spare. The old man
was like a ghost, as they only caught fleeting spectral glimpses of
their target.

Reznick stared out from his twelfth-floor room at the St. Regis
at the lights of Abu Dhabi. He had checked in with another fake
identity while Mac got a different hotel down the block. He had
unpacked a new tactical backpack that had been waiting in his
room, courtesy of Trevelle. He awaited their next crack at Crenshaw,
assuming that it ever came.

His mind replayed images of Crenshaw's chopper disappearing into the dark sky. It haunted him. They had gotten so close.
He wondered where Crenshaw was at this moment. Maybe he was
hunkered down in a Russian safe house in the city. Maybe he had a
villa or apartment here. Maybe he was under the protection of the
UAE government. Or perhaps he had moved on—next city, next
country, one step closer to disappearing for good.

A text from Mac asking if he wanted to meet up for a drink.

Reznick picked the second-floor terrace of the St. Regis Bar.
Mac joined him, slumping down in a seat. The Scot glowered,

silhouetted by the minaret of an imposing mosque in the distance. He had taken the setback personally. "We're fucking nowhere, Jon. Absolutely fucking zero."

"We're getting close," Reznick said. "Very close. We can't forget that."

"Are we? Close? I say we're grasping at straws, Jon. Jumping from pillar to post. City to city."

"It's frustrating, I know."

Mac winced. "Jon, I hate kicking my heels. I'm wasting my fucking time."

"If you want out, just say."

Mac shook his head. "You're not getting rid of me that easily. When I say I'm in, I mean it; I'm all-in."

"So what do you suggest?"

"We need a bigger team. We need more boots on the ground. And we need better intel."

"It is what it is. The intel is as good as it's going to get. As for a bigger team, you need to suck it up. It's just me and you. You don't like it, you need to walk."

"I don't walk out on jobs."

"I get that you're frustrated," Reznick whispered. "But Trevelle is trying to figure this out. We're not going to find the old man if you're bitching. Right?"

Mac shifted in his chair. "Fucking hate this. Hate this country."

"We have a job to do. I need to know that I can trust you."

"Yeah, you can trust me. One hundred percent."

"So let's agree that we won't bitch about this situation. It is what it is. We roll with it. We find this guy and put him in a box for good."

Mac rubbed his face before giving a sly smile. "I'm a pain in the arse, I know."

"I feel the same. So no more whining."

"Agreed." Mac checked his watch. "It's 0200 hours. Isn't it time you called Trevelle?"

Reznick picked up his cell phone.

"Hey Jon," Trevelle answered.

"We're twiddling our thumbs. We lost him earlier. This is a recurring theme. We need to catch a break. Fast."

"I know we do. What exactly happened?"

"The chopper took off and got away."

The line went quiet for a few moments. The sound of tapping on a keyboard.

"You still there, Trevelle?"

"Yeah, I'm still here."

"We're letting this bastard slip through our fingers. We need to find him quickly or it's over."

"I've been working on it."

"And?"

"I've been trawling footage from hotels in and around Abu Dhabi."

"I'm listening."

"Hang on . . ."

Reznick wondered what the delay was. "Trevelle, what is it?"

"I think I finally got something."

"Crenshaw?"

"Yeah . . . I've finally got a fix on him. At least I think it's him."

"Right now? Where is he?"

"Emirates Palace Mandarin Oriental. I've just viewed the surveillance footage from two of the helipads they have. The chopper landed on helipad one roughly three minutes after you lost him."

"So he landed there. Is he there now?"

"I'm working on it . . . Half a dozen security guys greeted him at his hotel suite."

Reznick determined if he and Mac should head there. It was tempting. "Anything else?"

"Suite 1822. But I can't confirm that he's still there. He went in there and I can't see anyone having left the hotel since then. No cameras in the room, obviously."

"We're assuming he must be inside?"

"Affirmative."

"Let's work on that assumption. But I want more. Harder intel. If anything changes, let me know."

Reznick ended the call and shared Trevelle's information with Mac. "What do you think?"

"The fucker is still hanging around the city? I find that a bit hard to believe. Why would he do that?"

"That's the intel we have. You think he might not be here?"

Mac leaned close. "If what Trevelle says is true, then it changes things."

"How do you figure?"

"I'm a gung-ho sort of guy, or so I'm told. My gut tells me to head over there. Right fucking now."

"Mine too."

"It might be it, Jon. Might be the last chance."

"Let's get to it. Figure it out on our way over there." Reznick grabbed his new tactical backpack from his room as Mac went back to his own hotel room and got his. They met up a few minutes later outside and caught a cab to the stunning, imposing Emirates Palace, asking the driver to drop them off a couple of blocks from the five-star hotel.

The hushed discussion in the back of the cab centered on the possible scenarios for getting to Crenshaw. Mac suggested setting off the fire alarm and getting the hotel evacuated, so they could gain access to the floor and room amid the chaos, ensuring Crenshaw and his bodyguards would have to leave too. It was a strong possibility. Reznick liked the idea.

Mac also talked of maybe attaching an improvised magnetic bomb to the target's car, if and when it was identified by Trevelle. But that would take more time, a lot more time, and they would need to source various electronic components. They considered trailing Crenshaw, if he was rushed away from the hotel, and following on rented motorbikes. Neutralizing a moving target. It was a sound idea.

Reznick was familiar with the motorcycle as a mode of transport for assassins. He discussed with Mac how he had used a similar tactic in the past, approaching a target's car from the rear on a motorcycle and then attaching an explosive device. He'd ridden away at high speed, remotely detonating the IED. Devastatingly effective. The collateral damage would just be the Wagner crew in the SUV. That wasn't a problem. The problem was the time it took to get a home-made magnetic bomb constructed and ready for delivery. Reluctantly, they discounted that mode of assassination as not practical.

The cab dropped them off at a street corner near to the hotel.

"Here's where I'm at," said Reznick. "I like your original idea. Set off the fire alarms, infiltrate the guests as they're leaving the hotel, and in the confusion, once we get a visual, take Crenshaw and the Wagner bodyguards out at close quarters."

Mac looked over at the hotel. "I can see that playing out. Different floors, stairwell approach."

"Maybe a bomb threat. Immediate rushed evacuation. Panic."

"Even better."

Reznick's cell phone rang, interrupting their discussion. He expected it to be Trevelle with a possible update. But it wasn't. It was a number he didn't recognize.

"Hey Jonny boy, how are you these days?" A raspy voice, maybe Californian. Reznick instantly realized who it was. *It was him.* The target. The man they were trying to kill.

Reznick said nothing.

"Long way from home, aren't ya, Jonny?"

"Who the hell is this?"

"Oh Jon, come on, don't play dumb. You're not a dumb guy. You're one of the smartest operators in the business. That's what they say."

Reznick switched the cell phone to speaker so Mac could hear, whispering in his ear that it was *him* on the line.

"I said who is this?"

"You ask a lot of questions, Jon. I'm flattered that you've come so far to find me."

Reznick wondered how the hell this cell phone number had been hacked. Had the heavily encrypted phone Trevelle had supplied him with been compromised? "One last time—who is this?"

"You know full well who I am, Jon. They sent you and the Scottish tough guy to neutralize me, right?"

Reznick's mind raced as he tried to figure out how such a serious security breach had happened. The whole point of using someone like Trevelle was that he was the best in the business at cybersecurity and hacking.

"Jon, listen to me, I'm going to level with you. Would it surprise you if I said I'm watching you right now, at this precise moment, in real time? But I'm not in Abu Dhabi anymore. I was. For a while. Bit of a fun game we're playing with you. I hope you're enjoying it."

Reznick studied the affluent area adjacent to the coast road. He spotted a phalanx of security cameras high up on a wall. He pointed to them and Mac shot a glance. It was at that moment, that terrible moment, that they both realized that they were indeed being watched by Crenshaw.

They were being played. Reznick didn't believe that Crenshaw wasn't in the city. He thought it might just be another bluff. But then again, maybe Crenshaw and his goons really had slipped out of the hotel.

"Ultra-high definition. 8K. They're miles ahead of us in so many ways, Jon. High-tech and futuristic. Light years, in some cases. So, talk to me. Or has the cat got your tongue, tough guy?"

Reznick stared at Mac, who shrugged.

"So here's the thing, Jonny. I hope you don't mind me calling you Jonny."

Reznick did indeed mind being called Jonny. He knew Crenshaw was fucking with him.

"I look at you standing there, Jonny, that look in your eyes, and I can tell you everything there is to know about you. I know all about your background. I know about your father. Patriotism is a fine virtue."

Reznick felt his nerve ends twitching.

"I'm very partial to Maine in the summer. Bit much in the depths of winter. I like the sun."

Reznick said nothing, keeping him on the line. He didn't know why. But he figured the longer he was talking to Crenshaw the better. Perhaps he'd get a clue as to where he was calling from.

"I'll tell you what, Jonny, let's cut to the chase."

"Yeah, why don't you?"

"Your little plan, or whoever's plan it is, has been burned to the ground. You are standing in the ashes of a ruin, so to speak."

"Do you want to get to the point?"

"Here's the point. This is an opportunity for you, and that shaven-headed Glaswegian thug, to go home. Get the next flight back to London, New York, Scotland—wherever you hang out these days. View it as a courtesy. Leave me and my friends alone, and I'll forget this. I'm prepared to let it go. Nothing personal, I get it. You see, I'm old-school, Jon. I believe in giving a man a chance."

"And if I don't go home?"

"Jon, I admire your defiance. Trust me, I think that's an underrated virtue. In all people. The problem is that defiance in and of itself is admirable. But when it becomes pig-headedness, and that's what you're displaying, especially in the face of technologically superior forces with a nation state backing them, it's a no-brainer. Don't start making dumb moves against me. It'll only end one way. See what I'm getting at?"

Mac began to pace the sidewalk.

"Are you finished?"

"Not quite. If you continue on this little adventure of yours, things will take a turn for the worse."

"Is what way?"

"Well, it means I would be forced to hurt you, Jon. And I'd have to hurt you bad. I abhor violence of any sort, Jon. I don't want to do that. I've got no beef with you. But my reprisal wouldn't be as direct as the one you're planning. It would be an asymmetric response. This little sojourn you've been forced to take smacks of being rushed. But that's the CIA all over these days. No one seems to take the time to do the job properly."

Reznick glanced up again at the cameras.

"You're sweating, Jon. That Abu Dhabi heat doing its worst? You're smart, capable, and very resourceful. So heed my advice: go home and forget this ever happened."

The call ended.

Reznick felt cold. It was as if someone had walked over his grave.

He waited until both Mac and himself were facing away from the cameras. "This whole thing has gone south. We need to regroup."

"We're flying blind. That fucker is getting into our heads. He's a step or two ahead every time. It's uncanny. That stunt he just pulled? He's enjoying the attention and toying with us."

Reznick took a few moments to compose himself. "The element of surprise is gone. The window is closing on us finding Crenshaw. That's why he sounds so happy."

"He says he's not in the city. But I don't know . . . maybe he's still in the fucking hotel?"

Reznick turned and looked over at the hotel again. "He might be."

Mac wrapped his arm around Reznick's shoulders. "I think he's still there. He's all bravado. Think about it."

"We'll get him."

"How?"

"We'll find a way."

"First we need to find him. Are we going to stay here in Abu Dhabi? We've no evidence he's here."

"We have no evidence he's *not* here. I say we stay in the city and watch and wait, in case it's all a bullshit bluff. He's a master of disinformation, after all. Getting into people's heads."

"You ever stayed at the Grand Hyatt on the Corniche?"

Reznick shook his head.

"Let's do that. Separately. And we can meet up for a drink in an hour. Otherwise I'm going to go out of my mind."

Nineteen

Trevelle was struggling to comprehend how Crenshaw had turned the tables on Reznick and Mac in Abu Dhabi. The old man had turned the entire operation on its head. Crenshaw was no longer the hunted; he was the hunter watching his prey. Trevelle sat at his bank of monitors, blinking manically, contemplating what had gone wrong. He couldn't understand it. The audacity of it took his breath away. But what was most worrying was that the operation had been jeopardized by an encrypted cell phone provided by Trevelle. The failure was his own.

He knew that Reznick would want answers. He needed to figure out what had happened. Had the military-grade encryption on the cell phone been broken? And if so, how?

Trevelle couldn't make mistakes in his line of work. A line of code, a breach from malware, was all it would take for the cell phone to have been compromised. And if it was true that the phones had been hacked, it would put Reznick and Mac's lives—not to mention the whole operation—in mortal jeopardy.

His professional pride was badly wounded. His clients came to him and paid top dollar because his knowledge gained through the NSA meant he was a world leader in the field. He was the go-to guy for Reznick. The black ops specialist had come to rely on Trevelle's mastery of cybersecurity and computer skills to guide his work as an assassin. Trevelle needed to figure out what exactly had gone wrong. But he needed to be scientific about it. Rigorous. Logical. Methodical.

He began the test. He ran his military-grade encryption software to detect any vulnerabilities in Reznick's cell phone. The initial test provided a clean bill of health for the device. He moved on to the next level of checks, remotely testing the three encryption packages that ran silently on the phone. He checked its configuration. The applications that were running. But each and every time, the results came back the same: the cell phone's encryption had not been breached.

While that was good news, it didn't identify how the penetration had occurred. He mulled over the options.

Trevelle's mind flashed back to where Reznick was when he'd gotten the call from Crenshaw.

Was that it? Did the location hold the key?

He tracked back to the call he'd made informing Reznick that Crenshaw was at the Emirates Palace Mandarin Oriental. The next move was Reznick and Mac leaving their hotels and traveling by cab to a location very close to the target's location. It was then, when they'd been standing outside in public view, that the call had come from Crenshaw. *Out in the open.*

Trevelle tried to picture the scene as he pieced it together. He knew Reznick's cell phone hadn't been compromised. But how had Crenshaw known that Reznick was there, and how had he known what number to call?

The United Arab Emirates, especially in the urban areas around Dubai and Abu Dhabi, was one of the most heavily surveilled countries in the world. The country had worked with leading American technology firms as well as NSA contractors to develop a network of digital surveillance of not only their citizens but everyone who visited.

Trevelle remembered his time at the NSA. A friend of his, a contractor who had just returned from the Emirates, had estimated that there were more than twenty thousand surveillance cameras in Abu Dhabi alone. In one city. It was a perfect way to track people's movements via cutting-edge facial recognition technology. In many ways, the UAE was the ultimate surveillance state. Orwellian. Big Brother was watching everyone, everywhere, all of the time.

He wondered if ultra-high-definition cameras on the streets had pinged Reznick's face. But it was one thing to find Reznick, and another to find his untraceable cell phone number, known only to him, Mac and Trevelle. None of it made any sense.

Trevelle began a series of remote activation tests. He wanted to determine if there were vulnerabilities in the crucial MAC address which assigned the device's private Wi-Fi address. He also checked the Bluetooth for any backdoor trojans inadvertently loaded, compromising the short-wave wireless signals. After a few minutes of testing and retesting, it was clear there was still nothing amiss.

"What the fuck is going on?" he asked, leaning back in his chair.

Trevelle tracked back further as he tried to piece together the sequence of events. He set up a timeline for Jon Reznick from the moment he'd stepped foot on European soil. Athens, Greece. Facial recognition systems might very well have pinged Reznick—a US citizen with a special forces background—as he'd arrived in Europe. Or upon his arrival in the Middle East.

He began his checks by remotely accessing the surveillance system within Athens International Airport. He quickly accessed their cloud servers, which backed up any footage captured on the airport's cameras. He was in. He watched Reznick arriving and going through security, second by second. Through the terminal as he caught a flight to Heraklion in Crete. Each and every frame was examined for any indication that something was wrong. Trevelle worked fast. Checking. Rechecking. Through the packed terminal in Heraklion. He watched the footage of Reznick returning to the airport a few hours later. But still nothing seemed wrong.

He turned his focus to Egypt. He was surprised by the advanced surveillance system deployed in Hurghada Airport at the Red Sea resort. From the moment Reznick landed, Trevelle could track him through the security gates. He slowed the footage down and rewatched it. Reznick headed through the terminal, dropped by one camera, then picked up by the next a step later.

Nothing. He watched it again. Slow-motion. Still nothing.

"Fuck!"

Trevelle shifted in his chair. He ground over what he was missing. He got up and fixed himself a fresh cup of coffee. He took a couple of gulps, caffeine rousing his system. He sat down and refocused on the footage. He needed to be forensically methodical. He couldn't miss anything. It was important to sort out this mess. Reznick was relying on him. The ex-Delta man needed him. Trevelle was his wing man.

He tapped a few more keys.

Within moments, he had penetrated the multiple layers of encryption shielding the surveillance system of Muscat International Airport from hackers like himself. He pulled up the footage. He went to the date and time of Reznick's arrival. And there he was.

Trevelle watched closely as Reznick headed through a metal detector and a body scanner. Travel backpack placed on a conveyer belt which would go through a scanner. A female security official behind a partition, mostly obscured from the camera's viewpoint, checked his bag. His hands were tested to see that he hadn't been touching drugs or explosives. His face was scanned to make sure he wasn't a wanted terrorist, almost certainly also scanning for individuals on "watch" lists shared among intelligence agencies.

Reznick headed through a metal detector arch, frisked by a couple of well-built security guys on the other side, before he picked up his bag and was on his way.

It all seemed fine. Textbook. Trevelle had monitored every step on Reznick's journey as he headed through the terminal. And yet . . .

Trevelle froze the footage. His gaze was drawn to the still image captured. He spotted a surveillance camera ten yards beyond the security woman behind the screen, situated at a higher viewpoint, with a bird's-eye view of the security hall.

He tapped a few more keys and accessed the footage, examining Reznick's arrival from a fresh viewpoint. The first thing he noticed was that the woman examining Reznick's backpack was virtually out of sight of public view, only the top of her headscarf visible.

Trevelle watched as she searched the backpack. The new angle allowed him to see the security area in greater detail. The woman behind the screen turned to a colleague, who was checking a separate scanning machine but also sat directly behind a screen. She held on to Reznick's backpack, then said something to her colleague, who nodded as if listening.

Then, slowly, very slowly, she took a craft knife, similar to a scalpel, out of a drawer. She sliced open the thick strap of Reznick's backpack.

What the fuck?

Trevelle watched the footage again, this time slowed down to a crawl. Then he rewatched it at full speed. Then slow motion. He zoomed in closer. He put together what she was doing. It was then he realized what was actually happening. He couldn't believe what he was witnessing. He felt a chill run down the length of his spine as he stared at her hands working expertly behind the screen.

"Motherfucker!"

Twenty

The following evening, the Lexx Bar, a deluxe lounge in Abu Dhabi's Grand Hyatt Hotel, was buzzing.

Reznick sat alone on the terrace, nursing a single malt on the rocks, waiting for Mac. He scanned the patrons sitting inside on the leather banquettes in the sprawling bar area. It was quite a cross-section. Business travelers wearing Italian suits, digital nomads wearing flip-flops, a local wearing a Nike tracksuit, another wearing a smart-casual button-down with chinos and loafers, and another wearing traditional garb, all mingling amiably. He checked his watch. Mac was ten minutes late.

Reznick nursed his Scotch and stared down at the lights of the cars headed along the Corniche, beside the beach. Earlier, he had bought a couple of burner cell phones from a pop-up iPhone shop close by. Purely as a precaution, he had dumped the cell phones Trevelle had given him and Mac.

Reznick was, to be honest, still in a state of barely suppressed anger at what had happened. He couldn't wrap his head around it. He couldn't figure out how the target had apparently hacked the encrypted phones. It had compromised the whole operation. Was there any point in continuing? The more he thought about it, the angrier he got. He refused to believe Trevelle had let him down. The ex-NSA expert couldn't possibly be the weak link; he was sure of it.

But he needed to find out what had happened. Had the operation been compromised in a different way?

Was it possible that the microphone in Reznick's cell phone had been activated remotely, turning his device into a bug?

Reznick checked his watch again as he wondered what the hell was keeping Mac. He considered whether he should head up to Mac's room, to see if Mac had crashed out on his bed, forgetting to set the alarm on his watch. But then again, he probably hadn't. He'd give him another ten minutes.

In the meantime, Reznick pulled out his new burner iPhone and called Trevelle.

"Yeah, who's this?" Trevelle's voice was tentative.

"It's Jon. Jon Reznick."

Trevelle sighed. "The voice recognition confirms it's you. I need two more bits of confirmation."

"What do you want to know?"

"Where was your father born, Jon?"

"Bangor, Maine."

"What is your blood group?"

"Rh negative."

"Copy that."

Reznick sipped the last of his Scotch. "I'm not a happy man."

"I understand."

"I'm not used to this sort of setback. I'm pissed. You need to know that. So I'm going to need answers. I'm going to need a technical explanation. This is not a blame game. It's just about establishing facts. We need to learn from our mistakes—and make sure they don't happen again."

"Agreed. First things first, this new cell phone of yours . . . I just remotely uploaded my latest military-grade encryption. It works without you knowing it."

"That was one of the reasons I was calling. We've been compromised. Big-time. How do I know the stuff you're uploading isn't compromised too?"

"You need to trust me. That's all I'm saying."

"Listen, Trevelle, I'm sorry to come down hard on you . . . but this is a fucking shitshow. I'm sitting here unable to do anything. You don't sound too worried."

"You think my encryption let you down? Tell me the truth. Is that what you really think?"

Reznick looked around the terrace. "Trevelle, I don't know," he whispered, conscious that there were other people ten yards away. "All I know is I got a call from Crenshaw, who was watching me remotely on an Abu Dhabi street via a surveillance camera, getting a real-time visual on both myself and Mac. Can you imagine how that felt? I can't have this. So, I want answers. And I want them now."

"And you'll get them."

"Give it to me."

"I've been running a series of penetration tests since that call from Crenshaw."

"Penetration tests? What the hell are those?"

"They're designed to probe vulnerabilities in networks, cell phones. I've been frantically trying to figure out how this happened. I can guarantee, after running these tests, that the encryption I use was not breached."

"Was *not* breached?"

"Correct."

"How can you be so sure?"

"I'm getting to that."

"Get to the point. I need to know how he got a fix on us."

"Crenshaw, or more probably the IT experts he has helping him—maybe Russians—have been tracking you since you got off the plane in Oman."

"They were following me? In person?"

"Not in person."

"What does that mean?"

"I checked out surveillance footage. Get this. The hand luggage you had, a travel backpack, was out of sight for five minutes and eight seconds."

"Security was checking it out."

"They certainly were. A female security operative at Muscat International Airport took your bag from the conveyer belt, out of sight, behind a screen. She then used a knife and sliced open the thick end of the left-hand strap of your backpack."

"She did what?"

"Bear with me. She then managed to insert a tiny GPS tracker—half an inch long, a quarter of an inch thick—inside the strap. Tiny thing. She inserted and sewed up this miniature tracker in just over five minutes. Job done."

Reznick sat dumbfounded. He had heard and seen some pretty crazy shit. But this was a whole new level. "That is pretty fucking far out there. So technically how is that possible?"

"Very simple actually. The tracker had a microphone inside it. Everything you said within earshot of the travel backpack, starting from the moment you landed in Muscat, would have been heard. And also the geolocation would be known too."

"Cute."

"Very."

"Tell me about the person at the airport. The woman. I'm assuming you tried to find out more about her and who's she working for."

"Correct. Here's where it gets interesting. I've done a bit of a deep dive into her background, trawling up all sorts of shit. The female security operative is a married mother of three. But here's the kicker, she's not actually employed at the airport. Not usually."

"So who does she work for?"

"Jahaz al Amn al Dakhly. Oman's Internal Security Service."

"Seriously?"

"Very skilled senior operative, obviously."

"Who asked for this to be done? Did someone tip off the Omani intelligence services?"

"I don't know. That would take a lot longer to find out. But that's a fair assumption."

Reznick's mind raced.

"First things first, you need to get rid of your travel backpack."

"I've already ditched that. What about Mac's?"

"Wasn't touched. That's fine."

Reznick ordered another whisky from a passing waiter. "The operation has been compromised?"

"Yes."

He shook his head. "Not a great start."

"It is what it is, Jon. But this is useful in one regard."

"What's that?"

"You now know, if you didn't already, that Crenshaw is a formidable adversary."

"He has to be an FSB asset."

"Either that or the SVR, Russia's Foreign Intelligence Service. He's a twenty-first-century Kim Philby. And remember what happened to him?"

"He escaped to Moscow and we didn't lay a glove on him. It was too late."

"Precisely."

Reznick could see the brilliance of the bugging plan. He had been tracked the moment he set foot in Oman. It pointed to a state power, or maybe private military contractors working on the state's behalf. It pointed to the Wagner Group. He had to assume it was either Wagner or Russian foreign intelligence who had been behind the order to the Oman intelligence services.

Reznick saw Mac headed toward him carrying a couple of Scotches on the rocks. "I'll update Mac. He'll call you with a burner for you to handle as well. One final thing, Trevelle. I need you to get me a solid lead on where the fuck the old man is. I don't know for sure if he's still in the hotel, holed up. I don't know if he's fled the country. It needs to be definitive. And another thing: I don't want any more nasty surprises."

Twenty-One

Petersen was shown into the office of the CIA Director. The door was shut behind her. She stood and waited patiently like a schoolgirl waiting for the principal to give her detention. Mendez glanced over the annotated notes on the briefing paper.

The large windows offered uninterrupted views of the woods that famously shrouded Langley, the beating heart of America's foreign intelligence service.

"Pull up a seat," he said.

Mendez appeared to be perusing her classified briefing on the progress in Oman and UAE—or lack of progress. He looked up and shook his head. "This is it? This is where we're at? He's fucking laughing at us?"

"Yes sir. As we knew, Crenshaw is no fool. The chances of getting him in the crosshairs are receding. When Reznick had a chance from a long-range position, circumstances dictated that the target couldn't be killed cleanly and then he was out of the line of sight within a split second. I want to stress again this is difficult stuff. SEAL Team 6 failed."

"Sure as hell looks like this left-field plan has failed repeatedly as well."

"I don't accept that, sir. There have been no innocent casualties so far. But that's not to say it's going swimmingly."

"Cut the bullshit. This operation is hanging by a thread. Maybe we need to cut that thread."

Petersen winced as she contemplated what she was going to say next. She had thought about all the reasons to get Reznick and Mac out of there. There were many smart, rational reasons for the operation to end. But the one compelling reason to keep them in the field was the obvious one. "Jorge, I don't think we can say that at this stage. We need to let this play out."

"Play out?"

"Let's not give up now."

"Fran, I've heard enough. It was a wild-card plan and it didn't work. That happens. He knows we're after him, and now he's calling Reznick and toying with him. We need to go back to the drawing board. So let's move on."

Petersen was quiet for a few moments, always attempting not to be too strident, too knee-jerk in her responses, especially to higher-ups. She found it difficult, as one of the most senior women within the CIA, to simply accept failure. Her father had imbued in her the importance of seeing a job through. "Sir, with all due respect, the plan has suffered a setback. I accept that. And I take full responsibility for the failures. However, I would disagree with your assessment of where we should go from here, sir."

"The whole scenario is an embarrassment. I want them called back with immediate effect."

"Sir, we have two highly capable operatives in the arena, ready to do what they have to do. I say we need to show some backbone now."

"Are you saying I'm not showing backbone?"

"Absolutely not. We have had a setback. But we do not retreat. Not now."

"Gimme a break. Crenshaw called Reznick. They're fucking laughing at us."

"They can laugh all they want. The goal remains the same. We must neutralize Crenshaw, one way or another. It's better to do it now, before he disappears forever."

"So why don't they do it now? I'll tell you why, because the operation has run aground. Give it back to Delta or the SEALs. Maybe even hand it over to private military contractors working in the Middle East. I believe there is a sizeable team from Chrome Security over in Dubai at the moment. Get them in on it."

"We've tried the conventional special forces way, and that was a disaster. I don't have any problems with the contractors from Chrome. But I don't want to throw in the towel just yet."

Mendez shuffled in his seat as he listened.

Petersen continued. "You remember our discussion after the SEAL Team 6 shitshow? We were fed disinformation, we acted on impulse, and we killed an oil minister. Think long and hard about that. The geopolitical tectonic plates are moving, mostly in the wrong direction. We hang in there with Reznick, and who knows, maybe he can see it through, allowing us to salvage the operation and complete the mission. If not, we have plausible deniability. Let's not abandon him. He deserves better. We need to give it time. I'm begging you, we need to stick with this!"

"How much time do they need? You said yourself they tracked him down, so why didn't they go in there and kill him? Or what about when they had him on the yacht?"

"We would have had a bloodbath on our hands. Innocent people killed. The Russians would have had a field day. They would be setting social media alight with the failed operation. American killers. The usual spiel."

Mendez stared back at her. "Your briefing note was interesting. Reznick got a call from Crenshaw on a supposedly encrypted cell phone. Who the hell is running this operation? How did that happen?"

"I'm running this operation. Listen, the encryption wasn't cracked."

"What are you talking about, Fran? It had to be cracked or hacked."

"No. I just heard from Trevelle, only within the last fifteen minutes, and he has proof that Reznick was tagged as soon as they went through security in Oman. They were waiting for him."

"Who tagged him?"

"The woman working security at the airport is actually Omani intelligence."

"So who the hell alerted them to Reznick's true identity?"

"A state actor, no question."

"Russia?"

"Who else?"

"The whole operation has been compromised. I want it off my plate."

"We're up against a formidable foe. You might remember my briefing about the Turla group."

"The Russian hackers?"

"Correct. Linked to Moscow, using the most advanced satellite-based hacking tools. There's a reasonable chance they might be involved in countermeasures to thwart Reznick."

Mendez pursed his lips tight.

"This hacking group has been linked to fifty-one devastating hacking attacks, including a French television conglomerate, the German Bundestag, and the Ukrainian parliament. They focus on diplomatic and government targets, especially in the Middle East. Which makes me think there's a fair chance they're responsible for this, or are at least advising in some capacity. Crenshaw is a Russian asset. A highly prized asset."

"The Russians also have assets all over Egypt. It's been a focus for them in the past."

"We have identified operatives who have trained with Turla in Saudi Arabia and Oman, areas where oil and gas are involved. Would it be too much of a stretch to imagine that this group has penetrated the facial recognition systems of airports across Europe and the Middle East?"

Mendez motioned for her to go on.

"If I were to speculate, I would hazard a guess that the problem occurred in Hurghada. We already know that Russian hackers have repeatedly infiltrated Egyptian systems. Have the Egyptians got spies and operatives within Omani intelligence who relayed the intel back to Russia? Oman and Egypt are not in NATO. Cairo has a decades-old relationship with Moscow."

"What a fucking mess."

"Think of what Reznick is up against. The easy move would be to pull the plug. I say no. It's compromised, sure. But we go again. Trevelle has indicated that Reznick and Mac are still on board. If anything, they're even more determined to see the mission through."

"The chances of success are rapidly diminishing."

"Maybe."

Mendez walked across to the windows overlooking the woods. "My background is the law. Your background is intelligence. Give me your best assessment. And no bullshit."

"The work we do is sometimes messy. It's sometimes infuriating. And there are setbacks. What makes this so raw is that Crenshaw was one of us. To become a bona fide Russian operative, spying on America, a country he served for so many years, is despicable. The worst. I think we need to suck this up and go again."

"I'm guessing this will put Reznick and his Scottish friend at greater risk."

"They know the risks."

"Very well. Let's stay on it. But we know Crenshaw is going to disappear. The clock is ticking. Let's get this done."

Twenty-Two

Reznick was lying on his bed in his hotel room in Abu Dhabi, wide awake, staring at the ceiling. His cell phone buzzed and he sat up. A text from Trevelle.

Give me a call.

He called the number he knew so well.

"I've got a fix on a phone belonging to a member of the old man's flight crew," Trevelle said. "The plane flies out later tonight."

"Shit."

"Doesn't give you long, I know."

"What else?"

"He lands at Bahrain International Airport and will be escorted into an exclusive terminal. It has eight private lounges. Designed for VIPs, that kind of thing."

Reznick got up from the bed and began to pace his room. "Where's the plane now?"

"Kuwait."

"So he's in Kuwait now?"

"Correct. I'm assuming Bahrain is where you need to head."

"It'll give us a little extra time. Not much. But it's better than nothing. Where is he in Kuwait?"

"I don't know."

Reznick felt his anger levels rising. "Trevelle, that is not what I want to hear."

"Jon, listen to me. I know how tough this is for you and Mac. But I am using every tool in the box to get a fix on him. He's like a ghost."

"I need hard intel. If we don't have hard intel, we're fucked. We have nothing."

Reznick ended the call. He decided he had been unnecessarily tough on Trevelle. He knew the kid was doing his best. He was just up against the apparatus of the Russian state.

Reznick needed to clear his head. He left the cool air-conditioned calm of the hotel and headed out into the steaming heat of the night. He walked over to some high-end shops and bought a new travel backpack. Then he headed back to his room. He first took out the weapons from the tactical backpack, in case the military bag had also been tagged while he was out, and transferred them into the brand-new travel backpack. He zipped it up and slung it over his shoulder. Then he headed downstairs to the lobby.

The concierge smiled at him. "Can I help you at all?"

"I'm fine, thanks. Waiting for a friend."

"Very good, sir. If you need anything, don't hesitate to let me know."

The concierge walked to the far side of the lobby as some new guests sporting expensive luggage arrived.

Reznick pulled out his cell phone and called Mac. He answered on the third ring.

"Hey Jon."

"We're on the move."

"Where?"

Reznick gave him the details about Crenshaw's next destination, Bahrain. "I think we should split up."

"Fuck."

"You been to Bahrain?"

"I have. And hated it. Tell you what. How about I drive north?"

Reznick considered that option. "It's risky. That would mean heading through Saudi Arabia."

"Life's better with an edge, right? I reckon I could be up in Bahrain by midday, after crossing over the causeway from the Saudi side."

"Very high-risk, Mac."

"Done recon work years back with the SAS. I know the lay of the land pretty good. If anyone can make it through there, it's me."

Reznick felt himself smiling. "It's direct, I'll give you that."

"That's me all over, Jon. Green light?"

"Do it."

"Excellent. What about you?"

Reznick looked at the concierge's desk. The helpful young man had gone outside to hail a cab. "I think flights would have me tagged, no question. Besides, the stuff in our backpacks wouldn't make it into the terminal."

"Agreed. By sea?"

"That's the plan."

"See you in Bahrain. We need to get lucky sometime."

"Our luck needs to change. Let's hope it's soon."

Twenty-Three

It was the dead of night in the oldest part of Abu Dhabi.

Reznick walked past the fish market and headed toward Dhow Harbor, opposite the Corniche. The smell of spicy cooking, the pungent aroma of fish, cigarette smoke, and the faint smell of hashish all blended in the air.

He looked along the line of dhows. Some tourist boats, but mostly working boats.

His gaze flew to a rickety old dhow, spewing out fumes from its diesel engine as if about to leave. It was laden down with wooden crates of dates and fish. A man and a young boy, along with a few scrawny deckhands swathed in traditional clothes, scrubbed the boat to get it ready for departure.

Reznick signaled to the man, who appeared to be in charge. "You speak English?"

"Yes sir, how can I help?"

"I'm looking for a ride."

"I'm sorry, sir, you'll want the other dhows. The tourist dhows. We are a working boat. I believe they open at seven in the morning."

"No, I'm wanting to head to Bahrain."

The man shrugged. "It is a long, uncomfortable journey."

"Are you headed there?"

"I am. But we're a working dhow, sir. It's not for the faint-hearted to be out on the Gulf on such a boat."

"Not a problem."

"Besides, we leave in ten minutes."

"Perfect." Reznick showed him two hundred-dollar bills. "For your trouble. Will that be enough?"

The man smiled, exposing his nicotine-stained teeth. "Well, of course, why not? But like I said, we're not very fast."

"Can you get me to Bahrain?"

"That's where we're going." The man shrugged. "Jump down."

Reznick jumped into the boat and handed over the hundred-dollar bills. The guy put the money in his pocket, pointing to a corner of the dhow. "That's the only free space. Make yourself at home. I'm in charge. I'm the captain by the way. So you must listen to what I say."

"Got it."

"Also, don't bother my workers during the journey."

"Not a problem." Reznick sat down under a filthy canopy, the backpack with the weapons at his side, partially hidden from sight. He got a few puzzled looks from some of the crew.

A few minutes later, the boat chugged slowly away from the harbor and the bright lights of Abu Dhabi, and gradually out into the dark waters of the Persian Gulf.

The vessel was a Shu'ai, a medium-sized dhow. The diesel motor sputtered, the lantern sails fluttering in the hot breeze, as it headed through the waters. Farther and farther away it traveled from the lights of the big city. The five-man crew all wore head-cloths, sarongs, and dirty robes. A kid with staring brown eyes watched him.

Reznick winked and the kid beamed. He checked his watch. It was just after three in the morning. He was taking the slow boat to Bahrain. It would minimize the risk of detection, but it would take him at least a day, maybe more, to get there. The risk was that Crenshaw would be out of Bahrain before he even made it. Mac would arrive first, if he managed to make it through Saudi land without being arrested. The truth was it was less than ideal having to take such slow modes of transport. Time wasn't on their side, after all. But after what had happened at the airport in Oman, it made sense. At least they were still in the game. Still on Crenshaw's trail.

Mac could arrive in Bahrain by midday, if he made it through the hell that was Saudi Arabia. It wasn't the place of twenty years earlier. The country was opening up. There were sporting events. Concerts. But under the veneer of creeping Westernism, the state was still, broadly speaking, a highly religious, traditional, and deeply conservative Islamic country. The police were not to be crossed. Neither were the feared mutawa—the religious police—who ran frequent random checks on foreigners. Mac had excellent fake passports—American, British, Ukrainian. He also had an ID showing he worked in the oil industry for a British company. It made sense in this part of the world.

However, the whole thing could be compromised if the Saudis started digging deeper. *Who do you work for? Where is your family? Come with us, we have some questions.* No one wanted to be detained in Saudi Arabia.

Reznick had heard horror stories of what happened to those who stepped out of line. The Saudis specialized in particularly ancient forms of torture. Public beheadings, the amputation of limbs for petty thieves, hundreds of lashes for "immoral" women, hangings for any number of trumped-up charges. Electrocution. There wasn't a torture method that had been invented that they didn't use.

He pushed those thoughts to one side as he hunkered down in the dhow. He took the satellite phone from a zipped inside pocket of the backpack and texted Trevelle. *Any updates?*

Trevelle texted him back in under a minute. *The old man is due to land in Bahrain at 4:40pm local time. He will check into Four Seasons, Manama. 5pm*

Reznick's mind crunched the times. It would be just over twelve hours until Crenshaw landed. Reznick would still be out in the Gulf. But there was a real possibility Mac would be in place. He texted back, *Let Mac know.*

Will do.

What else do we know?

I'm working on it, Jon. I'm tracking both your satellite phones. You taking the scenic route?

Anything, I mean anything, keep me in the loop. Could be a scrap of intel. I want to know about it.

Copy that. Mac is headed for the Saudi border, right?

Yup.

Better him than me. I'll keep an eye on his progress. Stay safe, man.

Reznick put the satellite phone back in the backpack. The kid approached him and handed him a wooden bowl of dates and a cup of sweet tea.

The boy bowed.

"Thank you," Reznick said and began to eat the fruit. It was moreish, and not too bad, washed down with the tea. "Very nice."

The kid grinned and walked over to a crate of fish, sat down, and began sorting them by size. A man beside the crate of fish was weaving a basket, but he didn't acknowledge the boy.

Reznick watched dawn break over the Gulf. A blood-red sun peeked over the far horizon, turning the inky black sky a cotton candy pink. He felt the rolling swell get more pronounced the farther out in the Gulf they got. Waves buffeted the dhow from both sides. The diesel engine growled as it powered the ancient wooden boat. Reznick felt himself getting drowsy as the sun beat down. He closed his eyes to the sound of the men praying to Allah.

The smell of tobacco and hashish filled the humid morning as he heard the faint sound of Arabic music. He felt himself drifting away. Somewhere far, far away. Deeper and deeper into a world of darkness.

He floated alone, out on the sea, staring up at the inky blue sky. Millions of stars like white pinpricks. He felt heat burning his skin. Deeper and deeper into a soothing, warm cocoon. Drifting away, miles away. The sound of voices in the distance. Farsi. Men were shouting. Screaming. Urgent voices.

Reznick felt himself being shaken awake. He sat up as he quickly snapped back to reality on the dhow.

The kid was staring down at him, fear in his eyes.

"What is it?"

"Iran!"

Reznick peered through a rip in the sails and off into the distance. A military patrol boat approached. More shouting. He didn't need to be told who it was. The Islamic Revolutionary Guards, patrolling the hostile waters of the Persian Gulf. His senses switched on. He reached into his backpack and took out the semi-automatic. He guessed the Iranians would be checking for weapons being smuggled into Saudi Arabia to be used against Iran or their allies. Or contraband. Or drugs. Or perhaps they were just looking for "foreign elements." Iran was obsessed with foreigners trying to foment uprisings to destabilize the regime—something America, and the CIA in particular, specialized in. The explosion of social media had connected a new generation of young people in the Middle East looking for a freer way of life. Iran was terrified of freedom for the young and freedom in general.

The boy signaled for Reznick to follow him to another part of the dhow. He crawled along the bottom of the boat, backpack and rifle in hand, past the baskets of dates and fish. The boy lifted up three planks of wood and pointed inside.

Reznick weighed the consequences of just using his rifle and killing the approaching Iranians. He could take them all out in seconds. He was torn. But then he reminded himself the mission was everything. It couldn't be jeopardized, unless it absolutely had to be. If he had no alternative.

He winked at the kid and crawled into the stifling space under the deck, backpack and rifle at his side.

Reznick would have to put his trust in the boy, the captain, and the crew not to inform on him. His (and their) fate would be decided by whether or not they could be trusted. His instincts told him to take the chance. He would be a bounty for the Quds Force, if that was indeed who was approaching. He got a whiff of diesel fumes and oil in the fetid, enclosed space. He lay motionless as the kid carefully laid the planks of wood back down, concealing him in darkness and hiding him from plain sight. Shards of light pierced the gaps between the planks until baskets of fish and dates were pushed over them.

Reznick lay quiet, sweat soaking into his linen shirt, his throat parched. He took his trusty Beretta 9mm out of his waistband, flicking off the safety. Far easier to neutralize at close quarters with a handgun.

He gripped the gun tight, hands sticky with sweat.

Crates of fish above; drips of warm, salty water landing on his skin.

The harsh Farsi voices got louder and more aggressive. He felt the vibrations of boots on the wooden planks. He realized the Iranians had climbed on board. Heavy boots kicked over crates and baskets; there was shouting. The sound of a heavy slap. More shouts and screaming. The sound of a boy crying.

Reznick felt his anger rising. He held his breath, finger on the Beretta's trigger. A basket above him was kicked over. A shard of light appeared through the cracked plank of wood. A beard and a flash of green fatigues. A succession of hard slaps. The boy was wailing. The cruel bastards were knocking the kid around. He had to use all his powers of self-control to stop himself busting out of his hiding place and shooting every one of them on sight.

He saw a skinny old man from the dhow. The elderly, frail guy stood up to one of the Iranians. But he quickly got gut-punched to the ground; groaning, moaning, and coughing up blood.

The Iranians were dishing out punishment. Beatings to scare. The shouting intensified for a few minutes, as another basket above him was kicked away. A shot was fired. The boy screamed.

The poor crew of the dhow were standing up to the Iranian thugs. Reznick could see their dirty, bare feet through the cracks. Tremendous bravery.

Another slap from the lead Iranian guard.

The boy wept again. The voices of the men on the dhow were raised.

The seconds felt like hours. He wanted to come to the aid of the kid and the guys on the dhow, but that would be fatal for not only his mission but perhaps the boy and the men as well. Another Iranian patrol boat would be quickly summoned by a guard upon hearing shots.

Reznick hunkered down, seething. The rage burned in him, ready to explode.

Another shot was fired. A silence hung over the boat. Heavy boots stomping across the planks of wood. Threats in Farsi. It all went quiet very quickly.

The sound of a boat speeding off, away from the dhow. A few seconds passed. The planks were pulled back. The boy blinked back tears. The kid's nose and ears were bleeding as if the Iranians had knocked him around badly.

The captain of the dhow pushed past the boy. "It is safe."

Reznick squinted into the sun and stepped out. "I'm so sorry." He thanked the captain for his discretion and nodded respectfully to the crew. They all look scared. The boy stared at Reznick, tears spilling down his face. Reznick picked up a cloth, dabbed it in a bowl of water lying on the ground, and carefully wiped the boy's face and skin, trying to wash off the blood.

The boy smiled through the tears.

Reznick cleaned the boy up as best he could. He patted him on the head. "I'm so sorry."

The boy nodded as if he understood.

The captain pointed at Reznick. "Stay out of sight. Sit over there, where you were. Do you understand?"

Reznick crawled back under the canopy. He sat, head bowed low. He felt rage that he couldn't help. The mission was paramount. More important than the boy or the crew getting mistreated. He watched as the boy was handed a cup of warm sweet tea by an older man.

The boy sipped the tea, hand trembling.

Reznick hunkered down against a basket of dates, pulse racing, black rage in his heart.

Twenty-Four

A neon-lit sign in Manama's old-town souk showed it was ninety-three degrees.

Crenshaw breathed hard, sweat plastering his shirt to his skin as he headed along the narrow, dusty street with his bodyguards in tow, a dark brown Italian leather satchel over his shoulder. He walked past Bab Al Bahrain in Customs Square in the former central business district of the city. Then he turned a corner before heading down yet more winding alleyways and side streets.

Dimitri turned and asked, "You OK?"

Crenshaw struggled in the oppressive conditions. "I'm getting too old for this shit. This heat is a killer."

"Humidity is very high too. You sure you're OK to do this?"

"Fine. Why wouldn't I be?"

"I just thought you seemed a bit more withdrawn than usual."

"Don't worry about me. Just all the heat, the traveling. I can't seem to cool down."

Crenshaw was worried too. And not only about the Bahrain summer heat. He also felt apprehensive about the meeting. He hadn't wanted to share his concerns with Dimitri. He had been especially on edge since learning the CIA had sent an assassin to take him out. He gave the impression to the Wagner crew that he was unperturbed, but deep down he was fearful. He wasn't sleeping well. His health was faltering. The fact was, he was getting older. Frailer. He needed to get out of this high-stakes game. He knew he would soon. But he grumbled if the Russians weren't right, as they always seemed to be. The warnings carried with them some weight. He would be a fool to dismiss such fears. The last thing he needed was the Russians losing patience with him and cutting him loose. No protection. He wondered if he should just hand over what he had. It might ease the situation. But he needed to keep the Russians on his side until he reached Jeddah. It made more sense, in Crenshaw's eyes—waiting until the agreed time and place, which had been planned months in advance.

He glanced up at the dark skies, imagining the lights of drones tracking him. But there was nothing. Just stars in the huge black sky. A pale moon.

Crenshaw walked on, throat as dry as sandpaper. The sooner his affairs were in order, the sooner he could get on with the rest of his life.

He was so close he could almost touch it. He would soon have his business affairs settled. And it would all be done.

He had recently purchased, via one of the offshore companies specifically set up for him by his lawyers and advisors in Switzerland, a stunning four-bedroom penthouse overlooking the Bahrain Financial Harbor. It also had a rooftop pool. Bahrain was a haven for those who wanted genuine privacy and security. An orderly country. It would be a change of scenery from Jeddah. A great winter destination for him to live in. Maybe not the best for summer. Summer was hell.

He turned down another alleyway in an area he knew well.

Crenshaw felt his stomach knot with tension. He was about to meet up with the most senior of his Russian handlers, Pavel, a former colonel in the KGB. It would be his third meeting with the Russians in quick succession. He feared they were going to neutralize him if he didn't hand over what he had. Pavel, after a lifetime of service to the motherland, had retired and moved to the Middle East. But he was still a player in the shadow world of Russian intelligence. Pavel's new job was to cultivate contacts in the British, American, and European expatriate business community, to develop intelligence links and business relationships with individuals and companies. He was a corporate figurehead—there had been no Western sanctions against him or his companies—but Moscow pulled the strings.

Crenshaw saw a sign for Haji's Café. He headed past the Tiffany blue benches outside, customers eating politely and quietly. He walked through arched walkways and went inside. A waiter escorted him to his favorite table in a private recess. He felt the air-conditioning cool him down almost immediately. It was a welcome relief.

He sat down and ordered a coffee as his men spread out around him. It was nice to take the weight off for a few minutes. A couple of old Bahraini men smoking cigarettes and drinking tea looked on. His Russian bodyguards prowled around, eyeing them suspiciously. The old men looked away as if sensing trouble.

Crenshaw lit up a cigarette as Dimitri and his men ordered lamb curries, goat stews, and rice from the owner, who knew them very well. He grudgingly admired the almost medieval ways of these new Middle Eastern autocracies in the twenty-first century. They were hyper-capitalist. But they were still imbued in the traditions of their ancient culture. Men and women had traditional roles. Crime was non-existent compared to American cities. A cursory glance at the stories in the Metro section of the *New York Post* on his iPad was enough to make him weep for his homeland.

It was hard to believe what America had become. In a matter of generations, he thought, it had gone to the dogs. The mentally ill roaming the streets, women being battered in the subway by savages as passengers pretended not to notice, glued to their phones. Refugees pouring into the city after being bused from the Texas/Mexico border and then housed in tourist hotels around the five boroughs. Filth, degradation, decay, all paid for by increasingly higher taxes. The working man or woman in America was buckling with the weight of this ailing behemoth. No one had blinked an eye when it was announced that the national debt was thirty-two trillion dollars.

Crenshaw was brought up strict. His parents instilled in him the need for hard work, sacrifice, and a strong sense of frugality. His heart bled for America. It was bankrupt—financially, morally, spiritually, caught in a death spiral of quasi-socialism masquerading as liberalism. Once-great cities like Chicago, New York, and Los Angeles were awash with crime, disorder, and dysfunction. Literally hundreds of thousands of homeless across the country, many starving and staring into the abyss. These were Americans. Left to rot. Left to die, no one lifting a finger to help them. By sharp contrast, Americans were expected to roll out the red carpet and largesse for the illegal newcomers. *Economic migrants*, they were called. Liberalism wanted to welcome them into the cities. Though Martha's Vineyard was off limits. That was a step too far even for liberals.

Crenshaw maintained that he saw it for what it was—the wholesale surrender of American society, subjugated to become top choice for the Third World. The unskilled, wretched men, women, and children who couldn't speak English but would willingly endure twelve-hour shifts for dog wages in fancy hotels in New York, taking the subway in from their hellish homes in the Bronx at all hours. How was that going to end?

The shining house on the hill was about to fall. But no one on Capitol Hill seemed to have noticed. What did they care?

Crenshaw's late father, who had also worked in counterintelligence under the infamously paranoid spy James Angleton, had talked about the "death of the West" constantly as the years rolled by. Crenshaw saw being white, Anglo, male, old, and smart as something derided by comedians on the TV. He looked around at the shit-for-brains storming out of colleges and universities across America—not as highly educated, smart people, thankful to be so lucky, but angry that the world and the country were so unequal. A generation of socialist activists who ended up working in NGOs. Young lawyers from good families throwing Molotov cocktails at the NYPD to support Black Lives Matter. Think tanks. Climate-emergency Marxists. Transgender crazies walking with supporters of Hamas.

More and more, Crenshaw saw it was over. Now here he was in fucking Bahrain. Once derided as a hellhole, now an enclave of financial districts in gleaming glass towers facing the sparkling waters of the Gulf. Embracing raw capitalism, embracing dynamism, not afraid of profit. Attracting businesses, remote IT workers, retirees. It was starting to feel like the early days of Dubai all over again.

Crenshaw snapped out of his thoughts as he caught sight of a familiar figure striding into the café. A tall, tanned, blue-eyed man with a malevolent visage and a scar above his right eye sauntered in. The scar was said to have been caused by a knife fight at school.

Pavel wore a white linen shirt, chinos, and boat shoes, and was smoking an unfiltered cigarette. He nodded to his fellow Russians, hardened mercenaries, and they patted him on the back like an old friend.

He sat down opposite Crenshaw.

Pavel stared at him long and hard. It was the sort of look that could unnerve many people, which was the purpose. "Didn't expect to see you again."

Crenshaw nodded. "A few odds and ends to tie up. Business."

"Ah, business. We'll talk all about that. But first, we eat. I'm famished. What are you eating, William?"

"I was waiting for you before I ordered."

"Let me deal with this."

Crenshaw always deferred to Pavel. He found it easier that way. Pavel was a sinister shadowy presence. Not a man to be trifled with. Crenshaw knew he had killed numerous internal and external enemies of the Russian state. But he also liked money. And women.

Pavel had been the one who had overseen Crenshaw's "transition" to the other side. His attention turned toward the mercenaries seated two tables away, scoffing food as if they were dogs. "It appears your countrymen are enjoying goat stews and a side of lamb and rice with flatbreads."

Pavel signaled to a waiter and ordered a selection of the house specials along with a couple of bottles of water and two famously strong coffees, all in fluent Arabic. Finally, he added a carafe of red wine to his order.

"Good to see you again, my friend."

"Likewise, William." Pavel poured a glass of red for himself and passed one to Crenshaw. He raised his glass. "To friendship."

Crenshaw clinked his glass with Pavel's. "Friendship." He took a small sip of wine. "That's very good."

"Bahrain has much to recommend. Being able to partake in alcohol, if you are a non-Muslim, is one of them. Small pleasures, right?"

Crenshaw nodded, cold sweat running down his back.

Pavel drank his glass of red wine and poured himself another. "We're concerned. You don't appear to be heeding our previous warnings."

Crenshaw looked around the backstreet café. He wondered how long he could hold them off. He again considered handing everything over now. The quiet, incessant pressure from the Russians was making him antsy. But his instincts told him that to hand over the final lot of intelligence documents ahead of schedule was not in *his* best interests. The handover at the last possible moment at a VIP departure lounge at Bahrain International Airport, as agreed, would give him extra security, before his planned departure to Saudi Arabia. Besides, he would be vulnerable if he handed over what he had ahead of schedule. He would have no cards to play. Bottom line? He didn't trust that the Russians wouldn't kill him when they finally had the priceless classified CIA intel he had carefully accumulated over the years.

"Time is running out. That's all I'll say. You need to think long and hard, my friend. Do you want to sail off into the sunset or do you want your fellow countrymen to find you?"

"I have what you want. Not here. Not now."

"Give me a flavor of this intel. The scale."

"Thousands of documents I scanned over the years. Notebooks."

"Interesting. What do these notebooks contain?"

Crenshaw picked up his drink and took a small gulp. "Hundreds of crucial agent names, handlers, dead drop zones, as well as highly sensitive photocopied documents, briefing papers. All sorts of goodies."

Pavel crossed his arms. "So, when can we see it?"

"Please don't press this issue."

"That's not an option. I must."

"A bit more patience. There's a whole lot more, buried amongst a mountain of classified data and projections. Intelligence budgets too."

"Intriguing. You've given me a lot to think about. And I want to say how thankful we are that you have helped us with building a greater understanding. But you need to know that our patience has run out. So we need to agree on a precise time. Within the next twenty-four hours."

Crenshaw said nothing. He wondered if the Russians were playing mind games with him. He couldn't be sure that it wasn't a theoretical threat. He stubbed out his cigarette in the glass ashtray.

Pavel stared back at him, long and hard. Eyes like pale blue gems.

"Let me sleep on it. You might also be interested in case files and cryptonyms of the CIA's most trusted Russian sources. You'll see that there are also the code names for projects and covert operations, and the addresses of diplomats, operatives, and sympathetic journalists who back US interests."

"We look forward to receiving this."

Crenshaw lit up another cigarette and inhaled the smoke deeply. "I promised you, didn't I?"

"Promises can be broken."

"I don't break my promises. I have it all. Years of painstaking work. A lot of Xeroxing in the middle of the night."

Pavel grinned. "How gloriously analog."

Crenshaw laughed softly. "Paper and pen. Dead drops. Sometimes the old ways are the best. Don't knock it. It's more time-consuming, but there's years' worth of intel I patiently gathered for you."

The conversation stopped as the plates of food arrived, steaming hot.

Crenshaw tucked in, enjoying the biting spicy flavors, sweat already beading his forehead. "This is quite excellent."

Pavel was cutting some goat and lamb. "Isn't it?" He turned and nodded to the Russian bodyguards gathered around. "They seem happy."

Crenshaw sipped his strong coffee. He sensed he had bought himself some time. He needed to make the right call.

"Have you had any problems with them? If you have, I'll be happy to sort it out."

"No problems at all. Good as gold."

"Excellent. They are very loyal."

"I wouldn't want to cross them in an alley in the middle of the night."

"Some of the most heinous thugs we have."

"I'm flattered. It's nice to have them around. Lends a certain spark of excitement to my life in my later years."

Pavel laughed as he wolfed down his food. "This must happen. I trust you understand my position. Don't fuck with us."

"No one is fucking with you. You'll get it. And soon. I promise." Crenshaw forked the sauteed slices of lamb, glad for the cool air-conditioning on his skin.

"Have you got any demands or requests I might be able to help you with?"

"Quite simple, really. Look after me. I want privacy. I want security. Discreet."

"We'll look after you. I don't want you to end up like fucking Aldrich Ames."

Crenshaw felt himself shifting in his seat. It was a touchy subject with anyone who worked in American intelligence. He had known Ames, the former CIA counterintelligence chief. The guy had been his boss at Langley way back in the 1980s. It was ironic that Crenshaw was now following in his footsteps. The betrayal. The money. The loneliness. The growing paranoia.

His mind flashed back to the day Ames was arrested by FBI agents in February 1994. The shockwaves had reverberated around Langley and the CIA for years. Then paranoia had set in. The hunt for Russian spies and foreign agents reached fever pitch. And there, hidden in plain sight, had been Crenshaw. An impeccable intelligence pedigree, just like his father. He had been questioned shortly after Ames was arrested. But his extensive training and knowledge of interview psychology meant he passed the interrogation with flying colors. No one had suspected a thing. Quite the opposite— they had apologized profusely that they had to even question him.

Pavel shrugged. "You need to think long and hard. I count you as a friend. And I say this as a friend. Don't end up like poor Aldrich. He will almost certainly die in prison. In disgrace. Alone. Unloved."

"Did you know him?"

"Aldrich Ames?"

Crenshaw nodded.

"I know the man who was his handler. He killed himself after Aldrich was arrested."

Crenshaw knew better than to ask sensitive questions about deaths and unexplained killings. He sat in silence, wanting Pavel to fill in the blanks.

"KGB found him at his apartment in Moscow. That's the official story."

"That's a most unfortunate coincidence."

Pavel gave an all-knowing smile. "And that's the final point I'd like to stress. Your work with us is not done. We are indebted to you. We will always help you or assist you wherever you are, because you are held in such high esteem."

"Very kind."

"So you need to hand over what you have. As soon as you can. Then you disappear."

Crenshaw had his own personal timetable he was adhering to. He was in the middle of extensive paperwork to unfreeze his various business interests—namely his numerous offshore bank accounts. "I believe my beachfront villa in Jeddah in that rather exclusive ultra-secure gated community is ready."

"The staff are already there. You just need to say the word."

Crenshaw closed his eyes. "I can just picture the Red Sea."

"Your jet will get you there in under two hours. No one can touch you after that. I've been doing some digging. I believe the gated community in Jeddah is home to a few crown princes and some European royals. You could play golf with them. You like golf, don't you?"

"Would you like to join me for a round or two when I'm settled?"

Pavel winced, as if in pain. "Not my thing, but thanks all the same."

"What is your thing?"

Pavel spread out in his seat, swishing the wine around his glass. "I like opera. I like reading. And the occasional drink."

"How very Russian."

Pavel finished his wine and shook Crenshaw's hand. "Until next time, my friend."

Crenshaw watched as Pavel stood up and patted him on the arm.

"Don't disappoint us."

The advice was a recurring refrain. Crenshaw needed to hand over the files to the Russians and then leave. But his business affairs were still not in order. He had been promised by his advisors in Zurich that it would be "soon." Until then he needed to be patient and stay put, until the legal and financial side of things had been taken care of. He wanted the peace of mind that Western governments couldn't reach out and extradite him on a legal technicality from behind the gates of the exclusive private community in Jeddah. Besides, the Saudis didn't want everyone to know that they were protecting Crenshaw. It wouldn't look good in Western circles. But they would just deny it. And that would be the end of the matter.

Crenshaw would spend the rest of his natural life hidden away from his pursuers. Like Idi Amin. He hoped he still had a good few years left in him, would maybe even live until he was ninety. His father had made it to ninety-two. A grand old age.

Crenshaw watched as Pavel made small talk with his crew of Russian protectors. Hearty laughs. Pats on the back.

Then Pavel turned and headed down the alleyway, into the stifling Manama night, to be driven back to the Russian Embassy, the latest warning ricocheting around Crenshaw's head.

Twenty-Five

It was nearly midnight out on the Gulf as the dhow chugged through the waters. Slowly but surely, the old boat was headed toward the Bahrain coast.

Reznick checked the GPS on his satellite phone. He still had hours to go. The journey seemed like it would never end. The crew slept as the captain chewed khat furiously, nodding his head to some Arabic music he was playing through a small radio. Khat was a plant that contained stimulant-like properties. The captain had not slept one wink throughout the journey, chewing industrial quantities of the stuff. The effect was the same as taking speed. The user became more talkative, crazy wide-awake, almost blissed-out.

Reznick got up and did some stretching exercises for a few minutes. The crouched position was making his joints and muscles ache. He gingerly stepped around some of the sleeping crew as he headed over to the captain. He sidled up to him and whispered, "I'm sorry again about earlier. The hassle. The violence on the kid."

The captain shrugged. "We occasionally smuggle. It happens. We need to live. Besides, they are animals. We are just poor people, trying to make a living."

Reznick handed him five hundred dollars.

"What's this for?"

"For your discretion. Your silence."

"It would take me years to make money like this."

"Share it with your men and the boy."

The captain hugged him tight, kissing him on the cheek, eyes glistening, chewing on the khat. "I love you Americans. I really do. Would you like some khat?"

Reznick chewed on some with the captain for a few minutes. The acrid taste was thick and rough. He washed it down with water, topping up the plant's stimulant effect in his bloodstream with a couple of Dexedrine. He stared out toward Bahrain, due south from their position. He wondered if they couldn't speed up a little bit more. He didn't know the true capabilities of the dhow. But he needed to make far quicker progress. "How long till we arrive in Bahrain?"

"A little while."

"What does that mean? How long?"

"Before sunup."

"And that's usually when?"

"About twenty past five at this time of year."

"So maybe around two, three, we might arrive in Bahrain?"

The captain grinned. "You want to get there for two?"

"That would be good. Very good. Tell me, where is your destination exactly?"

"Bahrain, I told you."

"No, I mean, where exactly will you be stopping and offloading your fish, spices, and dates?"

"Manama fishing harbor. Dozens and dozens of dhows disembark there."

"Perfect."

"I'll get you there. It might get choppy if I make it go faster than it can. The dhow has been in my family for generations. It has never failed us yet. It is safe, not speedy."

181

"Safe is good. Let's get a move on." Reznick headed back under the canopy and pulled up his satellite phone and texted Trevelle. *You got any update on Mac?*

Trevelle replied, *Still in Saudi. Ditched his vehicle before the border. Got a lift on a truck. Bribed the driver. And they're past Qatar, headed north. Now in Al-Khobar, headed toward the causeway. I figure he'll be at locale in one hour, maybe two if there are delays. But still not in Bahrain.*

The satellite phone rang.

"It's Trevelle. Any problems?"

Reznick turned away and whispered softly, "Apart from thugs from Iran boarding the dhow, knocking around a young kid on board, kicking around a few crates, firing off a few shots, nothing to mention."

"Close call. Listen, the current intel is just coming in. The old man—"

"Tell me you've found him."

"He's still in Bahrain. So that's good."

"That's something. Where, though?"

"An hour ago, I got a great fix."

"How did you manage that?"

"He visited the old town. I managed to access an unsecured Wi-Fi network in the café he was in. From there I activated the microphone of the cell phone of the one of the old guys who were sitting near the target."

"Fuck, that's crazy."

"It was some good luck for once."

"Tell me more about the location."

"The café is a favorite haunt of Bahrainis. In an alley in the old souk. Very traditional."

"And the old man was there?"

182

"He was there. And he was talking to a Russian guy. Voice recognition has identified the guy as Pavel Molokov, former KGB, now a businessman setting up agents and networks across the Middle East. Formidable operator, by all accounts."

"Excellent work."

"That's not all. Turns out the rear of a tailoring shop in the adjacent street took deliveries at a back door in the alley. It had a surveillance camera. I jumped onto that."

The dhow began to rock and sway as it plowed through the waves in the Gulf. It appeared to be picking up speed. "What did you see?"

"Crenshaw and a Russian intelligence agent."

"No handover?"

"Nothing. Crenshaw was carrying a satchel. But no handover."

Reznick thought they might be too late. He didn't want to keep on getting breaks that didn't end with the termination of the old man. He stilled the unwanted thoughts that he was just going through the motions. He sensed that they were getting a little closer. He was still in the game. Barely.

He needed not only a bit more luck, but for that luck to hold. Just for a small window of opportunity.

Reznick knew that Crenshaw was going to cut and run very soon and theorized the handover of, presumably, documents or intel was the final item on his to-do list. But maybe there was a whole lot more to this final tour of various drop-off spots across the Middle East.

The more he thought about it, the more he started to believe they would get one final chance. But first he needed Mac to cross into Bahrain without hassle. Then he needed to get ashore and try to figure something out. And quick.

"Trevelle, where is he now? Where is he staying tonight? A villa? Hotel? Is he catching a flight out of Bahrain? Is he even there?"

"I'm getting to that. First things first, I'm still doing a battery of facial recognition tests on the footage in the alleyway, to confirm it was really Crenshaw."

"Tell me he's not using a body double."

"Not quite. But what I did notice was interesting. And may, I emphasize *may*, be able to help us."

"What?"

"Crenshaw has a new smartwatch. A Hublot. Very expensive."

"And?"

"Which means, like any good smartwatch, it can receive and send messages, check his heart rate, oxygen in the blood."

Reznick realized the importance of that immediately. "I see where you're going with this."

"You got it. So, I accessed the watch remotely. I managed to gain control via a trojan."

"Go on."

"Via a keylogger program, it enables me to find out what Crenshaw is communicating. But I've also inserted another bit of cool tech I've been working on. And it appears to be functioning normally and unseen."

"So there's a vulnerability in the watch?"

"Like all smartwatches, it has vulnerabilities. I'm still doing tests, penetration tests, to make sure my tech is one hundred percent undetected, and we're fine so far."

"So that's your roundabout way of saying what exactly?"

"He's in a penthouse suite in the Four Seasons, Manama, enjoying a glass of champagne."

Reznick clenched his fist as the dhow rocked back and forth, speeding through the water. "There we go! That's what I wanted to hear. Excellent work, Trevelle. We need to get back into the game."

"You're back in the game alright. You just need to get to Manama."

"Who's with him?"

"I believe his chief bodyguard is there, along with three of the other goons, all inside the apartment on the top floor."

"Four Seasons . . . I think I might've stayed there five or so years ago."

"Very plush. Surrounded by Bahrain Bay—shops, cafés, restaurants, super-upscale condos."

"And he's there?"

"One hundred percent."

Reznick stared out over the dark waters of the Gulf. "We just need our luck to hold. The old man needs to hang around Bahrain for just a while longer."

"The window is closing. This might be your last chance."

"We'll get him."

"Why are you so sure?"

"Failure is not an option."

Twenty-Six

Dark, hard rain lashed off the windows on the seventh floor at Langley.

Petersen was in her office, rewatching the remarkable surveillance footage with audio that Trevelle had sent. It clearly showed Crenshaw and a retired Russian intelligence operative deep in conversation in a backstreet in Manama. She was blown away that he had managed to do what the NSA had failed to do—get a fix on the target. She ran the footage through the CIA's latest in-house facial and voice recognition software to check the authenticity. The results were conclusive; the old man was William Crenshaw.

She sent the encrypted digital file to the Director's office. She walked over and found him leafing through a pile of new classified briefings from Ukraine and Israel.

Mendez looked up from his workload, eyes heavy. Behind him, through the rain-streaked window, the floodlit woods shrouded Langley. "Yeah?"

"Footage of Crenshaw. I just sent it to you."

"Give me a second." Mendez opened the file and watched, rapt. The video was eighteen minutes and thirteen seconds long. His eyes were fixed on the ex-CIA operative. The footage, if nothing else, proved Reznick was on the right track. But it also proved, beyond a doubt, that William Crenshaw was a national security threat to the United States of America and its strategic economic, political, and military interests in the Middle East, and beyond.

When the clip was finished, Mendez leaned back in his seat, shaking his head.

"This is as bad as it gets," he said.

"Indeed."

"We sure it's him?"

"It's Crenshaw. I checked through our latest systems. And verified. So did Trevelle. It's him."

"When is this from?"

Petersen looked at her watch. "Three hours and twenty minutes ago."

"For fuck's sake, he could be out of the country by now."

Petersen was startled at Mendez's sudden flash of anger. She suddenly felt deflated that he had snapped at her for providing such excellent intel. It was a move in the right direction. But she knew he was under a ton of pressure from Capitol Hill and the press on how the CIA was reacting to the growing threat in the Middle East. "I can assure you, at this moment, he is not out of the country. Most definitely not."

"And this was in Manama?"

"Little café in the old town, tucked away."

"And we're sure? I can't get my hopes up again."

"He's still there. Penthouse suite at the Four Seasons."

"If I'm asked, either by the President or Homeland Security, *how* do we know?

"I'll tell you how." Petersen then told her boss about the remote hacking of the Hublot smartwatch.

Mendez nodded. "Now that is smart, if you pardon the pun."

She didn't acknowledge the light-hearted joke. "Bearing in mind, Trevelle is the best—the very best—at what he does. This is something concrete for Reznick to use."

"That's very good . . . very good indeed. And Crenshaw has no idea?"

"We don't think so. Certainly no indication at this stage."

"Playing devil's advocate . . . that's not to say that position will stay the same."

"True. But we have this intel. And until further notice, it means Reznick can be honing in on the target."

"We have to assume, I imagine, that Crenshaw has some smart people guarding him."

"He's got Russian intelligence around him. We know that. Handpicked killers. We believe that they will have at least one cybersecurity person on their team."

"How did Trevelle know to do this? How did he get the details of the watch? How did he detect this loophole in their security blanket?"

"I'm not sure. I think it began when he saw the footage. And he saw the watch. However he did it, he found a vulnerability to exploit."

"So the latest is . . . ?"

"Crenshaw is sitting on an outside terrace at the penthouse, surrounded by his gang of mercenary protectors."

"Have we got our operatives in place?"

Petersen sighed. "Not as yet. We believe Mac has just entered Bahrain. Reznick is en route."

"What's taking so long?"

Petersen felt herself squirm. "Reznick wanted them to avoid airport security. And that meant taking the scenic route."

Mendez pinched the bridge of his nose, seemingly exasperated with this problem. "Why the fuck is this taking so long?"

"This is a bare-bones operation. These guys are showing patience. They want to get it right."

"I've run out of patience, Fran. There's no point coming to me saying we now know definitively where the target is. We need our guys in place."

"That's easier said than done. We tried that before. These things happen on a wing and prayer. The best operations take weeks of detailed planning. I know that. You know that. But these guys don't have that luxury."

"What if this goes to shit as well?"

"As I outlined at the beginning, they don't work for us. They neutralize him, you get the plaudits. They fail, they're on their own."

Mendez said nothing.

"You're wondering how we realistically spin this if it goes to hell," Petersen said. "What do we say when we're asked questions. It has nothing to do with us. These are two renegades. We'll feed a line to the press that we believe, off the record, that they're assassins working as part of a Ukrainian special forces kill team."

"So, if these two get neutralized, that's the cover story?"

"That's the story."

"What if the Ukrainians deny it?"

"Who cares? The story will already be out there. It'll become the accepted narrative. Besides, you got a better cover story?"

Mendez shook his head.

"Think about it. This is a two-man operation carried out by hired killers working for the Ukrainian intelligence services who have been tracking the movements of the notorious Wagner mercenary group. Plotting retribution for crimes in their homeland. Some of these guys were responsible for countless massacres. Remember, the Ukrainians have carried out similar operations in Africa, specifically to neutralize Wagner men."

"Is this your suggestion?"

"Sadly no. My team has been bouncing ideas around. We enlisted the help of an old friend of mine, General Chas Torino, as we brainstormed."

"Torino? Special Operations Command?"

"Yeah, down in Florida. I gave him what he thought was a hypothetical scenario. Asked what would be a rational false flag cover story if, in the future, a rogue intelligence officer was selling government secrets, and the officer was protected by Wagner, and we wanted plausible deniability. He suggested our operatives could be acting at the behest of the Ukrainian government—a two-man kill squad. Motivation? Neutralizing the group who were linked to atrocities in Bakhmut."

"Ukraine is one of our partners."

"It's the name of the game. We cover our asses if this goes to shit. And we blame it on those hot-headed Ukrainians."

"Are we assuming this operation will go to shit?"

"I don't know, is the honest answer. The cover story is just a precaution. I know many people who have known Reznick for years. He knows how this works. And he can make this work. But this is a high bar for him to clear."

"Getting bronze or silver means nothing in covert ops."

"I know."

"Let's assume for a moment this fails spectacularly, and the Ukrainians say *this wasn't our operation*. What then?"

Petersen smiled. "We'll remind them quietly that we are pulling the strings in their country. And that they need to listen more and talk less. Failure to do so will result in not one more dollar being sent to aid their fight against the Russians. And that would be the end of Ukraine. This is a zero-sum game."

Mendez leaned back in his seat and stared at his monitor. "Crenshaw is a bastard. The similarities with Aldrich Ames are striking."

"This may be worse."

"How?"

"Crenshaw could get away with it, under the protection of Moscow and his powerful friends across the Middle East."

"I sense we're reaching the endgame. Either Crenshaw is about to disappear for good, or Reznick manages to get to him in time."

"The next few hours will be crucial. I'll keep you posted."

Twenty-Seven

The dhow chugged remorselessly through the dark waters of the Gulf, approaching the lights of Manama's waterfront.

Reznick was relieved the interminable journey was nearly over. He weighed his options as to how best to blend in when he arrived in the harbor. The last thing he needed was for an eagle-eyed harbor cop or a night security official to capture him as he stepped off a dhow in the dead of night. He was still dressed in his sweat-drenched Western clothes, jeans and a T-shirt. He decided to approach the captain and explain his predicament. The captain went over and spoke to one of the crew—a middle-aged man, lean and rangy, who was about Reznick's size. The guy walked over to Reznick and took off his dirty sackcloth, headscarf, and leather sandals. He was left wearing a sad pair of seventies-style underpants, a couple sizes too large for his frame.

Reznick stripped off to his boxer shorts and handed over his Western attire. He then put on the other man's clothes, sandals, and headscarf. The crew member put on Reznick's jeans and T-shirt and grinned. "Thank you," he said. Reznick handed him a fifty-dollar bill and the guy hugged him tight in return. "*As-salamu alaikum*," the man whispered. A traditional greeting among Muslims, it meant, *Peace be upon you.*

Reznick nodded respectfully to the man, but his shoulder also started to itch uncontrollably. He felt uncomfortable in the sackcloth, which smelled of fish.

He pushed those thoughts to one side when his satellite phone lit up. He checked the screen. A text from Mac. It read: *Safe and sound. I'll be waiting at harbor. Got a place three blocks away.*

Reznick felt a ripple of excitement. Mac was in position. The first part of the jigsaw was in place. His heart began to beat a little bit faster thinking of what lay ahead. Knowing that the target was still in Bahrain. He had half expected another setback, with Trevelle telling him that Crenshaw had caught a late-night flight out. But the operation was still on as they took it to the wire.

The captain expertly navigated the rickety dhow, dazzling lights all around. Reznick knew the risks of getting caught. It was not the best place to get caught spying, that was for sure; Bahrain's human rights record was atrocious. They certainly gave the Saudis a run for their money in that respect.

Earlier, Reznick had asked the captain to drop him off at an isolated spot farther along the coast. The captain wasn't having it, though. He didn't want to push his luck, especially after the encounter with the Iranian Revolutionary Guards. Besides, the captain and the crew couldn't have been any more accommodating under the circumstances.

So, Reznick had reluctantly stayed on the boat. He knew the layout of the harbor area from a previous visit. Despite it being the dead of night, he had to assume officers would be hanging around. Maybe a few stationed in the main security office. Perhaps just smoking, playing cards, drinking sweet tea, and watching and noting all of the arrivals. Hopefully the late hour would work in their favor.

It was 0203 hours when the dhow pulled up in the harbor alongside other dhows, away from the fancy yachts at the far end. The captain stepped ashore first and tied the boat in position.

Reznick hung back, waiting until the crew had disembarked before he stepped off the dhow. He said a few whispered goodbyes. Then he walked alongside them, tactical backpack slung over his shoulder, as they headed toward a waiting truck. It would be taking them to a backstreet hotel in the village of Karbabad, outside Manama. He walked on. Not a soul in sight. His heartbeat began to race as he strode through the open harbor gates and disappeared around the corner.

A motorbike pulled up, Mac grinning. "Hop on, you sack of shit!"

Reznick patted him on the shoulder, glad to be back on dry land. His joints felt stiff after sitting on the dhow for the better part of twenty-four hours. He held on tightly as Mac accelerated around the well-lit streets of downtown Manama before cutting down first a side street and then an alley.

Mac stopped the bike on a sidewalk, chaining the rear wheel to a metal railing. Reznick followed him down the alley, then up a flight of stairs to a third-floor walkup. Mac had found them a two-room apartment on Airbnb. He locked the door behind them. Inside, the apartment was cloaked in darkness. Reznick's eyes adjusted to his new surroundings. They kept the lights off.

"What the fuck happened to you, Jon?" Mac said. "You look and smell like shit."

"I was on a dhow."

"Fuck that." Mac handed him a carefully wrapped package. "Try it on. I bought you a new T-shirt, jeans, and trainers and underwear, just in case."

"I didn't know you cared."

Mac laughed. "Clean up, you stinking piece of shit. There's a shower next door, off the hallway. You smell like you've been living in a fish factory."

Reznick didn't need to be told twice. He left the backpack in the kitchen and headed to the bathroom, stripped off the rags, and turned on the shower. The water was tepid. He climbed in and washed and cleaned himself with a fresh bar of soap. He stayed in the shower for ten minutes. It felt good. After drying himself, he unwrapped the package and put on the clean clothes.

"Feeling better?" Mac asked.

Reznick threw the filthy clothes into a laundry basket in the bathroom. "Much."

"I didn't think you'd be so domesticated, Jon."

"Cheeky bastard."

Mac smiled.

Reznick sat down on a chair. "What's the latest? I've lost all track of time."

"Three minutes ago, I got a message from Trevelle. Crenshaw was due to fly out of Manama airport tomorrow. But he's moved things forward."

"This is not what I want to hear. Do we know why?"

"Maybe he got cold feet."

"So, when is he due to leave the hotel?"

"In just a few hours. Nine a.m. is the time logged on the plane's flight plan to Jeddah."

"He's not hanging around now. This is it."

"We need to intercept him before he's gone for good."

Reznick checked the luminous screen on his watch. It was 0239 hours. That didn't give them nearly long enough to plan an operation. Just over six hours until Crenshaw's plane left. They were going to have to improvise.

He picked up his cell phone and called Trevelle.

"You made it!"

"Listen—where is the old man now, at this very moment?"

The sound of Trevelle tapping his keyboard. "He appears to be moving around his hotel suite."

"Well, at least that's something. Doing what?"

"Chatting to some of his team. Watching TV. Killing time."

"What else?"

"I think you're going to like this. Programmed into his smart-watch is a power walk at four thirty in the morning. That could be your chance."

"Today?"

"Less than two hours from now."

Reznick saw the obvious opportunity. It was one they might never get again. "Is he crazy? Why take that risk now?"

"Maybe cockiness," Trevelle mused.

"What route is he taking?"

"The King Faisal Corniche."

"Makes sense. Where exactly on the corniche? It covers a wide area."

"Between Bahrain Bay and Bahrain Financial Harbor."

"0430?"

"Affirmative."

"But it might also be disinformation, right?"

"We can't rule it out."

"I'm assuming that, on this outing, he'll be surrounded by the Russian crew."

"No question."

"So a power walk at 0430 and then a flight out at 0900 hours?"

"That's correct, Jon."

"Does this guy ever sleep?"

"Negative. Everything I've found about him indicates he's awake most of the time. Insomniac."

"Copy that. I'll be in touch."

Reznick ended the call and relayed the latest intel to Mac. "What do you think?"

"We've got to do it now. This is it. No question."

"We need to think through scenarios."

"It's a tricky one."

"It's got to be rough and ready."

"Here's what I know," Mac said. "The corniche will almost certainly be deserted then."

"So makes sense for an early morning, predawn bit of exercise before the flight. Then he's off."

"Jon, we could take him out with a rifle from a rooftop or a parking garage?"

Reznick saw that as a very realistic and probable solution. "What other options or outcomes?"

"Problem is, Jon, those fucking Russians. They're not dummies. They'll be surrounding him—armed, waiting, and ready. So maybe we need to get a lot closer. A passing motorcycle, rake them with fire."

"Possibility. Not bad at all."

Mac stared at him, arms like lamb shanks. "Talk to me, Jon. What's your thinking? Where's your head at?"

"Let's start with what we know and don't know," Reznick mused. "We don't know how many of the Wagner crew will be with him. I suspect minimum ten. Maybe more. There might be half a dozen spread out around him."

"I think this is a guy who has a ring of steel around him, no matter what. The Russians will insist on it. He's a valuable asset, after all."

"So it might look like a hardcore group providing an inner ring. And an outer-ring shield?" Reznick posited.

Mac wiped the sweat from his brow with the back of his hand. "We don't know the fucking first thing about what the setup will be."

"Let's focus on the positive."

"What ideas have you got?"

Reznick's mind had switched into scenario mode. He was devising the best strategy to neutralize William Crenshaw. He tried to picture the scene: the old man, walking, presumably not too fast, surrounded by a phalanx of killer bodyguards. "I'm guessing he might be wearing a bulletproof vest. Right?"

"Wouldn't put it past him. He's a highly intelligent man."

"Unless . . ."

"Unless what?"

Reznick felt the first flicker of a plan fill his mind. "Can you think back a few years? 2016?"

"What are you talking about?"

"I'm thinking corniche, wide pedestrianized corniche, what happened then, in 2016, can you remember?"

Mac shrugged.

"It was July 2016. You remember what happened? In France?"

Mac went quiet for a few moments. "Jesus Christ. Oh yeah. The terrorist attack down in Nice."

"You remember?"

"A lone jihadist in a truck. Horrific. It's low-tech, maximum-impact, devastating if executed properly."

"There's two of us."

It was Mac's turn to get quiet.

"See what I'm getting at?" Reznick said.

Mac groaned. "No guarantees. But it could look like a terrible accident. And that would work in our favor."

"On the corniche?"

"That's how they could spin it the authorities."

"Which direction should we take? Should we come from behind them?"

"I think so. I figure they'll start at the east side of the corniche. Head west. Then turn back."

"Or they might just walk east to west and get some vehicles to pick them up." Reznick grimaced, doubt rolling in. "We need to hit them as they head east to west?"

"We might have it wrong. They might be dropped at the west side."

"Maybe."

"Fuck it. Hit them east to west. Problem is there's a high probability they're going to shoot, taking one or both of us out."

"I say one of us drives and one provides cover and mops up," Reznick said.

Mac was grinning. "I like it! That could work!" He pulled out a map from his back pocket and unfolded it, illuminating it with his cell phone light. He flattened out the map and pointed at the approach roads to the corniche. "This route is maybe fifty yards from the start of the corniche. We'd have to smash through some clumps of palm trees."

"Big truck, no problem."

"I don't mind driving into those fucks."

"Have you driven a truck?"

"Are you kidding me, Jon? I know vehicles inside out, including trucks. I'm a trained mechanic."

"I didn't know that."

"Tank transporters, heavy goods vehicles, tankers, logistics vehicles, I've driven them all. When I first joined the British Army, I learned all that. You never forget that."

His Scottish buddy was on the edge, as if ready to explode. It was almost like he didn't care if he lived or died. And that made him very dangerous.

"You'll be in the firing line," said Reznick.

"I've been in the firing line my whole fucking life. I don't give a fuck. Never have."

"You want to drive? For sure?"

"I'm driving."

Reznick contemplated the chain of events. "OK. So we need to get moving. But first you need to get a truck. A big fucking truck."

Mac looked pensive. "So if they head out on the corniche at 0430 hours . . ." Mac pointed his finger at the map. "I need to know exactly where they are."

"We'll get Trevelle to be our eyes and ears. Earpiece in. He'll give you a real-time location for the old man."

"What about an escape plan? An exit strategy."

Reznick stared at the map. He drew his finger from the corniche north, across a stretch of water. "The corniche is opposite Reef Island."

"What's that?"

"I know this area pretty well. Been here a few times before. It's an artificially created island. I stayed at a hotel there. Luxury apartments, fancy restaurants, gyms. But . . ." He pointed to moorings opposite the corniche. "No guarantees, but I do remember a few small yachts were moored there."

Mac nodded. "So we grab one, if there is one. What if there isn't?"

"Plan B would be the dhows, which are located behind barbed-wire fences at the eastern end of the corniche, out of sight."

"A dhow is too slow."

"I know."

"Here's another problem," Mac said. "How the fuck do we get from the corniche across to Reef Island?"

"You're a scuba expert."

"I don't have scuba gear on me, Jon. No shops will be open to buy stuff like that."

"So we swim."

"Backpacks on?" Mac said.

"You've done it before."

"I have. And with a Bergen loaded with gear."

"It's a quarter of a mile across. We get in the water and we swim."

Mac's face flushed red. "It could work. But we're assuming there's a yacht or boat over there."

Reznick took out his cell phone and called Trevelle.

"Hey man, what's on your mind?"

"We need real-time visuals of the corniche and the surrounding area, particularly the marina on Reef Island. There's a stretch of water beside the corniche. Opposite that are fancy condos. Can you tell me if there are any yachts or boats moored there?"

"Right now?"

"Affirmative."

The sound of tapping on a keyboard. "Give me a few seconds . . . I'm into the systems of a gym on Reef Island on the waterfront. Directly opposite the corniche. Right now, there are two medium-sized boats."

"Copy that. And you're one hundred percent on that?"

"I'll hook up to a surveillance system on the apartment blocks opposite. And they're showing . . . yup, same two yachts, moored on the wooden berths on the opposite shore."

"And the corniche itself, are there are any boats right next to the corniche at all? All down the length of it?"

"Nothing."

"What about dhows?"

"I can't see dhows—"

"They're there, but farther east, at the start of the corniche."

"Copy that. I'll check that out too."

Reznick ended the call. "Two yachts there."

"So, assuming we get out of there alive, and survive swimming through that shitty water, and we get one of the boats working, that's the exit strategy?"

"We could stick to land. Steal another motorcycle. Try and see how far we get."

"They'll lock down everything."

"OK, so we need to get the hell out of here, out of Bahrain ASAP. Then the yacht is a good option."

Silence stretched between them.

Mac stared at the map, breathing hard.

Reznick looked at him. "Are you ready?"

"Let's do this. Let's kill the bastard."

Twenty-Eight

William Crenshaw checked his watch as he sat on the huge penthouse terrace, the nighttime air like glue. It was 0345 Arabia Standard Time. He would soon have to get ready for his predawn power walk. He might've smoked all his life and he might drink more than doctors recommended, but he adhered religiously to his daily walk. Even if only for a mile. It allowed him to think, clear his head. A walk along the corniche, then off to the airport. He would hand over the thousands of documents, contained on a key flash drive, at the airport, as agreed. And not before.

His phone rang, snapping him out of his reverie. The caller ID was a number he didn't recognize.

"Billy?" said a faint voice on the other end of the line.

Crenshaw turned up the volume on his hearing aid. "Sorry?"

"Billy, is that you?"

Crenshaw knew who it was instantly. The only person that called him his childhood name was his private banker in Zurich, Bruno Siegfried. "You're working late. Do you ever sleep?"

"I was going to ask you the same thing."

"What time is it in Switzerland?"

"Let me see . . . It's a quarter to three in the morning. I'm just putting the finishing legal touches to link all your accounts. Between the offshore accounts, you have fifteen in total. Just making sure that you're going to be good to go so you can access your wealth at the touch of a button, without a chance of assets being frozen."

"We nearly over the line? I hope so. This is taking a long time."

"I know. You'll be pleased to know the end is in sight. I just assigned the final bank account for a new shell company I've set up on your behalf, based in the lovely British Virgin Islands."

"And that's it?"

"That's it."

"What's the total amount of assets I have?"

"It's looking pretty fantastic actually, Billy. Eight hundred and thirty-two million US dollars, give or take for currency fluctuations as and when you sell. That's in addition to your property portfolio. I have that estimated at one hundred and forty million dollars. So you're a dollar billionaire, give or take. No one can touch any of those assets."

Crenshaw checked the heart rate monitor on his watch. The device also showed his blood pressure hiking up a notch with the news.

"You happy?"

"Looking forward to my new life."

"How do you feel?"

"A lot better, now I know this has all been taken care of."

"It's legal. That's the best part. It's watertight under international law. It's secure. It's private. You're looking at a beautiful retirement, Billy."

"And your fees?"

"The figures I gave you are net of my modest fee."

Crenshaw laughed. "*Modest*. Good one."

"Billy, you are all set, my friend."

"Good work."

"It wasn't just me. A team of fifteen lawyers and accountants has worked on this for five months. Will you be needing any other assistance?"

"Not for a long time. Take care. And put your feet up!"

Crenshaw ended the call and swigged from a bottle of energy drink ahead of his power walk. He took a few gulps and felt the caffeine and sugar hit immediately. He checked his watch again. His heart was racing. He took a few deep breaths. Adrenaline was surging through his body. He was all set. The culmination of his work cultivating a new future for himself. His autumn years would be cocooned, surrounded by high walls and security teams hand-picked to protect VIPs in the gated community. Truth be told, he hadn't imagined his life turning out the way it did.

He had seen retired intelligence colleagues succumb to inertia, alcoholism, dreary golf trips abroad, depression, hospitalization, and the crushing realization that their lives amounted to a measly government pension. If they were lucky, they would get hired by defense contractors or think tanks and peddle the knowledge and contacts they had acquired to the highest bidder.

Crenshaw had done the same. Except instead of working for the private military-industrial complex in and around McLean, maybe picking up a six-figure salary for a few days of work a month, since the 1990s, the Russians had been reeling him in. Crenshaw had gambled away his salary. He'd found a savior and quickly gotten a taste for seven-figure bonuses from Russian oligarchs. With hind-sight, the approach by a man purporting to be from an organization called the Committee for a Democratic Russia had seemed inevi-table. He didn't realize it at the time, but the organization was a front for Russian agents to reach out and make contact with senior Western intelligence agents who had been compromised either by scandal or debt. He was showered with gifts. Holidays. There was a seemingly chance meeting with a young woman at a five-star hotel bar in Madrid which turned out to be a classic honey trap. Then they had him in their iron grip. He had been threatened with blackmail. Photos of him having sex with the Russian business-woman, a spy, along with his dire financial situation, were the final nail in his coffin. At the start he had felt bad. Regret. Remorse. And shame. But the money was like a drug. The more he got, the more he craved.

He had opened up a private security deposit box. Gold coins, small gold bars, Rolex watches, property deeds, all gifts, all discreetly stored away. Gifts from gas utilities in Siberia. It had all begun to mount up. Then he'd opened a larger private security box. Within a short while, he estimated, the gold, the watches, and the property portfolio had surpassed five million dollars. Three years after he began working for the Russians, he had moved on to an altogether higher plane. And from there, there was no going back. He was in too deep.

When he'd first given the Russians a taste of what he had, they didn't seem unduly impressed. Initially they were suspicious that Crenshaw was playing them, faking working for them. They suspected he might be a double agent for the Agency. But before long, the quality of the information, the outing of deep undercover CIA assets working overseas, especially in Europe—along with their code names—won the Russians over. They knew he was the real deal. He knew what he was doing. He was effectively signing off on CIA agents to be killed.

Crenshaw asked himself how it had all gotten so crazy. In the beginning, he had felt genuine, gut-wrenching pangs of remorse about betraying his country. But eventually, as his wealth began to accumulate, he didn't think about it as much. Now? He had long since stopped caring about America. He was looking after number one. As for conscience, the years had eroded whatever morality and ethics he had learned as a boy from his parents and the church.

The more he had realized how expendable he was, the more he pivoted toward a new life. He had begun to dream about life beyond the Beltway, beyond even the borders of the United States. He had spoken with colleagues who were more expert than him on geopolitics. What they said had concurred with his view. The era of the American empire was over.

The twentieth century had belonged to the United States. They had nudged aside the British Empire and expanded their influence around the world—economically, politically, and militarily. They had influenced elections or overthrown governments on a whim. Capitalism was king. Socialism and communism were signs of Russia's malign influence. Crenshaw had once bought into that. He couldn't allow the Reds to propagate and gather strength in America's backyard. But now? Russia was no longer a communist country; it was an authoritarian state. Disappearances, torture, and targeted killings were all part of modern Russian life. And Crenshaw was a profiting participant. He had come full circle.

The irony wasn't lost on him. He was working for the successor to the Soviet state. A state that had spawned monsters like Stalin. He pushed away thoughts about how he would feel in ten years' time. That is, if he lived to see that day. Would he be sitting in his waterfront Jeddah mansion, surrounded by the high walls and security guards, not knowing if his protectors would be paid to kill him? Russian foreign intelligence operatives were adept at neutralizing those who had outlived their usefulness. Was he going to be one of them? The truth was, he wouldn't know until it was too late. They had him until the grave.

He checked his smartwatch. He was on a schedule. He got up to change into gym gear and sneakers for his early morning walk. His joints ached and his bones creaked. But he enjoyed the endorphins that flowed after a serious hike.

Dimitri stepped onto the balcony and whispered in his ear, "Sorry to disturb you, boss, but there's a visitor in the hotel lobby."

"At this time? Who is it?"

"Captain Aleksandr Rostov, military attaché at the Russian Embassy here in Bahrain. He wants to talk to you now."

"About what?"

"He didn't go into detail. He requests a face-to-face with you. Now. As a matter of urgency."

Crenshaw was taken aback. Something was off. He sensed it. "Are you serious?"

"He said it's a matter of critical importance."

Crenshaw thought it was all very irregular. Why on earth would a Russian diplomat want to speak to him at this ungodly hour? It might alert Reznick or the CIA to his whereabouts if they learned a Russian diplomat was making a visit to a five-star hotel in the dead of night. "I'm not happy about this."

Dimitri shrugged as if there was nothing he could say or do.

"Who's with him?"

"It is just him. He is unarmed. No electronic devices. We've checked."

"This is ridiculous. I mean, he wants to speak to me now?"

Dimitri stared at Crenshaw. "My advice? Meet with him. He is worried about you. He has intel."

"Unless he has new intel pertinent to my personal safety—"

"That is what I believe he's here for. To warn you."

Crenshaw looked at his watch. "I'm headed out in half an hour."

"He says he needs five minutes of your time. That's all."

"Never a fucking break. Fine, send him up."

A few minutes later, Captain Rostov was ushered onto the terrace. He wore shades, a pale blue linen shirt, dark jeans, black shoes.

Crenshaw indicated he should pull up a seat beside him. He turned to Dimitri. "Lock the door to my suite until further notice. No one gets out at this floor until my guest has gone."

"Very good." Dimitri turned and shut the floor-to-ceiling glass terrace doors behind him.

Crenshaw watched as the Russian bodyguard then locked the penthouse suite, leaving Crenshaw and Rostov alone.

Rostov leaned close. "Thank you for seeing me on such short notice. I must apologize for my unannounced visit."

"It's a bit irregular."

"It is, I agree. I want to apologize for disturbing your plans. I know you will be on your way later this morning. I have some news. I received a message from one of our agents."

Crenshaw nodded. "Go on."

"As you know, two highly trained assassins, an American and a Brit, have been tasked with neutralizing you. We have learned that they are now here in the city."

"In Manama?"

"They avoided the airport. That's why we were blindsided."

Crenshaw wondered if he believed Rostov. It could be classic Russian disinformation to test how he would respond. He felt drained by it all. But then again, maybe that was the purpose. "Where exactly are they? Do they know my whereabouts?"

"The embassy has a team trying to locate them at this moment. We are concerned they might know where you are. I can't stress how serious this is. And that's why it was decided that I talk to you in person."

Crenshaw was unnerved. "I'm sorry, so you don't know where they are?"

"Not an exact location. We have strong intel which suggests they have entered the city."

"What does it matter? I'm going to be out of here in a few hours."

"William, shut up and listen for once!"

Crenshaw sat frozen in shock at the harsh tone of voice. He wasn't used to being spoken to like that.

"This is a final warning. I've been instructed to reach out to you."

"To say what?"

"Whatever plans you made, you will change them now. We do the handover immediately."

"You want me to change my plans at the eleventh hour? No chance."

"I must be honest, I'm alarmed at your blasé attitude, William. I'm here to help."

"Seriously? I've already agreed to my flight times with Saudi intelligence. They are not going to take kindly to any last-minute changes."

"We will deal with the Saudi end of things. You need to take action. Your arrogance will cost you dearly. You need to think long and hard about what I'm saying."

"Listen, I've got a small army of your fellow countrymen, hardened mercenaries, surrounding my every move. I'm fine."

Rostov shot forward and grabbed Crenshaw's jaw, hard. "When we give a warning, you take heed of that warning." He loosened his grip and sat back in his chair, staring at Crenshaw with an icy gaze.

Crenshaw felt sick. He couldn't believe Rostov had placed his hands on him.

"Moscow is getting concerned. That's how serious this situation is. When they get involved, you need to pay close attention."

Crenshaw nodded.

"These two men have been tracking you across the Middle East. We believe you will be killed if you do not adjust your plans. You won't make it to the airport."

Crenshaw studied Rostov's craggy features. "Do you have a specific idea of how they propose to kill me?"

"It doesn't matter. Our analysis shows these operatives are resourceful and will get to you in some way."

Crenshaw said nothing.

Rostov's focus was drawn to Crenshaw's smartwatch. He pressed his finger to his mouth, then reached over and undid the watch from Crenshaw's bony wrist.

"What are you doing now?"

Rostov pressed his index finger in front of Crenshaw's mouth and whispered in his ear. "Where did you buy the watch?"

"A mall in Oman."

Rostov made a fist, his face flushed, furious. "We need to dispose of it."

"It's just a watch."

Rostov slapped him hard around the face. "You fucking idiot!"

Crenshaw's face stung. He felt his eyes water at the shock and pain of the sudden smack.

"Your watch is also a tracking device. A listening device. You must know that sort of thing."

"How would they know about my watch?"

"They are very ingenious people."

"So what do we do?"

Rostov signaled Dimitri out to the terrace and handed him the watch, whispering, "Get one of your men to take this watch out to the desert and bury it. Do you understand?"

Dimitri nodded and put the watch in his pocket before he left them alone again.

Crenshaw stared at Rostov. "I thought it would be useful to monitor my heart rate and oxygen levels."

Rostov shook his head. "And it is. But they have learned that you have that watch and they have figured out how to access it."

Crenshaw felt stupid. And he wasn't a stupid man. Quite the opposite. But he had indeed grown blasé, arrogant even, about his security. "I still don't know how they could have known I had that."

"Doesn't matter. Your plan for today, what was it?"

"I'm going for a power walk and maybe a light jog before the flight. It helps me relax. Sleep better. Good for my heart."

Rostov shook his head. "You can forget that. We've got to assume they have accessed those plans."

Crenshaw sat in silence as he contemplated the latest warning. He just wanted to be left alone.

"So, what's it going to be?" Rostov said.

"What do you suggest?"

"That you let my team take over. We will get you inside the Russian Embassy. You can hand over the files you have long promised. From there, we can get you to Jeddah with no issue. We can transport you in a diplomatic bag, quite safe, don't worry."

"I don't know."

"This will happen. That's how serious I believe this threat is. It's critical."

"What guarantees can you give me?"

"I'm not in the business of offering guarantees."

"What do you want me to do?"

"Sit tight. I will speak to a couple of people. And I'll call you within the hour. We will get you out of here and over to the embassy. But do not move until then."

Twenty-Nine

Reznick pulled on his tactical backpack and slipped out of the apartment in downtown Manama under the cover of darkness. He headed through the winding streets and alleys. His earpiece buzzed to life. He checked his watch. It was 0402 hours.

"Talk to me, man," he said.

"Got a problem, Jon," Trevelle replied.

Reznick groaned. "What kind of problem?"

"The old man . . ."

"What about him?"

"He's just had a visitor. To his room."

"Who?"

"A Russian military attaché. Captain Rostov."

"Interesting."

"I don't know exactly what happened. I overheard Rostov mention the watch. The sound was a bit muffled. But within fifteen minutes of his visit, signs pointed to Crenshaw being on the move."

"What do you mean, *signs pointed to*?"

"The GPS on the watch showed his location as headed south into the desert along the King Hamad Highway."

"So why didn't you tell me?"

"I checked. It's not him."

"You're not making any sense."

"I've got access to surveillance cameras at all the entrances and exits, as well as the elevators, and he has not left the hotel."

"Not even in disguise?"

"No faces entering or leaving the hotel have been covered."

Slowly it dawned on Reznick what must have happened. "They got rid of the watch?"

"Correct."

"Fuck. I don't want to hear this kind of shit at the eleventh hour. Are you saying someone else has the watch and is driving south?"

"The person I picked up on a surveillance camera on the outskirts of Manama is one of the Wagner crew. A Russian psychopath who was locked up in a Siberian jail for fifteen years for killing and eating his sister before he joined up. Fidor Lizinsky."

"Jesus Christ." Reznick could see what was happening. "They're laying down a false trail. That's what it looks like, right?"

"Agreed. I think Rostov caught sight of the smartwatch and learned about the walk at 0430. And he sent the watch along with a Wagner goon out into the desert to throw us off his tail. Disinformation."

"But what brought this Russian military attaché to visit him in the dead of night?"

"You, probably. They know you're after the old man. They're making sure there are no last-minute hitches before he disappears for good."

Reznick sighed. "Have you told Mac?"

"I will."

"Where is Mac?"

"Sitting in an eighteen-wheeler next to a building site, half a mile from the corniche, waiting to rock and roll."

"Trevelle, I'm walking around in the middle of the night in fucking Bahrain . . . this is not what I want to hear. Get us eyes on the old man again."

"I couldn't have foreseen this, Jon."

"I don't care. Get this back on track now!"

"Copy that . . . Hold on . . . Seems to be . . . We've got movement."

"Talk to me, Trevelle."

"Six, I repeat, six SUVs have pulled up at the entrance to the old man's hotel."

"This second?"

"Right now."

"It could be another false trail. I need facts. Is he or is he not in this group of cars? Are they going to move him now?"

"I'm watching them . . . The Wagner crew are hovering around."

"Figure this out. I need to know for sure where he is. Get on it."

Reznick ended the call and walked on as he called Mac, relaying the latest developments. "What do you think?"

"He's either going to be in that group of vehicles . . . or he's not. I think the chances are he will be. Perhaps smuggled out."

"Who the hell knows? Here's what I want you to do, Mac. Follow them."

"In an eighteen-wheeler?"

"Correct. Trevelle can help you out if you lose them."

"What about you?"

"I'm going to hang around in downtown Manama until I figure out where the fuck the old man really is."

Thirty

Crenshaw felt uneasy as he paced the penthouse suite. Rostov sat watching him like a hawk. Crenshaw wondered if he could even trust him. Maybe the Russians were using this last-minute intervention as a ruse to spirit him away to their embassy, never to be seen again. It wouldn't be the first time.

The more he thought about it, the more he realized he had outlived his usefulness. Moscow might prefer that he was out of the way. But then again, maybe he was just feeling more paranoid than usual. In the shadowy world he had inhabited for decades, the line between fact and fiction was a thin one. Smoke, mirrors, disinformation—what to believe?

Rostov said quietly, "Don't be so agitated. We will sort this out."

"But I am agitated. I like feeling I'm in control. Everything has worked fine so far. This intervention of yours is a bit unnerving."

"How so?"

"I like order. I'm not a great fan of disruption in my life. I hate changes to schedules. Especially when the changes arrive in the middle of the night."

"This shouldn't come as a shock to you, William. You have been given repeated warnings to hand over what you still have, the last tranche, and disappear."

"It was all under control. I'm going to Saudi. That's the plan. That's always been the plan."

"Plans change. I'm not asking you to agree to my plan; I'm telling you. It's not up for discussion. Is that clear?"

"Captain Rostov . . . I appreciate you taking the time, even in the middle of the night, to give me your assessment. But it's getting tiresome. Can I speak frankly?"

"Of course."

"I don't like to be fucked around. Am I making myself clear?"

Rostov pointed a menacing finger at Crenshaw. "No one likes to be fucked around. You need to learn to shut the fuck up and listen for once. You need to trust me. You do trust me, William?"

Crenshaw bowed his head. "I just want some peace and quiet."

"You will have it. We will arrange the extraction to ensure you are taken to a secure location."

"I had plans . . . the plans had been carefully worked out."

"I don't care about your fucking plans! Here's what's going to happen. Decoy cars have left from the front of the hotel. Six of them will drive toward the airport."

"And what about me?"

"We have a plan just for you. We wanted to keep Reznick busy, caught in two minds."

"Can't we just get a chopper out of here?"

"We could have if you had decided to leave yesterday or the day before. But you've left it too late. The hotel won't allow landings on its helipad this early."

Crenshaw rubbed his face, adjusted his hearing aid. There was some distant crackle.

Rostov got up slowly from his seat. "Do you trust me?"

"I want to trust you."

"You can trust me. Here's what's going to happen. I will get my driver to take me back to the embassy. You must not leave here until either Viktor or myself have settled on a final extraction plan. We can formulate that very quickly. You're safe here. Is this all clear?"

"How long do I have to wait?"

"I said, is this clear?"

"Crystal clear."

"You'll be out of here soon, very soon. Within the next hour."

Thirty-One

Trevelle was running facial recognition software on everyone who entered or exited the hotel. If William Crenshaw left the building, through whichever exit, he would be alerted. So far, nothing. But he knew that complacency was the Achilles heel of any intelligence-gathering operation. He needed to stay on his toes and alert to any possibilities.

He followed cameras as they panned the hotel lobby, hallways on the penthouse floor, and the elevators, watching for the first sign of the American traitor. But without the smartwatch, he no longer had ears on the inside of the hotel suite Crenshaw had been holed up in.

Trevelle had tried to remotely access the Samsung Smart TV in the suite through the Bluetooth connection. It would have allowed him to use the camera and microphone in the TV to give him sound and visual on Crenshaw's palatial suite. But all the functions had been deactivated and deleted. Very smart, and presumably by Crenshaw's protectors.

He did have real-time camera footage of the inside of Mac's truck, which was following the convoy. He also had a current fix on Reznick. Jon was nursing a coffee in an all-night café in Manama.

Trevelle turned his attention back to the monitor showing various exterior shots of the five-star hotel. A small Wagner crew was huddled around the entrance, as if about to leave with their boss. They had been there for close to thirty minutes. But still no movement.

He knew he must be overlooking something. Trevelle hunched over his keyboard and tapped away at the keys, bringing up the footage of William Crenshaw in Muscat. No one else would have access to that. He had saved the surveillance footage to the ultra-secure and highly encrypted data servers onsite. He tapped a few more keys. He needed to look for clues he could use. A scrap of information. Anything.

He scanned Crenshaw's face and the features of the inscrutable Russian. Trevelle's eyes were drawn almost immediately to the smartwatch. He'd had a timely breakthrough there. Was there anything else he was missing?

He rewatched the footage again and again, slowing it down. Zooming in on Crenshaw's face. Trawling through it, frame by painstaking frame, one last time. At one point, Crenshaw turned slowly, as if to look down the street. Trevelle freeze-framed that moment. Was there a strange glint of light on the side of his face? Jewelry?

He checked Crenshaw's side profile. He didn't know what he was looking for. Was it an earring? He couldn't imagine Crenshaw wearing an earring. It was also hard to imagine that he would have missed that detail.

He zoomed in tighter on the side of Crenshaw's face. Trevelle's eyes were drawn toward the back of Crenshaw's right ear. That's when he saw it.

"What the hell?" The pixelation made it appear grainy. He quickly cleaned up the footage, turning it into an ultra-high-definition photo.

Suddenly, the image sharpened into clear focus. He saw what appeared to be a tiny, flesh-colored object discreetly tucked behind the ear. No bigger than two inches, and half an inch thick. A thin tube or wire led from the plastic casing into the ear.

"Son of a bitch!" How could he not have noticed it before?

His grandmother, who had died three years earlier, had worn something similar, though she hadn't had a Caucasian-pink device, but a light brown casing to match her skin tone.

Crenshaw was wearing a discreet hearing aid.

Trevelle knew a little bit about this kind of thing. His grandmother's partial deafness had been greatly alleviated by this type of hearing aid. It was a receiver-in-canal listening device. A new generation of technologically advanced hearing aid. The discreet casing behind the ear made it far smaller than traditional, bulkier devices.

His mind went into overdrive, connecting the dots. He had something. He knew this type of device allowed connectivity and audio streaming for everything from cell phones to TVs. They were also known as Bluetooth hearing aids.

"You cunning bastard," Trevelle said, staring at Crenshaw's image on the screen.

He tapped furiously at the keyboard. Within a few moments, Trevelle had found the previously hidden Bluetooth connection after he activated a Roku streaming stick in the side of the satellite box in Crenshaw's suite. He was then able to send and receive data via the short-range wireless signal to the hearing device, so long as it was within ten yards of the Roku. He then put on his AirPods Max headphones.

He waited and waited. There was a crackle of static for a few seconds. He had a definite fix on the hearing aid. The location too.

A short while later, it connected.

A patrician voice talking in clear, stentorian tones. "When should we go, Rostov?"

Trevelle's blood ran cold. It sounded like Crenshaw. He ran a quick voice analysis. A perfect match. He was in. But he couldn't get complacent.

He might have the GPS location and voice of William Crenshaw. He could, theoretically, guide Reznick and Mac to the target whenever they chose. But there were way too many intangibles. Were all the Wagner bodyguards gone? He found that hard to believe. He had to assume that several bodyguards were still either in the suite or in adjacent rooms, blocking all access to Crenshaw.

Trevelle buzzed Reznick's earpiece. "The old man is still in his hotel suite."

"How can you be sure?"

"I hacked into his hearing aid."

"That's better. A lot better."

"He's there. With him is the Russian guy, Rostov. I checked, he's based with the Russian Embassy in Manama."

"Get Mac to turn around now."

"Copy that."

"Tell him to dump the truck and head back to the apartment we were in. We need to figure this out very, very quickly."

"The Russians are going to smuggle him out. The question is how."

"They're fond of the old diplomatic bag trick."

"They're going to stuff the old man into a bag?"

"A diplomatic bag takes many forms. It could be a crate, marked as diplomatic luggage. Air pockets, ventilation, but locked. Then it's shipped off."

"Shit, of course. The Swiss IT spy, smuggled out of the Belarusian Embassy to Saudi Arabia by the Russians, right?"

"Trevelle, listen to me. I need a way to allow us to get close to Crenshaw without the remnants of the Wagner crew gunning down innocent hotel guests or taking them hostage. I don't want it turning into a Mumbai-style hotel massacre or a Hamas mass kidnapping or indiscriminate killings."

"I'm working on it."

"While we regroup at the apartment, look at what you've got, one final time. I want you to use every trick in the book, everything you know, Trevelle, to allow us to get to the old man. Leave no stone unturned. Stick with it."

"Leave it to me."

"I'm counting on you, man. Dig deep. Show me what you've really got."

Thirty-Two

The plaintive sound of the second call to prayer washed over Manama, echoing out into the stifling morning air.

Reznick headed down an alley and back to the crummy, airless apartment. It wasn't long before Mac returned with a street map of the city and a large bottle of water.

"What the fuck, Jon?"

"Decoy convoy. We had to at least get a tail on it."

Mac screwed up his face. "They're really giving us the runaround."

"So far. But things change."

"Where are we at? The old man was in his suite at the Four Seasons all this time?"

"One hundred percent. But this time with a smaller crew. Which could be *the* opening."

"Fair point."

Mac spread out the map on the concrete floor and sat down.

Reznick knelt and turned his cell phone light onto the map. A warren of crisscrossing streets veined the downtown area. "We've got to think, and we've got to think fast."

Mac took a red pen out of his pocket and marked an *X* to show their location. "This is where we are." He reached over and marked another *X* where Crenshaw's hotel was. "And he's there."

"We know that. What's your point?"

"My point is, if not now, when? I say let's get in there and wipe the fucker out. We might not get another chance."

"Collateral damage . . . we need to be careful. We know there's a hardcore cadre of Wagner bodyguards still hanging around there with the old man."

Mac bowed his head. "I don't like being hamstrung. It is so fucking frustrating that he's there. We had a plan for the jog. It would have worked."

"Plans change. I'm proposing we should head up to the hotel roof and access the penthouse from there. The element of surprise."

"That's interesting. It did cross my mind."

"Just thinking out loud."

Mac groaned. "While he's there, I say we go get him. Get access to the service elevator, rooftop, room service . . . maybe set off an evacuation, get everyone to leave the hotel. You know the drill. Let's shake things up."

Reznick listened as he pondered the various scenarios. "How about a package delivery? Inside we'll have made up a crude, home-made bomb. Fertilizer, a few wires, taped up a cell phone . . ."

"I fucking love that."

"The problem is time. It's intricate work. Have we got enough time? I'm not so sure we could execute that and ensure delivery."

"I can tell you from previous experience, working VVIP close protection, the floor he'll be on will be blocked off to the public. Maybe the floors below too."

"Act like a clueless tourist . . . and take out the guys at the private keyed elevator door with silencers. Then down the corridor to the suite. Knock on the door, saying we're hotel security."

"Promising . . . No frills. I can see that," said Mac.

"I want better odds. The old man is the target. He might be barricaded in a safe room."

Mac nodded, face bathed in the light of the phone.

"We need to improve our prospects. So that not only can we neutralize the fuck, but we have a decent chance of getting out of there alive. But I'm aware that we do not want a bloodbath."

Mac stared at the map. "The hotel sits on an island in Bahrain Bay. Three ways to get in and out."

"Right."

"Car over the causeway. Chopper from the helipad. And . . ."

"Water taxi to the Avenues mall, or a boat rental."

Reznick wondered if it was time to up the ante and risk it all. He usually prepared for operations with meticulous precision. It took time and patience. But this job was like nothing he had done before. It wasn't like Mossad's legendary hit in Dubai. They'd had a team. A large, multifaceted team. Their Hamas target had had no bodyguards in his hotel room. The Mossad agents had had a huge amount of intel and support. A clear run.

His burner cell phone rang. He picked up on the third ring.

"I think I might have come up with something that could, I stress, *could* work for you," Trevelle said breathlessly.

"Spit it out."

"The footage of the old man and the Russian in Oman, in the café—the voices of both Crenshaw and the Russian. A few yards from there, I hacked into a surveillance camera. It was situated at the back door in an adjacent alley, used by a tailoring shop. The deliveries entrance. So I could watch and listen to the conversation."

"Go on."

"The Russian is the old man's long-time handler. I've copied to my servers the cadence and rhythm of the handler's voice, the strong Russian accent. I believe we can trick the old man if he believes that his handler is calling him."

Reznick took a few moments to realize where Trevelle was going with this. "Voice morphing?"

"Exactly. I've uploaded a voice morphing program I developed a couple years ago, and it's on your cell phone."

"So when I call the old man, he'll believe it's his Russian handler. What's his name?"

"Viktor Mozorov. Crenshaw just calls him Viktor. So you could introduce yourself as Viktor. And it would sound exactly like Viktor."

"And that would work?"

"No guarantees in this game, Jon. You don't know how the old man will respond, or if he'll even take the call. But, to answer your question, it could work."

Reznick mulled the ruse as Mac studied the street map of the area around the Four Seasons.

"There's a landline in the old man's suite. I'll text you the direct number. From there, it's up to you."

Thirty-Three

When Reznick relayed the voice morphing ruse to Mac, the Scot grinned, eyes ablaze. He loved it.

"This fucker is a game changer, Jon," he growled in his inimitable brogue.

"What're you thinking?"

"What do you mean?"

"I mean, how would you work this? If you had to draw up a plan, what would it entail?"

"Get him out of the hotel, for starters."

Reznick felt a frisson of excitement. "Agreed."

"We can direct him to a location of our choosing."

"Go on."

Mac shone his cell phone's light on the map. He pointed to a stretch of water between the Four Seasons and the Avenues shopping mall. "There's a water taxi which crisscrosses here." He traced his middle finger to the boardwalk opposite, adjacent to the mall. "It rolls up at Gate Eight, if I remember."

"And then?"

Mac's finger moved to a building next to the sprawling, waterfront mall. "Multilevel parking garage. Sniper option. We take aim with our rifles as Crenshaw and his Wagner pals are on the water taxi making their way across here."

"It's direct, I'll give you that. And there's a good probability we could neutralize them."

"We gotta do what we gotta do."

Reznick stared at the map as doubts began to crowd his racing mind.

"Talk to me, Jon. You've gone all quiet."

"If they're asked to be exposed out in the open, on the water taxi, it might set off alarm bells for the Wagner crew. They're not stupid. They'll want to keep Crenshaw safe."

"I see that."

"Listen, I like the plan's simplicity. Its directness."

"But?"

"I don't know."

"Tell me your thinking, Jon."

"Here's what I think. I would prefer to contain the target and the bodyguards. Unseen. Out of sight. Maybe get them up close. But private. So it's just us and them, minimal chance of innocents being mown down."

Mac nodded. "Jon, I know you've done your share of hotel hits on foreign soil."

"What's your point?"

"I say we take Crenshaw and his goons out, long-range. And get the fuck out of there. Let the chips fall where they may."

Reznick contemplated the options. "We need to strip this thing back to the basics before we get to the game plan. We're assuming the voice morphing works. We're also assuming that Crenshaw plays ball and follows instructions."

"We're also assuming that he doesn't actually call his Russian handler to double-check that the orders are correct. There are permutations."

Reznick's mind raced faster and faster. "A lot of permutations. A lot of moving parts. You're right, this could fall at the first hurdle."

Mac shook his head ruefully. "It's a shame we haven't got some Semtex so we could attach a magnetic bomb to his car as he's driven to the airport."

"You old romantic!"

Mac laughed. He hummed to himself, seeking divine inspiration. "So have you got any plan that could keep them from being out on the open water? The only problem I could foresee is the water taxi is partially covered. Crenshaw could hunker down in a seat, away from prying eyes on the deck."

"Point taken."

"I've given you what I think is a decent plan. That would be my way."

Reznick was beginning to imagine how another scenario could play out. A germ of an idea was taking hold. "Well . . . I guess another option would be to direct Crenshaw and his Wagner crew to the parking garage you mentioned." He pointed to the location on the map. "How about if there are two shooters in the parking garage. Watching and waiting until they arrive. I could make the call, supposedly from the Russian, saying he'd be waiting. That Crenshaw has to move now. Stress the urgency."

Mac's pupils were like pinpricks. "Go on."

"But when he arrives in the vehicle, we delete Crenshaw. Them all. Each and every one of them in the confines of the parking garage. There are risks. But it would mean we could get in close. And make sure they're in the vehicle when we shoot them point-blank. So the bodies are inside the vehicle, and not lying out in the open on a water taxi. Then we can get the hell out of there. Gives us a head start. Maybe thirty minutes. Maybe an hour if we get lucky."

Mac ran his hands across his shaved head. "Fuck."

"What do you think?"

"They're both strong options," Mac said. "We have masks and gloves in our backpacks, to conceal our identities. What I would

230

like is if Trevelle could somehow access and remotely disable the surveillance cameras in and around the parking garage. That would be very helpful."

"Trevelle could do that."

Mac scratched the stubble on his chin. "I like it, Jon. I like it a lot. I suppose my next question is, what about us?"

"Getaway? I don't know whether the motorcycle option is the best, or just a plain old SUV, then dump and switch the vehicle on the other side of the city."

"SUV is a lot more common. No one would bat an eyelid."

Reznick referred back to the map. "So if we sit and wait at the Al-Hedaya parking garage not far from the mall, then when they pull up, we neutralize them, and drive off to here." He pointed to The Avenues parking garage directly adjacent to a shopping mall. "I figure that's just over a mile. Five minutes, six tops."

"So let's head over. Get in place. And make the call."

"I'll head over there first," said Reznick. "And then you follow. What about that truck you dumped? Would it be able to block exit routes, too?"

Mac patted him on the back. "Love the way you think, Rez! Let's do it."

Thirty-Four

It was just before dawn.

Crenshaw lit up another cigarette on the terrace. Dimitri stood next to him, both men watching the dark night sky slowly fold into color.

"I don't like it," Crenshaw said.

"What don't you like?"

"I don't trust him."

Dimitri raised his eyebrows. "You don't trust Rostov? He is a man of impeccable pedigree. Military, intelligence. He's connected. You need to listen to him."

"I don't know anything about him. He turns up, unannounced. Seems a bit strange."

"Why?"

"We usually work with Viktor, don't we?"

Dimitri turned to Crenshaw. "Rostov came here for a reason. I can vouch for him. I swear."

Crenshaw dragged hard on the cigarette, watching the blue smoke drift into the muggy early morning air.

"I'm guessing that, as we're in Bahrain, and this is Rostov's domain, he is leading on it," Dimitri said. "At least while you're here. I don't think there is any ill intent on his behalf."

"I don't like last-minute changes to schedules. It makes me uneasy. I smell a rat."

"You Americans worry too much."

Crenshaw shook his head. "You know the first thing I was taught when I joined the CIA?"

"What?"

"Don't trust a soul. No one."

"Not even your fellow intelligence operatives?"

"Trust is earned. I learned to trust colleagues over time. But it takes time. Learn to be circumspect. Look for patterns of behavior. When that behavior changes, it's important to take notice. I don't know Rostov well. I've heard of him. But suddenly he's in my life at the eleventh hour? That's a red flag for me."

"My job is to keep you safe. If Rostov says something, you listen. You follow orders. Simple."

Crenshaw smiled. "I hear you." He checked the time on his phone. "Not long now. Thank you for everything. For keeping me safe."

Dimitri's expression was sullen.

"What is it, Dimitri? What's bugging you?"

Dimitri sighed. "I'll be a lot happier when you're on the plane headed out of Bahrain."

Crenshaw felt the same. He nodded as they stood in companionable silence for a few moments.

"What are your plans now once your contract protecting me comes to an end?" asked Crenshaw. "Heading back to eastern Ukraine to kill some more of your Slavic brothers?"

"If necessary."

Crenshaw shook his head. "You guys need to sort that out once and for all."

"That's what we're doing."

"You go where you're told?"

"As long as the money is right, I go anywhere. Ukraine, Central African Republic, Mali, Sudan, Libya, doesn't matter to me. My family lives well because of my work."

Crenshaw leaned over the railing, checking the street below, absorbing the stillness.

"What about you, William?"

"What about me?"

"What will you do once you're not moving by plane, car, or boat every day? You will have so much time on your hands."

"I just want to enjoy the autumn years of my life. In peace. I think I've earned it."

"So you're just going to sun yourself?"

"I was thinking of writing my memoirs . . . I've sketched out a few ideas. I think that will be my focus."

"You think you'll get published?"

"I don't know . . . might be problematic for some New York publishers."

"Why?"

"A spy at the heart of the CIA? They don't want to condone that. But at the same time, the controversial nature would sell itself. And it would make money for them. That's what business is all about, isn't it?"

Dimitri grinned. "All about the money, right?"

"*Whoever loves money never has enough.* You know who said that?"

Dimitri shrugged.

"You need to read the scriptures more, Dimitri. It's from the Bible. Ecclesiastes."

"I didn't take you as a spiritual man."

"We're all spiritual. It's in us all. We just don't realize it until it's too late."

"Money, huh?"

"Isn't that your God, Dimitri?"

"I just do whatever has to be done, and to hell with the consequences."

"At the end of the day, money gets most of us up in the morning. The chance to make money, and the more the better."

"Won't you miss your country? I know I would."

"America?"

"Yes."

Crenshaw sighed softly. "The country I knew, the country I loved, is gone. When I grew up, it was a golden age. The 1950s. Now? Have you seen our once-great cities? It's pitiful. Decay. Slow death. It's no longer cyclical. Decade after decade. The city I was born in, Detroit . . . you ever been there?"

Dimitri shook his head.

"It's gone. Baltimore? It's almost like the Third World in swathes of the city. The infrastructure is old, inadequate for the twenty-first century. We're drowning in debt. We'll never be able to pay it back, even if we wanted to. And then there's AI. It'll obliterate millions and millions of jobs. White-collar, blue-collar, everything. What will we be left with? What will we be clinging to? And, to top it all, cultural Marxism is sweeping the nation's campuses. American students worry more about identity than they do about economics. About hard realities. Hard truths. They don't understand sacrifice. What it takes to remain the preeminent country in the world. You need to be tough. We need to rediscover our roots."

Dimitri nodded.

"You know what the great writer G.K. Chesterton said? He said, *When men choose not to believe in God, they do not thereafter believe in nothing, they then become capable of believing in anything.*"

"And that's what's happening in America?"

"In some parts of America. And in some segments of our society. We're losing faith."

"You believe there is a God, William?"

"Yes, I do. Somewhere along the way I took a wrong turn. Now? Only God can judge me."

"You paint a grim picture of America."

"That are some elements and states where freedom is cherished. Where the old values remain. But I fear for us. The republic."

"If you're from Russia, you see America in a completely different light. There are possibilities. I love New York."

"You've been to New York?"

"Ten years ago. Central Park, Fifth Avenue, Rockefeller Center, Empire State Building. It's fantastic."

"I love your optimism. Listen to me. Don't buy what Hollywood is peddling. The American empire is dying, Dimitri. All empires do. The problem for the American people is they don't realize their country will be on its knees in a few decades."

"I could never turn my back on my country. Never."

"I admire that."

"Do you like Russia?"

"Not particularly. I like Russians. No problem with the people."

"You think retirement in a place like Saudi Arabia will suit you? It is a brutal, medieval monarchy."

"That was part of the attraction," he said, half-jokingly. "That said, their infrastructure is among the best in the world. World-class golf tournaments, Formula One racing, boxing matches. You can walk the streets without being stabbed or shot. But who the hell knows?"

Dimitri pondered on that. "My wife wouldn't set foot in that country."

"Don't blame her. However, she might like to know that ninety-two percent of Saudi women can read and write."

"I don't believe that."

"Believe it. In America, it's eighty percent. Did you know that? A twelve percent greater literacy rate in Saudi women than American women. Think about that."

"That's insane."

"They also have fantastic health care. America? Fabulous . . . if you can afford it."

The phone in the suite began to ring.

Crenshaw's heart sank. "What now?"

Dimitri looked at him. "Do you want me to answer it?"

"Of course."

Dimitri went inside and answered the phone. He nodded, covering the mouthpiece. He signaled Crenshaw inside.

"What the hell is it now?" Crenshaw groaned and ambled into the suite. "Who the hell is calling?"

"Viktor."

"Viktor? At this hour?"

Dimitri shrugged. "He has an updated schedule for you."

"This is getting fucking ridiculous. Gimme that phone." Crenshaw grabbed the phone from Dimitri. "Viktor, I wasn't expecting to hear from you. What the hell is going on? My head is spinning with all this."

"We need you to move. Right now."

"I know. I'm waiting to hear."

"You need to move right now! We have fresh intel that came in minutes ago that says you will be in imminent danger if you stay in the hotel. You need to move right at this moment. Do you understand?"

"Right now?"

"Yes!"

"Move to where?"

"My team is waiting on level seven of the Al-Hedaya parking lot. Block 305. It's five minutes away. My team and I are waiting for you."

"You're there? Right now?"

"Yes, along with my team of specialists. We will escort you to a secure place. This is time-critical."

"Viktor . . . Captain Rostov was here just over an hour ago. He told me to sit tight. What you're telling me is diametrically opposed to that."

"Are you listening? You must go! Right now! The threat is imminent! The assassins will soon arrive at your hotel."

"And Dimitri comes with me?"

"Yes. Do not tell a soul. Just Dimitri. So it'll be you in the back with Dimitri, and the driver too. Three maximum. Got it?"

"Yes."

"You're on the move! Now!"

The line went dead.

Thirty-Five

Reznick reversed the Mercedes cargo van into the empty parking spot on level seven. He had stolen the van from three floors below. He wound his window down and looked over the concrete parking space. Huge air-conditioning units growled on a nearby wall, vibrating heavily, like the sound of static amplified. He checked his watch. He estimated that Crenshaw would just be about to leave. But he had to get confirmation from Trevelle.

Three minutes later, Reznick got a text: *Surveillance cameras across the parking garage have been remotely deactivated.*

His earpiece crackled into life. "Still no sign of life, Jon."

"Copy that."

"You think he's getting cold feet?" Trevelle asked.

"I sure as hell hope not. I made the call. He seemed to buy it. But I guess we'll just have to wait and see."

"More waiting."

Reznick scanned the near-deserted parking garage.

"Hang on . . ."

Reznick tapped his fingers on the wheel. "Got a visual?"

"Copy that. Movement on the penthouse floor."

"Have you got a visual?"

"Affirmative. The old man and two of his senior Wagner bodyguards, including the thug Dimitri."

"What else?"

"They are . . . on the move."

"Give me details."

"Heading down in the private keyed elevator. It will take them straight down to the parking lot in the secure basement, accessible only from the highest floors."

"Copy that." Reznick once more checked the parking garage. It was just him. He needed Mac in place. Mac had said he was getting a large truck, similar to the one he had stolen earlier. The purpose? To provide cover. But it would also block any escape and stop any other vehicles inadvertently stumbling onto the kill zone. "Talk to me, Trevelle."

"I repeat, two bodyguards, and the old man. Oh, hang on . . ."

"What is it?"

"I'm zooming in. Gimme a minute."

"What do you have?"

"The old man is wearing a bulletproof vest under his linen jacket."

"Copy that." Reznick winced. It was another complication he could have done without. "Anything else? You got eyes on the car?"

Trevelle gave him the license plate. "A black limo . . . BMW 7-Series, if I'm not mistaken."

Reznick tried to picture Crenshaw in the car at that moment. "Where is the old man sitting? Front or back?"

"Back seat, left side, one bodyguard driving, Dimitri in the rear right."

"So target in rear left, yeah? Old man rear left?"

"Confirmed. A 7-Series . . . Fuck."

"What?"

"This could be a problem."

"Talk to me, Trevelle."

"I'm just checking the specs of this car. It appears the car is fully bulletproof, both windows and bodywork."

Reznick considered whether they would have to blow out the tires with gunfire. But more importantly, where the hell was Mac? He needed to be here. "Copy that."

"I'm assuming that complicates your job."

"Everything is problematic or complicated in my line of work. Listen, where the hell is Mac? He's going to miss the party."

"He's half a mile away . . ."

"He's what?"

"Half a mile."

"So he's on the way?"

"Correct. Why?"

"I need him here! Now! It's ready to go down."

"Copy that, I'll text him."

"Right fucking now!"

"I hear you. Anything else, Jon?"

"Don't lose them. Keep me updated."

"Be good. And stay safe."

Reznick pulled on his mask and his gloves. He was on his own. He took the submachine gun out of his tactical backpack and laid it on his lap. He watched and waited. The target would arrive in a matter of minutes.

It was then, in that moment, that his thoughts turned to how to neutralize Crenshaw when they got him in the kill zone.

Thirty-Six

The limo pulled away from its parking space underneath the Four Seasons and drove up a ramp and out onto the street.

Crenshaw stared straight ahead. Dimitri sat in the back seat with him as they had been instructed. It still felt off. But, as he was realizing—and should have realized from the outset—the Russians were calling the shots now. They always had done. "Do you know when Viktor arrived in Bahrain?"

"No idea."

Crenshaw thought that strange, knowing the symbiotic relationship between Dimitri and Viktor. He was reminded of what Viktor had said about Dimitri when he had assigned him for lead protection duties. *Dimitri I would trust with my own family's life.* Crenshaw didn't know if he really believed that. But that's what he'd said. "I'm surprised."

"Why?" Dimitri watched the street as he spoke.

"I would have thought you'd know that. You and he are very close."

"That's true."

"And yet . . . he didn't let you know first? Isn't that the way it usually goes with you two? He runs things by you and you convey the message to me?"

Dimitri shrugged. "I don't know what you're getting at."

"What I'm getting at is that I thought, based on how things have worked previously, that he would have reached out to you."

"I'm guessing he thought it best to speak to you directly."

Crenshaw wasn't convinced. The protocols observed previously seemed to have disappeared. He knew from experience that interactions with Viktor were invariably planned well in advance. Had been since the start. This sudden call was not his usual modus operandi. It all seemed rushed. Ad hoc.

He questioned what had spooked Viktor so badly. Viktor was smooth, cultured, his mannerisms and sophistication palpable. Old-school KGB officer. Cold. Distant. Always on point. Crenshaw thought back to the phone call. Viktor had sounded more hassled and on edge than Crenshaw had ever heard him. And why hadn't Viktor just headed straight to the hotel with his men if he was that worried? Was there something else concerning him? Was the reason he hadn't reached out to Dimitri first because he felt he couldn't trust the feared mercenary? Was Dimitri the cuckoo in the nest?

The car accelerated as they sped around a corner, snapping Crenshaw out of his thoughts. "I guess Viktor will answer all my questions when we arrive."

Dimitri didn't answer.

Crenshaw studied his features, the Russian's face drawn and tense as if he was deep in thought, preoccupied.

"So, this garage, where is it? I just want to get out of here."

Dimitri pointed farther down the highway. "Just over a mile down this stretch of road."

Crenshaw's cell phone rang. He pulled it out of his jacket pocket, pressing it tight to his hearing aid.

"William?" The stern voice of Captain Rostov.

"Rostov?"

"Why are you not in your hotel suite as I instructed? Didn't I tell you to sit tight before extraction?"

Crenshaw couldn't believe what he was hearing. "What are you talking about? There was a change of plan. That's why I had to move."

"A change of plan? What change of plan?"

"I got a call from Viktor."

"Viktor? What are you talking about?"

"He instructed me to move with immediate effect. Viktor called me. Didn't he tell you?"

"William . . . I have no idea what you're talking about. I don't know about any call from Viktor."

Crenshaw ran through various scenarios in his head, from the Russians playing mind games, fucking with him, to something more ominous.

"I told you to wait in your hotel suite and I would be back to sort it out. Didn't I tell you that?"

"That's right. But after that, Viktor called me."

"When?"

"Ten, maybe fifteen minutes ago."

"I have no idea what you're talking about."

Crenshaw looked over at Dimitri, who turned back to him, eyes black.

"Tell me what happened," Rostov barked. "What did Viktor tell you?"

"He told me to get the hell out of there as soon as I could, and make my way to a parking garage. He said he'd be there. We're almost there."

"That's impossible."

Crenshaw's patience was ready to snap. "Do you think I'm making this shit up?"

"No . . . But Viktor isn't in Bahrain."

"I beg your pardon?"

"Viktor can't be in Bahrain."

"Why not?"

"Viktor is still in Oman. I was talking to him about three hours ago."

"I guess he flew in from Oman."

A silence expanded, filling every gap.

"Are you still there?"

"William, what you're telling me does not make any sense. Look, I'm going to contact Viktor and ask for an explanation. I'm the lead contact in Bahrain. Everyone knows that."

"So do I. But Viktor is my go-to guy . . . he pulls the strings. He's your boss, isn't he?"

"Not directly . . . but he has seniority."

"Viktor has been dealing with me all these years. I trust him."

"I know you do. But this doesn't seem to tally with how Viktor operates. He makes sure we all know and are in the loop."

Crenshaw felt a knot of tension in his stomach. Waves of paranoia washed over him. He felt uneasy again, his gut doing flips. He glanced again at Dimitri. The Russian had gone back to staring straight ahead.

"I'm going to call him."

Crenshaw sighed. "Whatever. Sort it out between yourselves."

Dimitri pointed to the silhouetted multilevel parking garage, looming in the distance. "We're nearly there."

Crenshaw ended the call, shuddering at the thought of what on earth had gotten into them all.

Thirty-Seven

Reznick adjusted his mask as he lay spread-eagled on the concrete, in a blind spot in the parking garage. AR-15 gripped tight, locked and loaded. Perfect line of sight. The waiting would soon be over.

His earpiece buzzed.

"Jon . . . the limo is close by." The voice of Trevelle. "Three minutes ETA. I repeat, ETA three minutes."

"Copy that. Where the hell is Mac?"

"There were a couple overnight road closures not far from the corniche. But he's on his way."

"When?"

"That's the first reason I'm calling. He should be there in three minutes forty seconds, by my estimate."

Reznick was concerned that Crenshaw would get cold feet if he didn't see Viktor or his entourage. "And the second reason you're calling?"

"I was checking out the specs on this particular BMW limousine."

"Bulletproof, you said?"

"A whole lot more. It's the latest model. It's a best-in-class pro-tection vehicle, used by diplomats, VIPs. Here's the kicker, Jon. It's made of armored steel. And the glass can survive hits from an AK-47."

Reznick had imagined raking the vehicle with rapid gunfire and moving in for the kill, piercing the bodywork of the car.

"In addition to that, the floor of the vehicle and even the car's roof can stop a grenade attack, roadside bomb, you name it. This is a beast of a car."

Reznick contemplated his next move.

"Just over two minutes, Jon."

"Trevelle, get Mac on the line so we can talk."

"Go ahead, Jon. He's listening in."

"Mac, we got a problem."

"I heard the end of the conversation."

"Where are you?"

"I think I'm being tailed. Cop car and high-end SUV right behind me."

Reznick felt himself tense up. "You need to lose them!"

"Easier said than done when driving a fucking concrete mixer."

"You need to stay away from the target area until you lose them."

"Copy that. Listen, I've got an idea. Shopping center around the corner. Parking underground."

"Mac?"

"Do what you have to do, Jon."

The call was cut off. No sign of Crenshaw's SUV. He could hear his heart beating. He lay still, listening. Watching. Waiting. The seconds dragged by.

"Trevelle, you still there?"

"Yes, Jon. I think you're on your own. Mac has turned around and is headed in the opposite direction."

"I hear you. Crenshaw?"

"He's stuck in a traffic jam. But he's on the move. Slowly."

"ETA?"

Trevelle groaned. "Couple minutes, Jon."

Reznick scanned the parking garage. Heard the sound of voices. Arabic voices. Male. He saw a security guard appear from a stairwell. *Shit.* The guy was speaking into a walkie-talkie, smoking an unfiltered cigarette. The guard shone a flashlight up at a surveillance camera. Reznick wondered if the guy had been sent to check why the cameras weren't working. It was the last thing he needed. Crenshaw would be here soon. He wanted a clean shot, no bystanders in the crosshairs. Line of sight.

The guard turned and shone the flashlight around the rest of the level.

Reznick held his breath as the guy babbled away into the walkie-talkie, then shone the light at another surveillance camera at the far end. He wondered if he should take the guy out before Crenshaw arrived. But he figured that if the guard was talking to the control room, and suddenly he wasn't responding amid the sound of gunfire, they would call the cops.

The seconds felt like minutes. *Disappear, man. Get the fuck out of here.*

Then the guard stopped as if he had heard something. His gaze wandered around the parking garage as if he sensed something was off. He looked up again at one of the surveillance cameras, fixed on the wiring behind him. He took out his cell phone and photographed the fixed wiring, as if to show his boss that the cables were untouched.

After what seemed an eternity, the guard finally shuffled off and into an elevator, the doors closing behind him.

Jon's earpiece came to life again. "That was a close call. OK, showtime. Crenshaw's vehicle approaching slowly from the east."

"Copy that. Where the hell is Mac?"

"Not long now. He's on his way."

Thirty-Eight

The limo turned up the ramp into the parking garage. Crenshaw sat quietly in the back seat as Dimitri fidgeted with his watch. "Are you OK?" Crenshaw asked. "You seem kinda antsy."

"You're right. It's not like Viktor. This was not part of the plan."

"I suppose Viktor is responding to real-time threats. Just wanting to ensure my safety. I trust him."

Dimitri nodded. "I do too." His cell phone rang. He reached into his pocket and pulled out his phone, switching it to speaker. "Yeah, who's this?"

"It is Viktor."

"Sir . . . we're on our way to see you. We've just got here."

Silence for a few moments. "What are you talking about?"

"Your call."

Crenshaw leaned forward, raising his voice. "Viktor, it's William."

"William? Have you lost your mind?"

"Viktor, what's going on?"

"You were instructed to wait for further information from Captain Rostov. Why have you disobeyed him?"

The limo edged higher until it reached level seven. The driver parked tight up against a concrete wall. Dimitri looked around the parking garage for Viktor or his team. But no one was around.

Crenshaw shouted into the phone, "What the hell are you talking about? I'm here! We just arrived where you wanted me to go."

"William, shut up and listen to me! Where are you?"

"What the hell do you mean where am I? You know where I am! The parking garage, level seven. You told me to—"

"No, no, no!"

"What? But you called me!"

"William, listen to me very, very carefully. I never called you. I'm in Oman. How can I be there?"

Crenshaw was dumbstruck as it suddenly dawned on him that he had been played. "So who called me? I swear it was you."

Silence in response.

"Viktor! What the hell is going on?"

"Get out of there! Now! It's a setup! Get the hell out of there now!"

Thirty-Nine

Reznick lay completely still, eyes fixed on the imposing black BMW limo. The vehicle was positioned directly across from the ramp where cars entered and exited the level. But no one was getting out. He figured there would be an opportunity if one of the bodyguards decided to step outside of the car's protective shell.

His earpiece buzzed. "I'm on my way, Jon," Mac said.

"What the hell is going on?"

"Long story. I had to throw those two cars off my tail. So I had to dump a load of wet cement behind me so they couldn't follow."

"You've got another problem . . ."

"What? Crenshaw changed his plans?"

"Negative. It's the vehicle. Crenshaw's vehicle."

"What about it?"

"Bulletproof, bomb-resistant, glass the same," Reznick said. "We could rake it for countless rounds but it might not do the trick."

"Only one thing for it, Jonny Boy."

"What's that?"

"They go high-tech, we go low-tech."

Reznick grinned behind the mask as it slowly dawned on him the type of surprise that Mac had in store. It was the only way.

"You know what to do?" Reznick said.

"Oh yeah. Let's do it."

Lying there, Reznick had a clear visual on the BMW, his rifle aimed at the rear passenger window. The whole operation was in the balance. His mind knew what needed to be done. Mac knew exactly what was required. But the question was, would the impromptu plan actually work? A deafening silence hovered over the garage. Not a sound. No voices. He wondered how long Crenshaw and his team would hang around.

His earpiece buzzed. "Mac has just entered the parking garage." Trevelle's voice was barely a whisper, as if he sensed how precarious the situation was. "He's headed up the ramp and moving beyond level three."

"Let Mac know," Renick whispered, "the limo is directly opposite the entrance ramp for level seven. Directly opposite. So it will be right in front of him as he approaches."

"Copy that."

Reznick held his breath, the limo in the crosshairs of the rifle. It was a matter of seconds.

He felt the heavy vibrations on the concrete floor of the garage. He knew what it was. Mac was on his way. The sound of a heavy monster truck making its way up. Revving hard as it climbed the levels.

Reznick watched it unfold as if in slow motion. He checked the rifle sights. And there it was. A colossal cement-mixing truck, accelerating, tires screeching as it headed directly for the limo. Reznick could see Mac behind the wheel, wearing his mask. He was staring straight ahead, his eyes ablaze like a maniac.

Forty

The limo was rammed from the rear with an almighty crash. It plowed forward, smashing through the concrete perimeter wall.

Crenshaw felt a terrifying shooting pain in his neck as his head was jolted back from the impact. Whiplash. The sound of metal and the roar of an engine. The limo was violently forced forward through a steel guard rail, grinding metal twisting a gaping hole. His life flashed for a split second. He felt gripped by blind terror. The seconds were like hours. He began to panic. And shake.

The limo was hit again and again. The airbag inflated. Blood rushed to his head as the car tipped forward, hanging in the air, and he stared through the tinted windshield, over the edge to the road below.

"What the fuck?"

Crenshaw tried to release his seat belt but couldn't reach. He tried to scream but he was paralyzed with shock and pain.

Dimitri shouted, snapping Crenshaw back to reality. They were still being tipped over the edge, high up in the parking garage. He turned around, groaning at the excruciating pain in his neck, and looked up through the back window. They were practically hanging by a fender. "Shit!"

The huge cement-mixer truck had rammed into them once more. Crenshaw was jolted forward, his neck whipped back again.

Searing pain in his back now. Face smashed into the driver's headrest. Unable to breathe. The smell of smoke filled the limo. He was choking. Coughing.

Crenshaw sensed he was seconds from death. The truck had them. It was inching them forward, bit by bit. The sound of grinding metal on concrete. The smell of oil and fire. The driver slammed the limo into reverse.

Dimitri screamed, "Locked! Open up! Get us out!"

But the truck was immense, pushing and pushing them. Crenshaw began to convulse with shock.

Dimitri lunged forward and tapped the driver on the shoulder. The limo driver was motionless, blood from his nose, head hanging loose. An alarm blared.

The central locking mechanism wasn't opening.

Crenshaw turned again. He peered through the smoke billowing out of the rear of the limo. The driver of the truck wore a ski mask. He hammered into them a fourth time.

The limo lurched forward, center of gravity gone. Dimitri pulled out his Glock handgun and fired at the lock, trying to open the rear door. But nothing was working.

A final terrifying, crushing impact from the rear.

Crenshaw felt the limo tip over. He squeezed his eyes shut. Dropping through the air as if in slow motion. His world turned upside down in a terrible, split second. He felt his neck snap.

He felt the cold chill of death as the limo descended into the void. His body tensed up on impact. First the crash, then the explosion.

He tried to move. Shooting pains in his leg and back, but otherwise paralyzed. It was like needles piercing his back and his legs. Pain erupted in his head, as his life flashed in front of him, until he saw himself as a boy.

Forty-One

Reznick burst through a stairwell door and bounded down the steps two at a time. Heart pounding, mask up, AK-15 in hand, he kicked open an emergency door and ran toward the burning, overturned limo, its wheels spinning in the air. Flames and smoke billowed from the shattered windows.

He raked the rear window with sustained fire. A crack appeared in the glass. He fired again and again.

A side window blew out, shards exploding across the street.

Reznick approached the limo, crouched, watching for any movement. He sensed someone was behind him. He turned.

Mac was grinning as he advanced, AK-15 in hand.

Reznick signaled for him to go around the other side of the smoking limo. The Scot sprayed the rear passenger window with a hail of gunfire.

Reznick smashed open the cracked window. He peered inside the car. A bloody, tattooed bodyguard, covered in glass, hand outstretched, made a move. Reznick shot Dimitri twice in the head. Double tap. He smashed the rest of the glass until it caved in.

The old man's neck was twisted as he lay crumpled, bleeding out. He was covered in shattered glass, face torn to shreds. Crenshaw wore a bulletproof vest. He opened his mouth as if about to speak, Glock slowly raised in his bony fingers. Teeth clenched, tears in his rheumy eyes.

Reznick fired off two shots to the forehead. The brain and blood splattered the dead bodyguard nearby.

Mac shot off the lock and window on the driver's side. He reached in and pulled out the driver. He drilled five shots into the tattooed man's face and neck.

Three down—Crenshaw. Dimitri. Driver.

"Clear!" Mac called out.

Reznick gave a thumbs-up. He took out his phone and took multiple photos of the bloody corpse of Crenshaw. The target was dead. The intelligence chief who had betrayed his country. A man who had raked in millions and millions through treachery. A traitor. A spy. Reznick reached inside the limo and rifled through the old man's jacket pocket. He pulled out a cell phone and put it in his pocket. He checked Crenshaw's belt. Keys hanging. He ripped off the leather belt loop they were attached to. Inside one of the keys, a metal USB memory stick. He slid it carefully into his pocket. "We're done!"

Mac gave the thumbs-up and they headed back through the emergency exit and bounded up the stairwell.

Reznick followed Mac quickly to the third level. "You looking for a car?"

Mac pointed to a motorcycle, chained up. A security guard approached, radio in hand. Mac trained his rifle on the guy. "On the fucking ground! Now!"

The guard threw himself to the ground, whispering, "Please don't hurt me. I have a family."

Mac grabbed the guy's radio and smashed it on the ground. He fired one shot which cut through the chains on the bike. Then he neatly folded away his gun, shoving it into his backpack. He zipped it up as Reznick did the same with his weapon, placing the backpack strap over his shoulder.

Reznick climbed onto the bike and started up the powerful engine. He ripped off his mask. "Hop on!"

Mac climbed onto the bike, pillion style, holding a steel support behind him. "Go! Go!"

Reznick accelerated away down the ramp and out onto the streets of Manama, the city slowly waking up at dawn. The sound of police sirens rose and fell in the distance. He revved harder as they sped through the streets. It wasn't long before Reznick and Mac had disappeared into a warren of alleys and side streets.

Forty-Two

The minutes that followed were a manic sped-up blur. Adrenaline flowed through Reznick's body like an electric shock.

They needed to get the hell away from the city. From Bahrain. And fast. Skidding and screeching through the downtown streets of Manama, Reznick's mind was in a heightened state of alert. He rode the motorcycle hard, accelerating, cutting corners as Mac held on for his life.

"So what's the plan now?" Mac yelled.

Reznick shouted, "We need to dump the bike. And switch."

"Let's do it."

Reznick sped past a handful of street stalls which were just opening. Up ahead, he spotted a police car. He slowed down, turned a corner, and they headed along a narrow alley. Through puddles of filth, they emerged onto a potholed side road. He accelerated fast and found himself on the freeway. He rode even faster for a few hundred yards. Then he spotted a neon-lit sign for The Avenues parking garage.

"This is it!" Mac shouted. "Get in there!"

Reznick turned up the ramp and headed into another multi-level parking garage. He accelerated around the bends and corners, all the way to the roof. They came to a stop and both dismounted from the bike.

Mac slapped Reznick on the back and declared, "That was fucking great!"

"We're not out of the woods yet." Reznick spotted a beaten-up old Mazda. He quickly took out a knife and pried open the lock. He tore off the underside of the steering wheel and checked out the frayed wiring. A few moments later, he had the engine purring to life.

"Nice one, Jonny boy."

Reznick slid into the driver's seat, backpack thrown in the back seat as Mac sat up front with him. He reversed out of the parking space, skidding as he turned quickly. He needed to get to an isolated marina or dock.

His earpiece crackled into life. "Jon, what's the plan?" It was Trevelle. "I got you, buddy."

"I need to get a boat. A fast boat."

The sound of Trevelle tapping away on his keyboard. "Marina, speedboat hire. Two miles due southeast. Yeah?"

"Got it." Reznick knew the area, having studied the map earlier. He hit the gas and drove fast toward the nearest coast.

"Keep on this main road, then I'll tell you when to move."

Reznick skidded around a corner and wove in and out of the light traffic. He saw Mac had taken out a 9mm Glock and was checking the handgun. "Keep it down!"

Mac slid the gun into his waistband, his T-shirt concealing the weapon. He pointed to an off-ramp. "Ten o'clock, due northwest, that's where the boats are. Right down there."

The earpiece crackled, "Yup, that's it! Take this left turn and straight into the marina."

Reznick drove on for another half mile. He plowed through a chain-link fence and into the marina. Three boats were tied up next to a young Bahraini dude in a Yankees hat, who was smoking. Reznick pulled up beside the kid and shut off the engine. Then he got out the car, backpack in hand, and walked up to the kid. "What's the fastest boat?"

The kid pointed to the middle one. "That is a fast boat. It belongs to my uncle."

Reznick reached into the backpack and pulled out a wad of cash. He handed the kid one thousand dollars.

"That is too much."

"We're not renting it. We're taking it."

The kid threw the keys to Mac, who started up the speedboat. They edged away from the shore, past a dhow floating aimlessly in the water.

Reznick turned the twist-grip forward and opened the throttle. The boat picked up speed and they sped out to sea. Faster and faster, skimming across the waves. Hundreds of yards out.

Suddenly, a boom from back on shore.

Reznick glanced behind them. A couple of cops were aiming long rifles at them. "Get down, Mac!"

Shots ricocheted off the boat.

Mac screamed as he was hit in the chest. He collapsed onto the wooden deck.

Reznick slowly pulled the throttle back. He rushed to Mac's side, looking to staunch the bleeding. He ripped off Mac's T-shirt and tore it into strips. "Don't check out on me, pal!" He pressed the bloodstained cloth to the bullet wound.

"Motherfuckers!" Mac screwed up his eyes.

Reznick crouched down as more shots whizzed overhead. "Don't move, Mac."

Mac clenched his teeth tight, in terrible pain, losing blood quickly.

Reznick stared down into the Scot's eyes. "We're going to get you out of here. You need to hang in there. You understand? You need to suck this pain up."

Mac grimaced as if in agony. He nodded. "Get me out of here!"

Reznick held his hand. "Hang in there, buddy." He got back in the driver's seat, slowly opening the throttle as they gathered speed. The boat accelerated almost to the maximum, skimming across the inland waters of Bahrain toward the Persian Gulf.

His earpiece crackled. "Jon, what the fuck just happened?"

"Mac's been hit. I repeat, he's been hit. Chest wound. Major blood loss. I need to get him medical help. Trauma team. He needs it now!"

"Copy that, Jon. Give me a few minutes. I'm working on some stuff."

Mac writhed on the deck as they powered through the waves and choppy waters.

"Trevelle, you need to get us out of here. He's losing blood fast. We're running out of time."

"Jon, I'm working on it."

"Well, work on it faster. He's bleeding out."

"OK. I have an idea."

Forty-Three

Fran Petersen was burning the midnight oil, sitting at her desk, staring at another grisly image on her screen. Numerous explicit photos of William Crenshaw. He was dead, drenched in blood. Bullet wounds in his forehead. She had ordered the hit. She had initiated and orchestrated this operation. The decision had been hers. The payoff was immense. The assassination of an American spy. High risk, high reward.

She should have felt elated. The operation had been successful. But inside, she felt a familiar emptiness. A fellow American, who had walked the same corridors as her many years earlier, had needed to be neutralized. She felt a tinge of sadness thinking of Crenshaw's final minutes. But it was just for a fleeting moment.

The phone rang. She let it ring, savoring the victory.

Petersen had learned over the years to compartmentalize such decisions and their outcomes. It was a cold-hearted business. No one needed to know. Besides, Americans were blissfully unaware of the serious risk to their national security that had been eliminated, thousands of miles from home.

She tried to not think about whether she had grown colder as the years passed. Nowadays every "foreign" hit just seemed to wash over her. She didn't mind jihadists being taken out, watching remotely on screens as drones killed dozens. But despite his disloyalty to his country, the killing of William Crenshaw, an American, was not something she would crow about. She would have to internalize it. Know it had happened. She couldn't unsee the bloody, bullet holes in his head. Dead and gone.

Her cell phone stopped ringing. Then it started again, snapping her out of her introspection.

Petersen picked up her phone. "Yeah?"

"Fran, it's Koninsky." It was a senior CIA analyst who specialized in the Middle East. "Turn on Al Jazeera."

Petersen picked up her remote control and turned on the TV, switching to the Doha-based channel. The footage showed a live broadcast from Manama, Bahrain. A burning limo, smoke billowing from it, a reporter behind police tape at the scene.

"Our sources within the Bahraini government tell us that this appears to be a tragic accident," said the reporter. "The vehicle driver, a Russian citizen, accelerated instead of braking in the parking garage, before plunging one hundred and twenty meters to the ground. But other sources are now indicating that there was another vehicle involved. A truck. And in the truck it is believed that two Ukrainian passports were found."

It was messy. It was making headlines. But the first draft of history was being written. It was incorrect. But it didn't matter. The reporter had gotten a heads-up from a source within the Bahraini intelligence services after a tipoff from the State Department. The cover story meant to keep the focus away from the United States had taken hold. The Ukrainians would take the fall. It was their operation. They would deny it, of course. But by then the fictitious narrative would have taken root in the public consciousness.

The reporter pressed her finger to her earpiece. She turned to speak to a Bahraini senior police official. "Sir, what is the latest information you can share with us?"

The man stared at her, stony-faced. "We are a peaceful, prosperous nation, a friendly people, a very low-crime country. Make no mistake, we will establish what happened. If there are perpetrators, they will be punished."

"Can you talk about the Ukrainian special forces' involvement in this? I'm hearing that two of the men in the vehicle who died were Russian citizens. Some are speculating that they were Russian mercenaries who had been involved in massacres in eastern and southern Ukraine. Is this true?"

"I'm not prepared to speculate at this stage. Bahrain will deal with this in the fullness of time, once we have established all the facts."

Petersen's phone rang again and she muted the TV coverage. "Fran speaking."

"Ms. Petersen, it's Trevelle."

"Trevelle . . . Hey . . . I'm just watching the TV coverage of this."

"Forget about that! We need urgent help!"

"What kind of help?"

"We need a medical evacuation. Extraction. They're headed toward the Persian Gulf and Mac is bleeding out. Reznick is driving a fast boat. But they need help."

"I'll handle it."

"It needs to be now!"

"I'm on it. Tell Reznick we've got his back."

Forty-Four

Reznick pushed the speedboat's throttle to the max as he slammed across the waves toward the Persian Gulf, eyes on the maritime GPS map on the screen. Mac still lay moaning in pain on the deck, the bloodstained ripped T-shirt pressed to his chest.

"I'm not going to make it, Jon!" he shouted. "Too much blood."

Reznick figured he was about eight miles out of Bahrain. He cut the engine, picked up his backpack, and went over to Mac, kneeling down as he tended to his tough friend, whose complexion was pale, almost gray. He felt warm blood on his skin. "Mac, you need to hang in there."

Mac's eyes rolled back in his head. "Jon, listen to me, I'm not going to make it."

Reznick tilted a bottle of water to his friend's lips. "I'm not going to leave you."

"Jon, get yourself to safety."

"I'm fine."

"These bastards will come looking for us."

"We're out of Bahrain." Mac was fighting to stay conscious. "You need to stay awake! Don't slip away! Do you understand?"

"Shut the fuck up and get back to the driver's seat. Get us the hell out of here! Don't fucking stop!"

Reznick gripped Mac's hand tight. "You stubborn son of a bitch."

Mac smiled, tears in his eyes. "We did it, Jon, didn't we?"

"We got him. We got them all."

Mac gave a weak laugh. "I knew we would."

"Hang in there!"

Reznick was loathe to leave Mac's side. But he had to. He strapped himself back in the driver's seat and opened up the throttle again, edging the boat forward. It careered through the water. Farther and farther from land, hurtling through the ethereal dawn light bathing the Gulf. He picked up his satellite phone and called Trevelle. "Have you still got a fix on my position?"

"I've got it. I can see exactly where you are."

"Buddy, I need some backup, fast!"

"It's on the way. Help is closing in."

Reznick glanced behind him. Mac seemed to have gone quiet, as if slipping out of consciousness. "You better get a move on. If you've got a fix on my GPS, where do I head?"

"Head southeast from your position for ten minutes. Can he hang in that long?"

"I don't know. This is touch-and-go."

"An American amphibious assault ship twenty miles out also has a fix on your position."

"Copy that. What's the plan?"

"Chopper from the ship is flying out. It'll pick up you and Mac. Rendezvous point due southeast as I indicated."

"Tell them to get a fucking move on. Mac is bleeding out fast."

"They know all that, Jon."

"Well tell them again! We need a full medical team."

"You'll get it!"

Reznick ended the call. He entered the precise location into the navigation system as they headed southeast, navigating the course toward the rendezvous point. A suitable blood red bathed the sea. Mile after mile, the boat arrowed through the water.

Mac moaned with the pain. He needed urgent medical help. Reznick turned and looked at him. "Hang in there, man."

Reznick felt helpless. He checked his watch. Seven minutes until the chopper would be in sight. "Stay with us, Mac! Help is on the way!"

Mac suddenly shouted, "Jon! Boat fast approaching on the stern side."

Reznick spun around. In the far distance, cutting through the waters toward them, a military patrol boat. He switched off the engine and held up a pair of binoculars, scanning the water. An Iranian fast boat. He knew they constantly harassed ships, boats, and tankers across the Gulf. He took out the foldable semiautomatic from the backpack, locked it into place, and spread-eagled himself on the deck. He zeroed the sights on the boat, tracking its movement. "Stay down, Mac!" he shouted.

He stared through the crosshairs as the patrol boat approached at high speed. A machine gunner stood on deck, watching and waiting.

Reznick knew all about the fearsome reputation of the Iranian Quds Force. He fired off three rapid shots, taking out the machine gunner. Two of the man's colleagues rushed to take his place, shouting and screaming, gesticulating. Reznick took aim and fired off a hail of bullets, mowing them down. He checked through the sights for any other sign of life. Nothing. He zeroed in on a large gas tank located at the back of the boat and fired off a dozen shots or more. The engine caught fire, then the boat exploded and was engulfed in flames.

Mac punched his fist in the air, gritting his teeth. "Take that, you fuckers!"

Reznick turned. "What do you think?"

Mac laughed, coughing up blood. "Good work. Now let's get the fuck out of here before the Iranian navy get after us."

Reznick strapped himself back in the driver's seat and powered them on for a few more miles. He realized after a short while that Mac had gone quiet. "Talk to me, Mac! You still with me?"

Mac was silent.

Reznick kept one hand on the steering wheel as he called Trevelle again. "We're still hanging on, Trevelle. Where the fuck is the cavalry?"

"ETA two minutes, Jon. Keep heading southeast. Help is on the way. I'm tracking them and you. Hang in there."

Reznick ended the call as he pushed the speedboat to the max one more time. It was then, somewhere in the distance, that he heard a familiar whirring and roaring. The sound of a chopper fast approaching. A few seconds later, in the distance, he spotted a Black Hawk swooping low, a winchman already dangling from the side. He turned and shouted across to Mac, "Hold on, buddy, we're getting you out of here!"

But Mac didn't move, or say a word.

Forty-Five

The minutes that followed seemed like an eternity.

Mac's eyes were closed as he was strapped down and winched up by the navy medic. He rose unconscious up to the chopper. A few moments later, Reznick was winched up as well.

Reznick strapped himself in as the helicopter banked sharply to the right, turned, and flew away fast from the speedboat. He looked across at the medics surrounding Mac, who was hooked up to a morphine drip as a nurse and doctor tried to stem the bleeding with Celox gauze and bandages.

The doctor shone a penlight in Mac's eyes. "Pupils not dilating!"

Reznick could only watch as the nurse started hard chest compressions. *One! Two! Three! Four!*

"Come on, come on!" the nurse implored Mac.

The doctor took fresh bandages from a first-aid kit and pressed them tight to Mac's chest. "We need to plug this! We're losing him!"

The nurse checked Mac's pulse as she pressed the bandages down. "Faint pulse, and he's breathing."

The doctor quickly took out a blood plasma bag and hooked Mac up to another intravenous drip, inserting a needle into his arm. "Fixed!"

The nurse shouted, "Stay with us, Mac! Mac, can you hear me? Stay with us!"

Reznick watched as they fought hard to save David McCafferty. He was on the thin line between life and death. He thought of Mac's son back in Scotland with his ex-wife. He had wanted Mac on the mission the moment he knew he was only allowed one special forces operative to join him. He said a silent prayer as the chopper skimmed low across the Gulf, then unbuckled his restraints and crouched down beside Mac, gripping his cold hand tight. "Don't you dare give up on this, Mac! Do you hear me? You hang in there! Come on, I know you can hear me! Stay with us! You're getting blood. We're getting you out of here! Stay with us!"

The nurse was unrelenting in the compressions. *One! Two! Three!* She checked his vital signs. "Pulse slowing!"

Reznick felt Mac's right hand begin to shake. He gripped it tighter. "I got you, Mac. We're here. Just hang in there, man. You need to fight this! Do you hear me? Stay with us!"

Mac's life lay in the balance.

The minutes stretched endlessly, as if the flight would go on forever. The doctor felt Mac's neck for a pulse. "That's better! Stick with us, Mac!" He opened up a fresh pack of medical gauze and bandages, strapping the dressings tight to Mac's bare torso.

A few moments later, slowly, miraculously, Mac's eyes opened. His pupils were like black pinpricks. His steely gaze fixed on Reznick.

"I'm here, Mac. It's Jon." He squeezed his hand again. "Hang in there, man. We're almost there. You need to fight to stay in the game, man! Don't you dare check out on me!"

Mac's eyes rolled back in his head.

Reznick slapped his face. "Mac, don't fall asleep. Not now! You're not fucking bleeding out on me. Do you hear me? I said, do you hear me?"

Mac managed to open his heavy eyes, which darted around the interior of the chopper. Then his vacant eyes stared at the nurse compressing the fresh bandages.

She looked down at him. "Almost there, sir," she said. "Just hang in there."

Mac reached out and gripped the nurse's hand.

"I got you, sir," she said.

"You look like a girl I used to know."

The nurse blushed. "Don't talk, sir."

Mac turned and faced Reznick.

"I'm right here, buddy."

"We nearly there, Jon? I'm really tired."

"Stay with us, Mac. We're nearly there, Mac."

"What a fucking trip!"

"A crazy few days. You're going to make it. You just need to stay in the fight. Stay with us. Stay in the fight!"

Mac gave a wan smile. "I'll stay in the fight. Don't leave me."

"I'm not leaving you. I'm staying with you all the way."

Forty-Six

The chopper descended and landed softly on the destroyer, the sun's rays beating down as it edged higher over the Gulf. It was already one hundred degrees. Mac was lifted out, laid on a gurney, and rushed to an operating room in the ship's sick bay. The hours that followed were going to be crucial for Mac.

Reznick was escorted to an airy private quarters on board the ship. He showered, still full of adrenaline, flashbacks erupting in his mind. The look on Crenshaw's face as he took his last breath. The breakneck bike ride to the parking garage, stealing the Mazda and on to the Bahrain marina to seize the speedboat.

He took his time, gathering his thoughts. He dried off and was given a fresh set of clothes.

Trevelle called on the satellite phone. "How's Mac?"

"He's alive. That's all I know. Did you access Crenshaw's cell?"

"Copy that." The sound of tapping on a keyboard. "I got it. I'm taking a copy of the contents for Petersen."

"Anything else?"

"You did good, Jon. Real good."

Reznick ended the call. He slumped into an easy chair in his cabin. He knew the job was done. But it was a classified operation.

No one, even those on board, could know the true nature of their mission.

A sharp knock at the door snapped him out of his thoughts. A naval intelligence officer arrived carrying a brown satchel along with a tray of coffee and some sandwiches. The officer pulled up a seat beside him.

Reznick knew he needed to be on his guard. He couldn't afford idle talk.

"How you feeling?" The officer pointed at the tray. "Eat up. It's for you. You must be famished."

Reznick's stomach rumbled; he was starving. Ham sandwiches, hot coffee. Perfect. He wolfed down the first sandwich, loving the feeling of the caffeine in his body slowly invigorating him.

"Feel better?"

"A lot better, thanks."

"My pleasure, Jon. You don't mind me calling you Jon, I assume?"

Reznick shook his head. He knew this was the soft start to questioning. He understood the rationale as to why the officer would want an explanation for why an American and a Brit had needed to be rescued off the coast of Bahrain, one with life-threatening gunshot wounds. The explosion of the Iranian fast boat would be known to him too.

"Great, Jon. I'm wondering if you can help me out."

"Depends on with what."

The officer reached into his briefcase and pulled out a notepad and pen. "You OK if I take down a few details?"

"Go right ahead," Reznick agreed, wanting to appear cooperative and amenable.

The officer scribbled a few details including the time and date. "Great. You see . . . we were debating . . . or more precisely, I was wondering . . . I mean the American navy is just wondering, what were you doing out there, Jon? It's all very strange. We're just trying to get a handle on this."

Reznick picked up the second sandwich and began to eat in silence. He wasn't going to answer any questions. It was a secret mission. Period.

"Help me out here, Jon. I've got this paperwork to complete."

Reznick ignored the guy, who was already beginning to annoy him.

"We know a bit about you. So it's best if you tell us what you were doing out there."

Reznick shrugged.

"America has very good relations with the governments of the Middle East. Shared values and interests. This is an incredibly volatile time. We can't have misunderstandings leading to confrontations. Do you know what I'm saying?"

Reznick continued to eat in silence.

"The Bahrainis, who are usually very circumspect, have called in our ambassador for a dressing-down. They want answers. They believe, privately, the United States might be involved in a provocation."

Reznick took a long gulp of coffee. "How is my friend?"

"The ex-SAS guy they brought in?"

"How is he?"

"He's in the operating room. That's all I know."

"What's his condition?"

"I don't honestly know."

The intelligence officer pulled his chair even closer to Reznick, lowering his voice. "Jon, don't take me for a fool. I need to know what you were doing in the Persian Gulf."

Reznick slowly finished his sandwich. "Delicious. Thank you."

"Are you taking the Fifth?"

"I'm not in a courtroom, am I?"

The guy just shook his head. "Who are you working for? You working for the CIA? Because you know what? I asked, and they say you don't work for them."

"I'm not on trial, am I?"

"No, but it's a simple question. Who are you working for? Military contractors?"

"Listen, I'm just interested in making sure my friend is OK."

The officer pressed his face tight up against Reznick's. "Things can go south if you don't help me out, Jon."

"Listen. I don't know who you are. I love your enthusiasm for the job. But I'm more concerned about my friend. Now why don't you fuck off and annoy someone somewhere else."

"Security in this part of the world is essential to America's energy security. Do you understand?"

Reznick laid the tray on the ground and spread out in the bunk. "Nothing personal, pal, but I need to get some rest. You understand?"

"Is that it?" the officer said.

"I guess so. Wake me up when my friend is out of the operating room. And thanks again for the food. Delicious."

The officer shook his head again, picked up the tray, briefcase, and pad, and walked out, not saying another word.

Reznick began to smile. He felt himself drifting away. Falling into a black void. He sensed he was floating on an endless, winding river. The strong current was pulling him farther and faster downstream. Deeper and deeper he was being pulled down a dark river. Then it all turned black . . .

He was back in the hellish inferno that was Iraq. Suffocating heat. Smoke drifting through the azure blue sky. But why was he cold? He looked down and realized that he was floating on an endless river of blood. He turned his head, gripped by fear. Parts of bodies drifted past in the murky waters of Baghdad's Tigris River. He tried to scream. But nothing. He turned his head again. More dead bodies and parts of bodies. The victims of the sectarian tit-for-tat killings. Shia death squads. Sunni death squads. Reprisals. Corpses floating in the ancient waters of Babylon. The sound of the call to prayer could be heard amid the horrifying screams of widows. The suffering drove people mad. Mad with fear. Mad with anger. Consumed by hate. Sanctified in blood.

He tried to move as he gulped down water. Slowly drowning. Gazing at the darkening skies. But he was paralyzed, floating on a river of death. The corpses, blueish-black skin peeling off, eyes drilled out by sectarian and religious psychopaths, only ghosts and their spirits inhabiting the river for eternity. Maybe they would be found. Maybe they would just float, unbothered by the madness and cruelty which had been delivered to their country.

Reznick awoke, heart pounding, bathed in sweat. Staring down at him was a female surgeon. He checked his watch. He had been sleeping for six hours.

"Are you OK?" she asked.

Reznick nodded as he came to, getting his bearings. He sat up in his bed.

"Your friend? David McCafferty?"

Reznick was still half dazed by the nightmares and dreams of the past.

"Sir, did you hear what I said?"

"Yeah, of course. Mac. How is he?"

The surgeon cocked her head. "Why don't you see for yourself."

Forty-Seven

Mac sat up in his bed in the sick bay, his chest and shoulder heavily bandaged. He was eating a sandwich, grinning like a crazed jackal. "This is tremendous, Jon. Club sandwich on rye. Phenomenal."

Reznick laughed as he approached his indefatigable friend. "Seriously? You get shot up, bleed out, and here you are eating a sandwich. That's ridiculous."

Mac shrugged. "What can I say? I'm ridiculous."

Reznick shook his head.

"What a few days, Jon, huh? Still, beats working for a living, right?"

Reznick turned to the surgeon. "So I'm taking it the operation went well?"

"Better than we expected. Half an inch and he would have been a goner. He has tissue damage and ligament damage. But in the overall scheme of things, it went very well. He's a super-fit man and he has somehow bounced back within a few hours of coming out of the operation."

"Appreciate everything you've done."

Mac winked at her. "Tell me, Doc, when do you get some shore leave?"

The surgeon blushed. "Give me a break. I'm getting married in a couple months."

"So we've still got time. What do you say?"

She chuckled. "Your friend is incorrigible."

Reznick cleared his throat. "You can say that again." He looked down at Mac. "That's enough, Casanova." He turned to face the surgeon. "Tell me, when can we get out of here?"

"We're docking in Doha in three hours."

"That works for us. And he's free to go?"

The surgeon winced. "It would be preferable if he rested up for a few days on board."

"What do you think, Mac?"

"No can do. I'm out of here. Got things to do. And Doc, that offer is still on the table."

The surgeon shrugged. "We have medication for you to reduce the pain. Five-day supply. I'll get you another script in case you need to go beyond that."

Mac gave the thumbs-up sign to her. "Perfect."

Reznick shook her hand. "Appreciate everything you've done."

"What happened?" she asked Reznick.

"A long story."

When the destroyer finally docked in Doha, they were driven to a sprawling US military base where they were both checked over by more doctors. Then they were escorted onto a British transport plane that was headed to Cyprus.

The Scot popped the morphine tablets he had been given and chatted up a British nurse who was cleaning his wounds. A few hours later, they touched down at RAF Akrotiri, a British military base in Cyprus.

The base's English commanding officer met them as they descended the stairs of the transport plane. A fierce summer heat hit them as they stood on the asphalt under the unrelenting

Mediterranean sun. "We've been expecting you." There was awkward small talk for a few minutes.

Reznick spotted a Gulfstream and made his excuses to extricate himself from the formalities. He recognized the registration number as a CIA plane. He turned to Mac and pointed across at it. "I think that's my ride. You want a lift over to the US?"

"Sounds like a plan," Mac said. "But I think I'll hang out here for a week or two. Bit of sun, rest, recuperation. Brits love Cyprus."

"You need anything? The money arrived in your account?"

Mac laughed. "I just checked. My bank manager won't believe it. The most I've ever had at one time. I've already sent over a million to my ex and my son."

"That's a nice touch."

"I wasn't the best husband. Or father."

"Well, you're trying to make up for it now. And then some. Besides, you earned every goddamn cent, man."

Mac stepped forward and hugged Reznick tight, almost too tight. "What a trip. What a fucking trip."

"That it was." Reznick extricated himself from the Scot's bear-like grip. "We got him. Sorry about you getting hit."

"We're here. We're alive. And we have many more years to go, God willing."

"Amen to that, brother. I'm going to miss you."

Mac studied Reznick's features. "You like the way I tipped those fuckers over the edge?"

Reznick laughed. "It's what I would have done in the circumstances. Bulletproof vehicle, bombproof."

"But it wasn't *falling-from-a-great-height proof*, was it? They hadn't thought of that."

Forty-Eight

It was nearly midnight when Reznick was shown to a seat near the back of the Gulfstream. A CIA medic handed him a couple of Ambien and a small bottle of water.

Reznick sat down, relieved there was no small talk. He liked it that way. He buckled up, closed his eyes. It was a long, long flight from the eastern Mediterranean, across western Europe and the huge expanse of the Atlantic Ocean.

When Reznick opened his bleary eyes, he looked out the window to see a cotton-candy dawn bathing rural Virginia. He felt a wave of calm wash over him. The plane banked sharply to the left as it descended, swooping low over the familiar woods surrounding Camp Peary. He was nearly home. He had slept all the way back to America.

Reznick felt his muscles relax, glad to see his first glimpse of home soil after more than a week away. He gathered his thoughts. The mission had been completed. It had gotten messy and problematic. But the job he had been sent to do was done.

The plane touched down and taxied to the far end of the runway. The aircraft door opened and stairs dropped down before being locked into place.

Reznick thanked the staff on board before he headed down the steps, shielding his eyes from the harsh glare of the morning sun. A waiting armed guard escorted him to an SUV, and he was driven to the camp's office buildings he'd been in just over a week ago. It seemed like months, so much had happened. He hadn't had time to decompress or process exactly what had transpired.

Reznick was shown inside.

A CIA operative who didn't introduce himself shook his hand. "Nice to have you home, sir."

"Thank you. And you are?"

"I was sent from Langley. Ms. Petersen is on her way. She wanted you to know that."

Reznick was escorted through a series of hallways until he was shown to his quarters. A towel on the bed and another change of clothes.

"We thought you'd want to freshen up before you met Ms. Petersen."

"Appreciate that."

"If you need anything, just let me know. I'll be waiting outside."

Reznick quickly showered, changed, and was escorted by the CIA guy to the office he had originally been interviewed in.

Petersen was sitting behind a large desk, alone, smiling, her hands clasped.

The CIA guy said, "Ma'am, do you need anything else?"

"We're good, thank you. Shut and lock the door, Thomas."

The door was locked, leaving Reznick alone with Petersen.

"Take a seat, Jon."

Reznick slumped in an easy chair. "So here we are."

"Here we are, indeed. Quite a week you've had."

"It was eventful; I'll say that."

"Maybe more eventful than you intended."

"Quite probably."

"Glad to be back?"

"Always glad to get back and in one piece."

Petersen smiled. "I've got to say, it was a bit of a shitshow over there."

"Not enough time, not enough intel, not enough boots on the ground. But it is what it is, as they say."

"The Bahrainis are not happy."

"The Bahrainis are never happy. And the Iranians? They can't have been too happy with their guys being obliterated in the Gulf."

"Well, they're going to make life difficult. They're talking about bringing this incident up at the UN Security Council. Russia and China have indicated they would listen favorably to their analysis. This causes us a bit of a headache."

Reznick shrugged. "Not my problem, right?"

"This was very unorthodox, even by your standards."

"Very effective, I would argue."

"I'll give you that. That pal of yours . . ."

"David McCafferty."

Petersen arched her eyebrows. "He seems quite a character."

"You can say that again. He's larger than life. And he played a crucial role in this mission coming to a successful conclusion."

"Good choice. Jon, can I clarify the chain of events? McCafferty was driving the concrete mixer and rammed the bulletproof limo, which tipped them over the edge of the parking garage, right? Just that I need to confirm the details for the Director."

"Mac was at the wheel. Rather ingenious what he did, I thought."

"Could the operation not have been cleaner?"

"Probably. But it wouldn't have been successful. Sometimes you've got to just roll with the hand you've got. It's a dirty business we're in."

"Shooting up the Iranian Revolutionary Guards in their boat . . . that is problematic."

"Fuck it. Taking some of their own medicine."

Petersen said nothing.

Reznick took the cell phone he had retrieved from Crenshaw's jacket pocket and the USB memory stick, and put them on the desk. "These belonged to William Crenshaw. You might want to examine them. Trevelle has copied the data remotely from the cell phone. But you can forensically examine everything about it. The memory stick has, I believe, all the classified files he was about to hand over to the Russians."

"I was going to ask you about that. That could be very helpful, thank you."

"You're welcome. Anything else?"

Petersen stood up and reached across the desk. She shook his hand. "Astonishing work, Jon."

"I have my moments."

"What are your plans now?"

"Me? Get home. Shut the door. Call my daughter and tell her I love her."

Petersen smiled. "You're a big softy, aren't you?"

"Am I free to go?"

"Enjoy some downtime. You've earned it, after all."

Epilogue

Three months later, Reznick was driving a convertible south through Florida's Lower Keys, sun blazing down, the car eating up the miles, when his cell phone rang. "Yeah, who's this?"

"It's Petersen."

"Hey, what's happening?"

"The fallout is what's happening. The Director will be appearing on Capitol Hill in a closed session later today. People want answers."

"And is he going to give them?"

"The story is already in play."

"The Ukrainians?"

"You got it. But the ramifications of what Crenshaw did, there's going to be a major mole hunt underway. A team has been assembled. It's going to get very murky. It doesn't reflect well on the Agency."

"You suspect there are more?"

"We believe someone was protecting him. Maybe in government. Maybe in another intelligence agency. Maybe in the CIA. We're still running background checks on a few people that were in and around Crenshaw's inner circle. Spending patterns, lifestyle red flags, drugs, that sort of thing."

"Best of luck with that."

"Sometimes these things take on a life of their own."

Reznick drove on, adjusting his sunglasses. "Anything else?"

"Just to say thank you once again."

"For what?"

"Neutralizing a man who cost an untold number of American lives."

"You've got Mac to thank for that as well."

"I nearly forgot . . . The real reason I'm actually calling."

"Is he OK?"

"Mac? He's more than OK."

"Where is he? Is he back in Crete?"

"Not as far as I know. Last I heard he was still in Cyprus. Here's the thing. We were checking through some records about David McCafferty . . ."

"Why?"

"Why what?"

"Why were you checking his records?"

"What you did, with his help, made us want to know more about Mac."

"You want him to help you out in the future?"

"You're very perceptive, Jon."

"Like I said, I have my moments."

"We learned that Mac, a couple years back, applied for a Green Card. He wanted to settle down permanently in America."

"Really? I didn't know that."

"Apparently he was turned down."

"Why?"

"We're still trying to piece together what happened. I don't know if it was an administration error, immigration problem, some kind of infringement—we don't know."

"Why the hell did America turn down someone like that? A stellar career in British special forces."

"We don't think it's fair that he was turned down. So I've put in a good word. So has the Director. We just heard last night he's going to be offered a Green Card. Ex-wife and son as well. In light of his crucial role in this operation."

Reznick was bowled over. "That's terrific; I really appreciate that. He'll be thrilled."

"We believe he can also be useful going forward. His knowledge and background are incredible."

"So Mac could soon be roaming around North America?"

"Very probably."

"God help us all!"

Petersen laughed. "Just thought you'd want to know."

"Appreciate that."

"What about you?"

"What about me?"

"Where are you?"

Reznick drove past a seafood truck. "Down in deepest Florida. Off the beaten track. Bit of R&R."

"Sounds like a plan. Well, behave yourself."

"Until the next time."

Reznick drove across the Seven Mile Bridge. The sky was pale blue, water all around. He went past Big Pine Key and then Cudjoe Key. The hot sun burned his neck as he clocked up the miles. Impossibly pastel blue skies, turquoise waters, and beautiful little hamlets and communities dotted along the roads. Beach bar shacks by the side of the road. Fishing bait stalls. It was a part of the world he loved. The expansiveness. The sense of a life outside the norms of the strictures of American society. Maybe he was looking at it through rose-tinted glasses. But he always thought of the area as not only having a more relaxed pace, but that the people who made it their home lived life on their terms. Americans who wanted to be left alone on the last frontier. Ninety miles from Cuba, but the first taste for many escaping the island for true freedom. A raw, tropical slice of old America. Unbowed. Unashamed.

He headed on, past Big Coppitt Key. It wasn't long before he passed a sign for the sprawling American naval base on the outskirts of Key West.

Reznick drove down US-1 over still waters. He headed along North Roosevelt Boulevard, a nod to President Roosevelt who had vacationed in the town. A town which had previously been wiped out by a hurricane more than one hundred years earlier. A place Hemingway had called home for a time.

A party town where the great playwright Tennessee Williams had cruised the bars. Where Jimmy Buffett had started out. The original Margaritaville.

The sun warmed his face as he turned down a palm-lined street. Familiar roads. The first smattering of tourists, some from nearby cruise ships which had docked, taking photos of everything around them. The closer he got to Mallory Square, the busier it was.

He pulled up outside a bookstore, switched off the car's engine, and got out.

Reznick brushed past a group of sailors as he walked over to Captain Tony's Saloon. It was a favorite haunt of his when he was in town. Inside, the usual idiosyncratic touches gave the bar character. It had been built around a tree, an actual hanging tree that had been the gallows in a courtyard a century earlier. The tree was located right in the center of the bar. Impossible to miss. Plastered on the walls and ceilings were dollar bills, bras—who knew why— and God knows what else stuck on every available surface. Sitting at the bar, a few thickset tourists wearing smart polo shirts, jeans, and flipflops laughed, smoked cigars, and drank beers and shots.

Reznick sat down on a stool at the far end of the bar. He looked around. On the tiny stage in the corner a guy strummed an acoustic guitar, playing punked-up country blues.

A bartender came over. "What you having?"

Reznick ordered a Heineken and a double Scotch on the rocks. He thought of Mac, glad he would soon be able to move to the States. He took stock of the decor around the bar. Newspaper clippings from decades earlier framed on the wall. Photos of the previous owner.

A redhead chewing gum was playing pool with a gray-haired, red-faced geriatric and a portly tourist who wore a beer-stained T-shirt with *Nebraska* emblazoned across the front.

The bartender slid his drinks across. "A beer and a double Scotch. Always a good way to get the party started."

Reznick handed him a fifty-dollar bill. "Keep the change."

"You sure, man?"

"Absolutely."

The guy shook Reznick's hand. "Out of sight, man."

Reznick took a long gulp of the cold beer. He loved hanging out in dive bars. Bars with character. Bars with characters. Real people. Unvarnished. Down to earth. The real America. Not the kind who inhabited social media night and day. The ordinary men and women of the United States who treasured the simple things. A good bar. Nothing fancy. Not caring about likes on social media sites. No digital nomads talking about relocating to Vietnam.

He knocked back the Scotch, feeling the amber nectar warm his belly. God, it was strong. His thoughts again turned to Mac. The unassuming Scot who had been on the crazy mission with Reznick. Mac hadn't needed to be persuaded to risk his life. Or risk his life for America. He'd just done it. Instinctively.

Reznick admired that fuck-it philosophy. The bravery. The selflessness.

His gaze was drawn to the redhead playing pool. She stared across at Reznick and smiled. "Hey stranger."

Reznick smiled back, not saying a word. Out of the corner of his eye he saw a familiar face. He turned and saw Trevelle walking in. "What the fuck? Are you kidding me?"

Trevelle ambled over and sat down beside Reznick at the bar. "This where you're hanging out, man?"

"What are you doing here?"

"I was going to ask you the same thing." Trevelle looked around the interior of the bar, shaking his head. "What the hell is this place?"

"This, my friend, is a slice of a bygone America. Enjoy it while you can."

"I saw you were headed down to the Keys . . ."

"Are you stalking me?" Reznick asked.

"Just wanted to meet up and say hi. And say well played."

"What do you want to drink?"

"Cold beer, whatever."

Reznick ordered two cold beers and two double shots of tequila.

Trevelle looked around the bar again. "I mean, really, what the fuck is this place?"

"This, my friend, is where none other than Ernest Hemingway drank when he lived in Key West."

"The actual place?"

"The actual place. You got it."

"That's pretty crazy."

"He was pretty crazy."

"Didn't he kill himself?"

"He did. In the end."

"And to think, he drank in here." Trevelle's gaze continued to edge around the quirky, eccentric interior. "What's with the goddamn tree in the middle of the bar? Talk about crazy."

Reznick told him the grisly backstory of the gallows tree.

"That's some dark shit."

"It's Florida. Remember, it's a swamp."

Reznick picked up his shot of tequila and Trevelle did the same.

"What are we going to toast to?" Trevelle asked.

"Absent friends."

Trevelle knocked back his tequila. "Absent friends," he said, screwing up his face. "That is strong."

Reznick downed his own shot and felt the booze rush to his head.

The redhead looked over. "You play pool?"

"Me?"

"Yeah, you."

"Not so much."

"Twenty dollars if you can beat me."

"A hustler, interesting."

The girl grinned back at him. "Honey, do you like your odds or not?"

Reznick finished his Scotch. "Maybe another day."

"What about your friend?"

Trevelle looked uncomfortable. "Me? I don't know the first thing about pool."

"Let me show you. Come on. What've you got to lose?"

Trevelle took a large gulp of his beer and shrugged. "What the hell."

Reznick ordered more drinks and sent one over to the redhead.

"Thanks," she said, flashing him a pearly smile.

Then Reznick turned and faced the bartender. "Just another day in paradise, right?"

About the Author

Photo © 2023 Robbie Bald

J. B. Turner is a former journalist and the author of the Jon Reznick series of political thrillers (*Hard Road, Hard Kill, Hard Wired, Hard Way, Hard Fall, Hard Hit, Hard Shot, Hard Target, Hard Vengeance, Hard Fire, Hard Exit,* and *Hard Power*), the American Ghost series of black ops thrillers (*Rogue, Reckoning,* and *Requiem*), the Jack McNeal Thriller series (*No Way Back* and *Long Way Home*), and the Deborah Jones crime thrillers (*Miami Requiem* and *Dark Waters*). He has a keen interest in geopolitics. He lives in Scotland with his wife and two children.

Follow the Author on Amazon

If you enjoyed this book, follow J. B. Turner on Amazon to be notified when the author releases a new book!

To do this, please follow these instructions:

Desktop:

1) Search for the author's name on Amazon or in the Amazon App.
2) Click on the author's name to arrive on their Amazon page.
3) Click the 'Follow' button.

Mobile and Tablet:

1) Search for the author's name on Amazon or in the Amazon App.
2) Click on one of the author's books.
3) Click on the author's name to arrive on their Amazon page.
4) Click the 'Follow' button.

Kindle eReader and Kindle App:

If you enjoyed this book on a Kindle eReader or in the Kindle App, you will find the author 'Follow' button after the last page.